STICK

other books by andrew smith

The Marbury Lens

In the Path of Falling Objects

Ghost Medicine

Andrew Smith

STICK

FEIWEL AND FRIENDS • NEW YORK

A Feiwel and Friends Book
An Imprint of Macmillan

Library of Congress Cataloging-in-Publication Data Available

ISBN: 978-0-312-61341-9

Book design by Barbara Grzeslo

Feiwel and Friends logo designed by Filomena Tuosto

First Edition: 2011

10 9 8 7 6 5 4 3

macteenbooks.com

For Laura Rennert

FIRST:

saint fillan's room

What would you hear
if my words could make

sounds?
And if they
did,
what music would I

write for you?

They call me Stick.

I am six feet tall, an inch taller than my brother, Bosten, who is in eleventh grade.

I'm thirteen, and a stick.

My real first name is Stark, which, in my opinion, is worse than being called Stick. It was my great-grandfather's name, and I suppose my parents were all into connecting with our roots or something when they decided to put it on me. My great-grandstick lived and died in Ireland and never once set eyes on me in his entire life. But I'm pretty sure he'd call me Stick, too, if he ever had.

A lot of times, after people learn my name, they'll say things like, "Oh. What an *unusual* name," which, to me, sounds the same as, "Look at that poor, deformed boy."

And when they learn that I don't care to be called Stark, they'll offer some consolation.

"I'll bet you come to like that name when you're grown up."

The only things I can think of that people like more after they grow up are alcohol and cigarettes.

My parents smoke all the time.

I am as unremarkable as canned green beans.

It bothers me when people stare at me. Most of the time, they can't help doing it on account of my missing right ear.

Besides that, with first names like ours, my brother and I may just as well walk around waving signs saying LOOK AT US. At least where we grew up, in Washington State, boys were all pretty much expected to have names like "Chip" or "Robert."

But not Bosten and Stark McClellan.

Stick.

The world sounds different to me than it does to anyone else.

Pretty much all of the time, it sounds like this.

Half my head is quiet.

I was born this way.

Most people don't notice it right away, but once they do, I see their faces; I watch how they'll move around toward that side—the one with the missing part—so they can see what's wrong with me.

So, here. Look at me.

I'm ugly.

When you see me at first, I look like just another teenage boy, only too tall and too skinny. Square on, staring into my headlights, and you're probably going to think I look nice, a handsome kid, even—green eyes, brown hair, a relaxed kind of face (from not smiling too much, probably). But then get around to that side, and you see it. I have what looks like the outline of a normal boy's ear, but it's pressed down into the flesh, squashed like potter's clay. No hole—a canal, they call it.

Nothing gets into my head that way.

I can't easily hide it because my dad won't let me grow my hair long. He yells at me if I wear a hat indoors. He says there's nothing wrong with me.

But I'm ugly.

You see what I'm doing, don't you? I am making you hear me.

The way I hear the world.

But I won't do it too much, I promise.

I know what it can do to you.

I know what it can do to you to not have that hole there.

Humans need that hole, so things can get out.

Things get into my head and they bounce around and around until they   find a way out.

My mother never talks about my ear. She hardly ever talks to me at all.

I believe she is sad, horrified. I think she blames herself.

Mostly, I think she wishes   I was never born.

EMILY

On a Friday afternoon in March, everything started changing.

Next to Bosten, my best friend was Emily Lohman. She was in eighth grade, too, and she was the only kid I knew who never made fun of me.

Her perfection amazed me.

It was the end of winter.

We lived by the sea.

When Bosten was younger, the three of us would walk from my parents' house down to the beach. We'd go beneath the pier and tip over rocks, catching crabs that we'd bring home in coffee cans dotted with rusty scabs; and then wonder at how they'd die so quickly in our care.

At sixteen, Bosten said he was too old to hunt for crabs with me and Emily anymore. I believed he still wanted to, sometimes, but there were other pressures on him now, other things my brother was looking for.

He was wild and rebellious, like a horse that would rather die than submit to being ridden. He could make me laugh, too. Real laughter that tickled me inside and made my eyes wet. And over the years, Bosten got too many bloody noses by sticking up for me.

I never cared about being picked on even a fraction of how

much I cared about seeing my brother take a beating on my behalf.

There is something in the late winter gray of the Washington sky that makes you feel wet inside, buried under cold rotting leaves, like you can't ever get dry and warm.

My jeans and boots were soaked with seawater. Somehow, grains of sand had migrated inside my socks, settling in, between my numb toes.

Coming home with wet feet always meant trouble from Mom. I was already devising a plan to stop somewhere in the woods so I could throw away my socks.

"I hate winter," Emily said.

She walked on my left side; never said anything about that habit. We headed north, away from the pier, the black, saw-toothed water of the Puget Sound pushing me toward her whenever I had to escape the occasional wash of the sea.

"So do I." I watched as my words turned into fog in front of my face. "Here's a good one."

A fat, dark purple crab with yellow claws spidered out onto the muddy sand from between two jagged lava boulders.

There is a trick to catching crabs. If they see you, they will usually run and wedge themselves in impossible cracks between the rocks. And you need to get them quick, confidently, from behind and above, at a perfect angle of attack.

My angle of attack was off that day.

The crab pinched right into the tender flesh that webbed between my thumb and first finger.

I yelped like a Chihuahua with a stepped-on paw and flailed my hand.

The crab went airborne toward the water.

Emily laughed.

I said, "Shit!"

Then I laughed, too.

She was the only person, besides Bosten, that I was never ashamed about anything in front of.

We walked across a jagged field of gray and white driftwood, toward a line of dark trees where Bosten and his best friend, Paul Buckley, had built a plywood fort with me two summers before. The fort was half-buried in the ground, a subterranean bunker that protected us from everything we imagined was out there.

It began to rain.

Emily tipped her coffee can at the water's edge.

"I'm letting them go," she said.

We only had two. But they were big ones.

I zipped my jacket all the way up and pulled the wool cap down on my head until it made a horizon of black just at the top of my eyes.

I sighed. "Let's get under the trees, Em. My mom . . ."

"It wasn't supposed to rain today."

"Welcome to winter."

We hid in the fort, next to each other on a stolen redwood picnic bench, and I could feel the *tap-tapp*ing of the rain through the damp wood as I sat on my hands to make them warm.

It was Friday afternoon. There is a kind of drunken happiness that kids our age feel on Friday afternoons.

I needed to wipe my nose, and every so often the sound of the rain encircled me. And I listened.

"So. Next year. High school. You ever think about that, Stick?"

Most of the kids around Point No Point dreamed of things like growing up or places like California.

I sighed. "I won't have any friends. I'll be beaten up regularly."

Emily laughed. She knew I wasn't really afraid. "You need to learn how to fight."

I couldn't hear what she said, because of the rain and how we sat. It sounded like something about burning and night.

"If you just beat up one of those key guys, nobody would ever give you crap again," she said. "Look at you, Stick. You're the tallest kid in eighth grade."

"You keep a list of *key guys?*"

She laughed.

I shifted. My hand got a splinter in it.

She never made me nervous.

"I think I need to get home. Bosten and me are going to the basketball game."

"That's what I mean," she said. "You should play basketball. I've seen you play."

"I'm no good."

"Don't be dumb."

"Want to come with us?"

She smiled. She had a way of smiling that said *no* musically.

Emily didn't like going to high school games. And Bosten and I never played sports on teams with other kids, but we'd go see the games because Paul was on the team.

I began unlashing the rawhide ties on my boots.

"I need to throw away my socks," I explained.

"Oh."

She knew what my mother was like at times.

My feet were pale. They looked exposed and startled, like those salamanders without eyes you find living in the permanent night of sunless caves. And when I leaned forward to stretch that second sock away from my skin, Emily did something that would have made me run and scream in anger if it had been anyone else but her—or Bosten.

She pushed the edge of my cap up with the tips of two fingers and touched my ear.

The place on the side of my head where a normal boy's ear would be.

She'd never done that before.

And when I jerked like I'd been shot, she pulled her hand away and quickly said, "Sorry."

"What are you doing?" I couldn't help sounding annoyed. People don't touch me. I could feel it, the sound came around the other side and it mixed with the lightness of her fingertips and swirled, trapped, inside my head.

It made me shake.

"I'm sorry, Stick.   I just—"

I tied my boots so tight they hurt my bare feet.

I couldn't look at her; I was too embarrassed.

And she was perfect.

There was nothing between me and Emily that wasn't held steady by the anchor of our friendship.

I didn't think about girls the way other boys did. I didn't know that either of us was ready for that. We liked catching crabs and hiding in Bosten's fort.

Kids in eighth grade liked nipping at you. Worse than cornered crabs, even if you weren't missing any parts.

And for some reason, Emily wasn't like that. She never put up with the kids with claws.

But that day, Emily planted a miracle in me.

BOSTEN

"What are you all smiles about?" Bosten whispered. His eyes squinted when he wanted to joke around or play tricks on someone.

I didn't realize I had been smiling. I'm sure it wouldn't look like a smile to anyone else but my brother.

"Nothing."

He glanced back over his shoulder. He was looking for Mom. I stood, shivering and wet, barefoot in the mudroom. Bosten's cheeks were red. He skated toward me across the polished floor in his thick white socks.

"I should have come in the secret way. It was too muddy, though."

"That's why you're happy?"

"No. Don't be dumb, Bosten."

I took off my beanie. It dripped in my hand.

We called the storm doors on the side of the house our secret way into the basement. Sometimes, on summer nights, we would escape through them. We would only come back when the sky began to lighten.

Bosten said it was like being vampires, and I always liked that.

"Come on," he said.

We snuck down the dark and narrow stairs to the basement.

They creaked, no matter how softly we'd step, but she didn't hear us.

I was the only one in our family whose bedroom was down there.

"Take your clothes off. I'll see if I can put them in the dryer without her busting me."

Bosten carried my wet things, all wadded up in a heavy and twisted mass, across the open expanse of the basement's concrete floor from my bedroom to the little laundry alcove beneath the staircase.

I could smell the cigarette smoke drifting down from above us.

"Can I use the car tonight to take Sticker to the game, Dad?"

Whenever Bosten called me Sticker, I knew he was planning on doing something crazy. It was our code, the only thing Mom and Dad hadn't figured out yet.

We had finished dinner. It was my job to clear the dishes from the table.

"Not the Pontiac. The Toyota." Dad smoked a cigarette and still wore his tie. The Pontiac was the work car, for his realty clients.

Mom said, "Which one of you boys was using the dryer downstairs?"

She knew it was me.

She placed a lit cigarette in the ashtray beside her napkin.

She was not happy.

I looked at Bosten.

He said, "I did."

"No." I shook my head. "It's my things. I got wet walking home after school with Emily. Bosten just put them in the dryer for me."

My father exhaled smoke through his nostrils.

"Now there's dirt in the dryer." Mom looked disappointed. This was how she usually began tirades.

"It's a waste of electricity," Dad said.

I turned on the water and rinsed our plates so I couldn't hear. But some sounds don't get killed easily.

"I don't work seven days a week . . ."

I felt vibrations of footsteps on the floor coming up through my legs. I didn't turn around. It was better to play deaf sometimes.

My mother reached over and shut off the water. Then she put a white spray bottle of 409 and a rag on the counter beside my hand.

She held her cigarette backwards between her index and middle fingers. I liked how she did that. I always thought if I ever smoked that I would practice holding a cigarette like that, too.

"You'll have to clean out the dryer before Bosten and you can go to the game."

"Okay," I said. "Sorry."

"Don't do that again." Her voice was tough, cold, like left-over meat.

"I won't."

"Maybe they don't need to go," my dad said. "They're both big enough that we shouldn't have to be treating them like goddamned babies all the time."

Bosten began to plead, "But, Dad . . . Paul's playing. It's Friday night."

My dad inhaled. "You're not allowed to go anywhere else. I'll be checking on you two."

"We're just going to Crazy Eric's with Paul after the game. And his mom and dad," Bosten added.

I knew he was lying. Crazy Eric's was the burger place where the high school kids hung out. I knew we weren't going there.

My mom grabbed my shoulder, like she didn't think I was listening.

"And do something with your wet things," she said.

Mom and Dad liked everything to be perfect.

My wet clothes lay on the floor in front of the open dryer, scattered. I shook them out, carried them into my room to find corners, shelves, anywhere I could hang them so they'd dry. So they wouldn't make her mad at me.

The spot on the floor where they'd been dropped was covered with a cold, wet mark. I thought it looked like a map of Greenland.

I had to kneel down in the middle of it to clean the dryer.

There were dark rings on the knees of my jeans where they'd gotten wet on the floor, and I smelled like the bathroom at a gas station. The 409 made me sneeze when I put my head inside the dryer to wipe it down. I couldn't see any dirt in it, but I cleaned it anyway.

"Want any help?" Bosten stood at my bedroom door and watched.

"Naw."

I brushed off my knees and looked apologetically at my brother. I didn't want to make him late.

"You need to change your pants?"

"It's water, not piss."

Bosten smiled. "Okay. It'll dry. I'll crank the heater on you."

. . .

In the dark, with the driver's door open and his feet hanging out in the gravel on the side of Pilot Point Road, Bosten bent backwards with his head up beneath the dashboard and grunted.

I knew what he was doing.

We always did it.

It was the exact distance from home as a round-trip to his school.

And I couldn't hear the sound at all, but knew by the way Bosten's shoulders tensed and then relaxed that he had slipped the odometer cable out from the back of the dashboard.

We were free.

Dad never knew where we went after Bosten found out how easy it was to rig the car. The only risks were that my brother had no way of telling how fast we were going, because the speedometer would sit flat, and, sometimes, we'd forget to reconnect it and one of us would have to sneak out of the house in the middle of the night and slip the cable back into place.

Bosten climbed back into the driver's seat, slammed his door, and started the Toyota. Then he leaned all the way across the gear shift and said, "Let's rip it up, Stick."

"Okay. Let's."

He pulled a U-turn right across the wet highway and we headed back toward the high school, David H. Wilson Senior High.

I don't have any idea who David H. Wilson was.

Bosten grinned and reached his hand down under the seat between his legs.

"Look what I found."

He pulled up something thick and heavy, and dropped it in my lap.

Thud.

"Where did you get this?" I asked.

Bosten slapped the steering wheel and laughed, loud. "I found it in the Pontiac. It's Dad's."

There was something exciting and terrifying at the same time in holding on to the cool slickness of a *Penthouse* magazine. One that belonged to our father.

I opened it and flipped through the pages.

"Bitchin', huh?"

I gulped. My throat felt tight. "Yeah."

Bosten laughed again, and he kept looking over at the magazine in my lap as he drove.

My hands shook and my mouth hung open. I thumbed the glossy images back and forth, one after another. They showed everything, without shame, and the pictures were so big.

I saw a layout called "Three in a Tub." Two men and a woman were taking a bath together. The bathroom was real nice, like something you'd only see in a movie. I could almost feel the steam rising up in that room. The woman lay back in the tub. Her tanned breasts glistened with droplets of water, and her dark pubic hairs swirled beneath the surface like seaweed; naked men stretched out in the water on either side of her.

I didn't even have any pubic hair at all, except for a few under my armpits.

It was just one more thing that made me so self-conscious at school, because Mr. Lloyd, our PE teacher, would stand in the shower room and check off names in his roll book as he handed out towels that weren't even big enough to wrap around the smallest boy's waist, making sure every one of us took a shower after class. In eighth grade, most boys except for me were already getting hair around their nuts. And while just about every boy would dangle that school-issue towel in front of himself to cover his privates, I'd use mine on my head, over my hair, to hide my biggest embarrassment.

Then there was a picture, after the bath, of the men standing beside the woman, drying her off, their penises hanging right beside her hips, almost touching her. I knew what having sex was, but I never saw anything like this before.

I wondered if everybody took baths in threesomes after they got pubic hair.

I was curious about how the men got their penises inside her, too. They didn't look like they would go. I couldn't see anywhere on her where they'd fit. And I wondered if the men were on tranquilizers or something, because how could you stand next to a naked woman who looked like the one in this picture and not get a boner?

My pecker was already so hard just looking at her in a magazine.

Suddenly uncomfortable, I shifted, turned the page, awkwardly aware of what was happening to me. It kind of hurt, and I had to pull out the front of my jeans to make some room.

I was scared and thrilled at the same time.

Bosten kept laughing at me.

"What are you going to do with this?" I asked.

"Ha!" Bosten said. "What do you think I'm going to do? I'm going to keep it."

"Mom will find it."

"I'll put it in my locker at school."

"Dad's going to get mad."

Bosten giggled. He almost doubled over the steering wheel. "What's he going to say? 'Which one of you bastards took the magazine I bought for jerking off at work?' "

Even I laughed at that.

I flipped some more pages. I hoped Bosten might let me read it later, but I was afraid, thinking about being caught with it at home (they caught just about everything we ever did); and I needed to see more pictures first.

Bosten looked at me with a sneaky expression on his face.

"Do you ever masturbate?"

"What?" I said, like I didn't know what he was talking about. It just startled me that he asked.

"You know . . . jack off, dumbshit? Do you?"

"No," I answered quickly.

Bosten burst out laughing again. He slapped my shoulder so hard I nearly hit my face against the side window. "You're such a liar, Stick!"

I closed the magazine.

My hands shook. I knew I couldn't lie to my brother. It was stupid, anyway.

"Okay. Well, sometimes I do."

"Sometimes?" he said. "Ha-ha! I jack off at least two times every day."

Bosten grabbed the magazine from my lap and flipped it open. He steered with his knee. " 'Three in a Tub.' That's so nasty. One time I jerked off so many times in one day that I got a road rash. It was raw and bleeding."

"On your hand?"

"No." Bosten looked proud, completely unashamed. He was always fooling around with me and acting like this. "On my dick."

I laughed. "You're stupid."

"I'm not kidding, Sticker. I thought it was going to get infected or something. I was scared. I thought I'd have to go to a doctor and tell him I've been jacking myself off too much."

He slipped the *Penthouse* back under the seat. "But I had to stop doing it for a few days. Quitting was almost impossible, but then my dick finally got better. Relief."

The high school was just up ahead. I could see all the

headlights from the other cars as they pulled into the parking lot in front of the gym.

"I'd rather die than have to go to a doctor for jacking off too much," I said. "And, anyway, haven't you heard you'll go blind, or it will stunt your growth?"

"You don't actually believe that, do you?" he asked. "That's just what old people tell us so we don't jerk off all the time. How many blind kids did you ever see in your life?"

I couldn't remember ever seeing a blind kid. But Mr. Lloyd told us boys in gym class that masturbating does that kind of stuff to you. So, I thought, maybe it makes your ear fall off.

"It really *doesn't* stunt your growth and make you go blind?" I asked.

"Maybe that's why I'm shorter than you." Bosten pulled our car right alongside the Buckleys' station wagon. I looked outside, guiltily, like Paul's parents might be watching or maybe listening to us, but they weren't there.

"Besides," Bosten said, grabbing his crotch and adjusting himself, "I may be short and blind, but I'm happy."

"You are dumb." I laughed. I wasn't embarrassed or anything talking to Bosten about jerking off. I loved my brother too much to be embarrassed about anything around him.

I opened the door and got out.

And Bosten said, "Stick! Sticker! Help me! I'm blind! I can't see!"

I laughed again. Bosten got out and came around to my side of the car. He put his arm around my shoulder and whispered right into that one sound spot on my head, with his lips so close I could feel the heat from his breath.

"You know what I'm going to do later on, when we go home? When I get home tonight, I'm going to jerk myself off right into the goddamned dryer."

"You are totally sick, Bosten."

. . .

It rained that night.

We walked toward the gym—it gave off heat and noise and light—through puddles in the parking lot.

I pulled my hat down low. Bosten wore a cap that said DWHS.

At the game, we sat next to Paul's parents, Joy and Ian Buckley. They were close friends with our parents, so Bosten and I both knew we had to be careful about what we said around them.

I sat between Bosten and Mrs. Buckley. She was on my right, so I couldn't really hear her. Occasionally, she would put her hand on my knee to get my attention, and she'd ask questions or say nice things, so I had to make up replies, just to be polite.

How are your mom and dad, Stark?

She called me Stark.

We are so looking forward to having your family over for dinner on Sunday.

When she put her hand on my knee, it felt soft and warm. I thought about that woman in the bathtub. Mrs. Buckley made me get an erection right there, sitting in the bleachers at my brother's high school.

I loved basketball, but I'd never have the guts to play it.

How could I ever get out there on the floor with all those boys and their perfect and flawless bodies running around with me—being watched by so many eyes?

Wilson High was playing a team from Bremerton. Paul was out there most of the game, too. Well, at least what we saw of the game, that is.

Bosten and I got thrown out of the gym during the second half.

Mrs. Nolan, the dean of students, told us we were lucky we didn't get arrested, but it didn't matter. I knew Mr. and Mrs. Buckley would tell our parents all about what we did if they heard about it from the other kids at the game that night.

We'd waited until after halftime to go pee. During the break, the toilets get so crowded it's almost impossible to pee. Bosten stood in line to get a Coke and I went into the boys' restroom.

There was one other kid, standing in front of the urinal. He was an eighth grader I knew, named Ricky Dostal. Ricky was in the same gym class as me, and he had this tough little man-body he got from playing Pop Warner football and spending an hour every day in his garage lifting weights while his dad sat there and smoked cigarettes and told his son how great he was going to be. Ricky was also a year older than all the other boys in eighth grade. Mr. Dostal held him back just so he would be bigger and stronger for high school football. Personally, I'd rather have to go to the doctor for jerking off too much than spend an extra year in junior high. We always hated each other, so all I could do was ignore him and pretend he wasn't there.

It didn't work.

When he turned away from the pisser, he noticed I'd been standing a few feet away from him.

Ricky said, "Hey,

retard. How's the head wound?"

What could I do?

You can't do or say anything when you're standing there holding your dick.

Ricky reached out and swiped the beanie from my head.

"You sonofabitch!" I hurriedly zipped up and turned toward him. I remember that I was thinking about what Emily had said to me earlier—about how I needed to learn to fight back.

But I wasn't like that.

Ricky shoved me and I spun back and nearly fell into the urinal.

It was one of those ones that ran along the length of the wall, open, with no dividers, about chest high.

"What'd you say about my mom, freak?"

There's always piss all over the floor in school gym restrooms.

Ricky flipped my hat down into the piss in the bottom of the urinal. Then he smiled at me and stared straight into my eyes.

I hated it when people stared at me.

I figured I was going to get hit.

I looked down at my feet.

"Isn't that your beanie there in the piss drain, Stick?"

I didn't answer him.

That's when Bosten came in, holding a Coke. I didn't hear him.

Neither did Ricky, I guess.

"I think you should put it on, Stick. You need to cover that shit on your head," Ricky said.

I looked up. I wasn't scared of him.

Bosten casually set his Coke down on the sink behind Ricky and cleared his throat. And just when Ricky Dostal turned his face, Bosten punched him so hard, just below the eye, that I could feel the *whack!* of my brother's fist vibrating up through the yellowed restroom floor.

Ricky spun back toward me so fast that droplets of his blood splashed onto the tiles above the chrome water pipe that dripped a continuous flow all along the length of the wall's open urinal.

He was out before he hit the ground, completely unconscious, lying on his side with his face in the piss on the floor. There was a dark red gash that arced all the way across Ricky's cheekbone, and blood splashed everywhere across the floor, over Ricky's gray face.

It almost looked like somebody had been murdered in there.

Bosten didn't say a thing to me. He just took a sip through the straw in his Coke, set it back down on the sink, then stepped over Ricky, went to the end of the urinal, and peed.

I stood over Ricky, watching the pool of blood run through the grooves between the tiles on the floor, mixing with urine, finding its way, eventually, into the bottom of the piss trough.

"Want some?" Bosten offered me his Coke.

I was thirsty.

Ricky moaned, began to roll over. He was a mess, soaked in piss and blood.

"Wait a second," Bosten said. "Here."

Then he took off his cap and put it on my head.

"As long as I live, Stick, no one's ever going to do that to you again."

During the game, as we sat beside Mrs. Buckley, who didn't even notice that I was wearing my brother's ball cap, we saw the dean of students walking across the floor, scanning the bleachers for me and Bosten.

So he leaned over to me and whispered, "Come on, Stick. We might as well go turn ourselves in."

And that's how Bosten and I got thrown out of the game that night.

We waited in the car for the game to end.

I found myself feeling sorry for Ricky.

I was sure that at that moment, he was lying in a hospital emergency room, smelling like piss, while some doctor leaned over him and stitched up the cut my brother laid across his face.

I turned, so that I was looking out the window. The rain had stopped and I could see a few stars in the breaks between clouds.

I didn't want to look at Bosten, anyway.

"Do you want your hat back?" I said.

"No. Are you okay? I hope you're not mad at me."

That's when I felt like crying.

So I wouldn't look at Bosten.

He knew.

"I'm sorry, Stick."

And words like those, from my brother, were the kind of words that could get inside my head and whirr around like mad hornets trying to find a way out.

Sure he was sorry.
I knew what he meant.
He wasn't sorry he busted
that fucker's face open.
He wasn't sorry we got thrown out of a
goddamned basketball game.
Those were things to be proud of.
Those were things you'd laugh about
and tell stories about over and over.
Things like that make normal boys normal
boys.
But goddamnit, goddamnit, GODDAMNIT
I knew what Bosten was sorry about.
He was sorry about *me*, like he felt
some kind of responsibility for me being me.
Like he knew what she was thinking every time
Mom looked at me, so he was sorry for that.
Like he had to admit
that since nobody else was sorry for me,

he might as well do the job.
Just like cleaning out the goddamned dryer.
But it wasn't Bosten's job to feel sorry for me,
and GODDAMNIT
I AM SORRY
I DID THIS TO YOU, BOSTEN.
I AM SORRY.

PAUL

Cars started. People filed out of the gymnasium.

Bosten opened his door and got out.

"Mrs. Buckley," he said.

Then I couldn't hear anything.

He closed the door.

I watched him talking to Paul's parents until they got into their car and drove off. And Bosten just leaned against the hood of the Toyota, facing the gym, waiting for the players to come out.

"I'm not mad at you, Bosten," I said. "Why would I be?"

But he couldn't hear me, either.

I got out and stood next to Bosten when I saw Paul coming. I knew they'd expect me to ride in the backseat, anyway.

I shoved my brother's shoulder.

"What did you say to the Buckleys?"

"I told them we got thrown out. And that I punched a kid in the bathroom who was messing with you."

"Oh."

It would be trouble.

"Don't worry about it. It was me, not you," he said. "So I asked them if we could take Paul to Crazy Eric's before we went home. They said it was okay."

"Are we really going to Crazy Eric's?"

Bosten laughed. "Hell no."

He grabbed the bill on my cap and pulled it down in front of my nose.

Across the lot, Paul shouted good-byes to the other players.

Paul Buckley was just a bit taller than me, and solid—definitely not a stick. He carried a canvas bag slung over his shoulders. His hair was wet. I could tell by the way he walked they'd won their game.

He came up to us, smiling, red-faced, and slapped a hand into Bosten's.

"Nice game," Bosten said.

"Hey, Stick." Paul nodded to me and I nodded back.

"Buck."

"Well, to be completely honest," Bosten said, "we didn't actually see the whole game. We got thrown out before the end because I beat the shit out of Ricky Dostal in the bathroom."

"That was you guys?" Paul smiled; had a look of awe on his face. "I heard someone almost got *killed* in there."

"I busted him up pretty good for screwing with Stick."

I felt sick.

"You're going to get suspended," Paul said, but he was still smiling.

"I know." Bosten jangled the car keys. "So let's go have some fun and mess shit up before my mom and dad totally destroy Stick's and my life."

So much for Bosten trying to assure me it was going to be all on him.

I knew better, anyway. No punishments were ever exclusively limited to Bosten in our house.

Paul beamed. "Wait till you see what I got from Francis."

Francis was Paul's brother. He was in the army, stationed in Texas, and visited the Buckleys every few months. Whenever Francis brought surprises for his younger brother, it usually meant I was either going to have to watch Paul and Bosten attempt to smoke Mexican pot or blow things up.

That night, it meant both.

Bosten drove out to the short stretch of low bank beach at Pilot Point and parked.

He left the lights on, and I watched how the dashboard glow made him look green.

"You might need to drive us home, Stick," he said.

I already knew that.

And I'd seen seventh graders who could roll better joints than Bosten, but I loved to watch how completely inept he and Paul were whenever they got into their "danger mode."

Personally, I hated the smell of pot.

But I did wonder how Mom would hold a joint, if she ever smoked one.

Paul reached back between the seats and handed his baggie of weed and rolling papers to me. "Will you put this in my bag?"

When I unzipped Paul's gym bag, a fog of steam and sweat escaped. I almost gagged. It made my hand wet to slip his baggie back inside it. I touched something wet and clothy. I tried not to think about what disgusting article of Paul's uniform it may have been.

"Buck, the stuff in your bag reeks like armpit," I said.

Bosten laughed. Paul shoved the dashboard cigarette lighter in to heat it up. It ticked.

I tapped on the back of Paul's seat. "You guys can't smoke pot in the car."

Bosten's door opened, and Paul told me, "Grab my bag, Stick."

"I'm not touching it."

They spread Paul's gym towel out on the bank and sat there passing the joint back and forth while I walked down to the edge of the water.

The wind blew back. I couldn't smell their smoke, and I was glad for that. I looked out across the blackness of the Puget Sound and could see, through the fog, the lights of Seattle. I turned back and watched the little orange tip of the joint levitate and cross between two shadows, lying on their backs next to each other and staring up at the stars.

Bosten got up first.

Then he fell down.

Paul started laughing at him.

They were stoned.

"So check this out." Paul pushed himself up and dug a hand down inside his bag. He pulled out two things that looked like big green cans. And he pulled out a sock, too, which he let fall limply onto the ground.

"Number one

and

number two," he said. He dropped the second can and it rolled toward his feet.

"Don't tell me those things blow up," I said.

"What? My sock?" Paul flipped his wet sock back at my face.

I ducked.

Bosten started laughing so hard, I thought he was going to pee himself.

"Well, they kind of do blow up," Paul said. "This one's a smoke grenade. Green fucking smoke."

"Bitchin'!" Bosten crawled over on his hands and knees and put his face right down next to it.

"Francis says it will even go off underwater," Paul explained. "He told me you could put it in a pool and it will turn the water green and still make smoke, too."

"Are you going to throw it in the ocean?" I asked.

"Let's throw it in the pool at Wilson." Bosten laughed.

I shook my head. "You're going to get in trouble."

"I'm already going to get suspended for fucking up Ricky Dostal."

Paul grabbed my brother's shoulder. "But wait." He waved his hand over the second, slightly bigger canister. "This one's called a handpop. It launches a flare into the sky and it floats down on a parachute."

Bosten had an almost religious look on his face. "Oh my God. That is so bitchin'!"

"You guys are going to blow your hands off," I said.

They just laughed at that.

I stood back from them. I knew there was no way to talk Paul and Bosten out of doing something crazy. Something was definitely getting blown up at Pilot Point Beach tonight.

"You know what, Stick?" Paul said. "When we shoot this off, Francis says people are going to think it's a fucking UFO."

"Wow," I said, as unenthusiastically as possible. "That's exactly what I was hoping for."

Bosten scrambled to his feet. Paul's towel stuck to him and

trailed away from the seat of his jeans like some kind of comet tail, and he dug a hand down into his pocket as he followed his friend down the bank, toward the water's edge.

I heard a jangling sound.

Bosten dropped the car keys at his feet.

"Here. Go start the car, Stick."

What could I do? I tried telling myself it would be no big deal.

We'd blown stuff up before, only we never shot anything five hundred feet into the air that would light up like a goddamned nuke over Seattle.

I sat behind the wheel and watched Bosten and Paul laughing, bumping into each other down by the water. I put the shift into neutral and sighed and I turned the key.

Dad would kill us both if he knew how many times Bosten made me drive him home.

I saw Paul drop the handpop at his feet, and I thought, *Good, maybe it's rolled into the water and he can't find it.* They were just screwing around, anyway, laughing and wrestling with each other. I wondered how anyone could ever enjoy smoking pot, if all it ever did to you was make you act stupid.

I pulled the *Penthouse* magazine out from under the seat and studied the pictures by the light of the dashboard gauges. And just as I was settling back in wonder at that steamy bathtub scene, everything lit up, flashed by a sudden white-hot blast that was as bright as the sun.

Through the windshield, it looked like an old black-and-white science fiction film, a grainy and distorted clip of Bosten and Paul slowly backing away from the shore, their shadows cast down upon the wet ground with a complete pitch that was fierce, absolute. And beyond them stretched the twisted umbilical of smoke that corkscrewed away from the handpop as it ascended and then flared open like an eye, a swinging pendulum of phosphorus that dangled beneath a bat-shaped veil.

It was amazing.

The boys stood on the edge of the bank with their chins up, leaning into each other with arms hugging around their shoulders, as though they were watching something that could never be seen this way again.

I rolled down my window and yelled, "Come on, you dumbshits. Someone's got to have called the cops by now."

They turned and began moving back up toward the car, but it was like slow motion. Paul stuffed the gym towel into his bag and slung it over his shoulder. Bosten climbed into the backseat and Paul sat up front next to me. The bag was open and I could still smell the odor of Paul's sweat-soaked basketball stuff steaming out from between the teeth of the zipper.

I rolled the magazine up and dropped it on top of his clothes. "Here."

"*Penthouse?* What were you doing in here all by yourself with this, Stickie?" Paul laughed and pushed my shoulder.

"Nothing." I backed the car away from the beach bank. It jerked. I wasn't a very good driver. "We need you to hide it for us for a day or so."

"Yeah," Bosten dopily affirmed from the backseat.

I was having a hard time getting the gearshift up into first.

"But, Buck, you better goddamn give it back to us," I said.

Paul pushed his bag down onto the floor between his feet and opened his door.

"Wait," he said. "My sock. My fucking sock. I left it on the beach."

I reached across him to grab his door, to try to stop Paul Buckley from getting out of the car. When I did, I popped the clutch and stalled out the engine.

"You are stupid, Buck."

He slipped away and ran down toward the beach.

The UFO was sinking lower, dropping closer to the blackness of the Sound.

Then Bosten pushed the seat forward and slid out after Paul.

I sighed as I restarted the car.

They were both completely stoned, and I couldn't help worrying that we were going to end up in deep trouble.

I sat there for what seemed like half an hour with the engine idling, nervously watching the rearview mirror for the flashing lights of police cars. I was certain they'd be coming for us. And all the while, the glow from the handpop dimmed away as it sank into the sea. Finally, I turned the motor off and went outside to look for my brother and his friend.

I found them. They had fallen asleep on the wet ground of the bank, right next to Paul's stinking sock.

Bosten was lying on his back, a look of complete peace and contentment on his face; and Paul was sleeping with his head on Bosten's shoulder, using it as a pillow. I wished I had a camera so I could take a picture to show them how stupid they both looked.

I kicked Paul on his butt with the toe of my Converse.

He inhaled sharply and sat up.

"What?"

"Wake up, Buck."

"Huh?"

"You're high. Get back in the car."

Then I kicked Bosten, too.

"And don't forget your goddamned sock."

And Paul argued groggily, "That was one of my only team socks, Stick. And what if some cop found it and realized that a Wilson basketball player had been involved in the UFO incident? Did you ever think of that? Huh?"

"Wow," I said. "You really *are* smart, Buck."

Most guys would think that was enough, that it was time to go home. But not Bosten and Paul. Their short nap invigorated them, and once we got back into the car they demanded two things: that I drive them somewhere else where they could roll and smoke another of their ridiculous joints, and that the night could not end until they'd fired off the green smoke grenade in the water of the David H. Wilson Senior High School swimming pool.

Wilson was completely dark when we got there. On the drive, Bosten kept playing around with Paul's smoke grenade, just to annoy me. It wasn't a good idea because I drove the front wheels into the curb twice, which made Paul spill some of his pot down onto the plastic floor mats of my parents' car.

"Jesus. Isn't the street wide enough for you, Stick?" Paul complained.

And from the backseat, Bosten kept goading, "I wonder what would happen if I pulled this ring out while we were still driving?"

"We would all die. That's what," I said.

Swerve.

"But it would look bitchin', I bet," he answered.

"Did it!" Paul proudly held up a crooked and spit-sogged joint.

The second joint didn't make them as stupid as the first. Maybe they were getting numb, I thought. I knew I was. My hands were frozen stiff while I stood with Bosten and Paul out in the field behind the pool. I shoved them so far down into the cross-pocket of my sweatshirt that my fingers cupped beneath my crotch.

I didn't watch the boys while they smoked their weed, but I couldn't help being irritated by the annoying smell and the sounds of their strained and slobbered sucking on the joint. I kept my eyes on the pool. Even without any lights on at all, I could see the foggy gray steam from the water rising up above the top of the spiked iron fence that enclosed the swimming and diving arena.

I thought a warm bath would have been really nice at that moment.

"Time to go," Paul said.

He held the grenade in his right hand, cocked like a spring behind him, as my brother followed him to the edge of the fence. They must have choreographed this ahead of time, I thought, because while Paul held the canister at the ready, Bosten poked his finger through the wire ring.

Bosten said, "Ready?"

"Go!"

Bosten pulled the wire.

Smoke instantly swallowed Paul's hand.

He hurled the grenade up into the night.

It hit the top of the fence, with a sound like *dink!*

Hissing and spewing, it bounced back and landed in the grass between the three of us.

The last thing I clearly saw was Bosten, falling down in a heap of laughter. As the world disappeared into a noxious green haze, I could hear my brother giggling.

"Goddamn basketball player who throws like a girl!"

And Paul, laughing equally hard. "Shut up! That thing fucking scared me, and it's heavier than shit!"

I crawled out from the smoke on my hands and knees, crouching when I finally found my way into a patch of clear air.

"You guys are both so stupid. Can we *please* go home now?"

But Paul and Bosten just rolled around in the dark greenness, laughing like they'd never stop.

DAD AND MOM

It was just a few minutes before midnight when Bosten and I got home.

Dad and Mom were waiting for us.

They didn't see that it wasn't Bosten at the wheel, parking the car in its spot next to Dad's Pontiac. There was no way they'd know about how I snaked my hand up behind the dashboard and reconnected the wire to the odometer, or that I'd carefully shaken out the floor mats of all the marijuana Paul had spilled while trying to spastically craft a joint.

They didn't need to know any of that, because they knew enough already.

Maybe once per week things exactly like this happened in our house.

Dad had his belt off, folded in his fist, before we even came in from the mudroom. Mom stood just inside the doorway to the living room.

As soon as Bosten stepped into the house, Dad grabbed him, clawing the soft flannel shirt into a ball right between Bosten's shoulder blades. Dad pushed him into the living room, past Mom, and threw my brother down across the chair where Dad always smoked and watched television. And when Bosten landed hard and knocked over an ashtray full of twisted butts, I could tell it made Dad even madder.

Everyone knew what was going to happen next. It was always the same, just sometimes the actor would be different, and I'd be the star of the show; and, usually, the script would be different, too. But if you've seen it once, there's no need to see it again, in my opinion.

Dad hit Bosten across the center of his back. Hard. It sounded like the belt could cut my brother in two.

Bosten yelped.

It sounded pathetic.

And, like always, I thought I could somehow disappear, not be noticed, so I quietly turned in my socks and began to slip toward the basement stairs.

Everything smelled like smoke.

But my mother was right behind me. She grabbed me by my hair (they both liked to drag me around by my hair at times like this—and, usually, it would also remind them that I needed to have it all cut off the next day) and walked me into the living room, holding my head so I couldn't look away from Dad or my brother.

"Ricky Dostal's father called me," Dad said.

He hit Bosten again, not hard to hurt him, it was just a prod—something like you'd do to a horse, maybe—just his way of making sure we both knew the title of the story Dad was about to tell us.

Bosten tightened his arms on the chair, like he was hugging it, like he loved that chair so much. He wasn't about to try to move.

"Four hundred dollars!" Dad swung the slashing belt across Bosten again.

This time, he wasn't just trying to get our attention.

"That's what he wants me to pay him for the emergency room. Four hundred goddamned dollars!"

Then he hit Bosten across the back of his head.

I heard my brother cry out.

But it was soft, buried in the cushion of Dad's smoking chair.

I heard it anyway.

Mom's hand twisted. Like she was telling me I better not think about turning my face away.

"You think you're tough? Beating up a goddamned fourteen-year-old? How do you think I can afford to pay four hundred dollars?"

I didn't wish he would stop.

I knew how stupid wishing was.

Mom's hand dug tighter into my hair with each angry word from Dad's mouth. Dad grabbed the bottom of Bosten's shirt and pulled it up, baring my brother's pale and bony back. Then Dad slid both hands through Bosten's belt and jerked his blue jeans all the way down past his knees. I was terrified and embarrassed for my brother.

These things happened all the time, though.

It's just how the McClellan family did things, and me and Bosten never wondered if, maybe, there wasn't some other way out there for getting family things done.

Everyone was like this, right?

Then Dad began beating Bosten, dutifully cutting red slashes into the flesh across my brother's back and butt.

I tried shutting it out, but with each *whack* of the belt I felt electricity cutting across my own spine. I closed my eyes and swore at myself that I wouldn't cry, but I called myself an ugly bastard because it was all my fault that Bosten was being beaten.

I opened my eyes when Mom jerked my head.

My father hit him with the belt over and over, and Bosten took it, whimpering, shivering at times, until Dad, out of breath, finally stopped.

Mom's grip loosened.

Dad looked at me. I thought I'd be next, but his eyes fell away from me like I wasn't there at all. He casually fed his belt back through the loops on his slacks and picked up the pack of cigarettes from the floor where Bosten had knocked it down.

Bosten lay there, stretched across the chair, shaking. He

wasn't crying. I knew Bosten wouldn't ever cry in front of Dad and Mom.

He'd do it later.

Mom let go of my hair and Dad lit a cigarette, and then dropped the pack, again, onto the floor beside his chair. He hooked his fingers into Bosten's collar and stood him up. I was thankful that Bosten's shirt fell down and covered his nakedness and the bloody marks on his backside. I hoped, somehow, that the softness of the flannel made my brother not hurt so much.

Bosten tried pulling up his jeans, but my father wouldn't allow him to bend forward. He walked Bosten, manacled by his lowered pants, out of the living room and into the hallway. I knew what would happen next. Same as always. Bosten would get locked inside the spare bedroom—I called it Saint Fillan's room, I will tell you why—no lights, no nothing, not even any clothes; just a galvanized bucket to use for a toilet and a cot with one sheet. This would usually last for two days, sometimes more. It happened to me as often as it happened to him.

Everyone raised kids this way.

And Dad stopped before they'd gone too far down the hall.

"Say

good night, Bosten."

My brother whispered,

"Good night."

It was like a game, but it wasn't fun and there was no chance of winning.

Maybe a minute later, I stood there not knowing what to do, a door slammed shut down the hallway.

I stole away.

When I was at the top of the basement stairs, Mom called out,

"Good night,

Stick."

It was a game.

I didn't answer her.

"GODDAMNIT, I SAID
'GOOD NIGHT, STICK'!"

I tried to close myself inside my room.

It was a game.

Footsteps on the stairs.

Dad.

"Didn't you hear your mother? Get your ugly ass up there and say good night!"

He grabbed my hair and pulled me upstairs to the living room.

To say good night.

It was a game, and it always went like this.

There was a pipe that ran down a corner of my wall; a drain from upstairs to the septic tank for gray water. It descended along the concrete walls of the basement in the same corner where I kept my bed.

If I pressed my only ear to it at night, when the house was quiet, sometimes I could hear things from upstairs.

And with my head pressed like that into the pipe as I lay in my bed, I could hear nothing else.

The sounds would get into my head and there was no way they could ever get out.

I would lie there,
the top of my head resting against the rough concrete,
so I could
listen
to the upstairs.
I kept my eyes on the small window above my bed.
It was a perfect rectangle—golden—I'd measured it; and it sat
right at ground level.

In spring I could look up and see how the grass grew.
It was like being buried, and still able to watch and
listen
to the living world.
I heard Bosten crying
upstairs.
It sounded like coughing at first,
but I know my brother.
I kept a sixteen-penny nail
on the floor beneath the bedframe.
I tapped
on the pipe for Bosten
and sometimes
I believed he heard me.

Robert Beckett always smelled like urine.

It was the clearest memory I had from my first days at school.

They put me in the mentally retarded class for two years until I started talking.

The first time I spoke, I told Robert Beckett to stop pissing on himself, and he did. We became friends after that.

I liked the mentally retarded kids. One ear was enough for them.

In third grade they put me in with the normal kids. In third grade

they
put me in with
the normal kids.
Inthirdgradetheyputmeinwiththenormalkids.
Normal kids in third grade do not like

boys
without that hole.

I was no good
in most things, but especially bad in math.

Bosten and I were walking in the woods one day and he announced, "Stick, I did the math. Did you ever think about why there are no pictures from Mom and Dad's wedding? She was pregnant with me, that's why!" And he laughed. "I did the math. It was May when they got married. The announcement is in the scrapbook, just two pages before my birth certificate. August was only three months later.

Ha-ha!
What do you think of that, Sticker?"

I didn't know what to think. At least he was born whole.

EMILY

In the morning, I tried to sneak out while they were having cigarettes and coffee.

Mom stopped me.

"Stark McClellan." She said, "You are not leaving this house looking like that."

And I knew what *that* meant.

Dad glared at me. "You look like a god-damned bum."

I stopped at the top of the basement stairs. Mom came out of the kitchen, holding her backwards cigarette in one hand and the electric hair clippers in the other. A green extension cord dragged behind her.

"Take your shirt and undershirt off and

go get the broom."

I hated when she gave me haircuts.

I stood, stripped to the waist on the front porch, listening to the sound that came around that one side: the insect buzzing of the clippers, fascinated at how Mom could smoke a cigarette without using her hands at all; one hand held my head steady, while the other swept the teeth of the clippers up, up, up—mowing from the bottom of my neck, around that one ear, and over the dead spot on the right side of my skull.

I liked the way the blades nipped at my neck. But it was freezing cold outside, and I shook.

"Stay still."

Everything itched. My hair fell in spiny tufts over my chest and shoulders and found its way inside the waist of my jeans and down my legs. My arms locked tense against the tickling and the cold and the morning. I tried to blow the bits of needle hair from the end of my nose.

"Why can't you stay still?"

Mom was getting angry.

"Sorry."

She switched off the clippers. "There. Clean this up."

I made a broom of my fingers and tried to get as much hair as possible off my skin before slipping on my undershirt and tucking in my shirt.

There were rules about how we boys could dress at my house.

Dad made them:

We could never have hair longer than half an inch.

We always had to have our shirts tucked in before we left the house, too, and we had to wear white T-shirts under them.

Always.

We were never allowed to go outside wearing just T-shirts, like other boys did.

Dad said that was disrespectful, like walking around in public in our underwear, which also always had to be no other color but white.

And we never had pajamas, no matter how cold it got.

Dad said the boys don't wear pajamas to bed in his family.

Bosten and I never even once thought about the rules.

They were just rules.

"And you have to eat some breakfast before you can go anywhere."

"Yes, ma'am."

I'd sweep every last bit of the hair from the porch, and then clean out the bristles on the broom, too, before I could come back inside the house.

I rubbed my hand across my head. The nubs of my hair felt like coarse velvet. I liked that feeling, how I could hear the friction of my hand on the inside of my head. I traced my fingers over the spot where a normal boy would have an ear. That touch made a sound, too. Inside my head.

I hated my ugliness.

I looked at the door. Then I crept across the wet lawn and stood outside the window on the spare room. If they caught me here, they'd beat me.

Why wouldn't they?

I would expect them to.

I tapped with one finger.

Bosten peeked out from the edge of the dark curtain. He winked at me, and I winked back.

"Those bombs last night. They were really cool, Bosten."

I could tell by the squint in his eye that he smiled. He nodded his head.

I went back inside and made myself a bowl of Cheerios.

That morning, I went to Emily Lohman's house.

The Lohmans lived on the other side of the road from us, but it was a long walk through the woods to get there. I'd have to squeeze through a barbed-wire fence and cross a cow pasture where Emily's family kept two calves; and then follow the shore of their pond for a quarter mile before her house even came into view.

"Stick! Good morning!"

Mrs. Lohman swung the door open, smiling.

I thought she was the nicest person in the world, but not as pretty as Paul Buckley's mom. I untied my shoes and slipped them off on the porch. They were wet from the walk.

And I took Bosten's cap off my head and hung it on a brass coatrack when I stepped inside.

The house smelled like pancakes and flowers.

"Emily! Your friend's here!" Mrs. Lohman called out into the vastness of the house.

I liked the way it sounded when she called me Emily's *friend*.

Mr. Lohman sat at the kitchen table, wearing a stained T-shirt and pajama bottoms. He had glasses on his face, but his eyes smiled when he noticed me standing on the cool linoleum of their kitchen floor. He was reading the paper from Kingston, folded in one hand, with a glass of juice in the other. A big plate smeared with syrup and leftover crumbs had been pushed away from him toward the center of the table.

"Looks like someone got himself a haircut," Mr.

Lohman said. "You're lookin' overly handsome for a Saturday morning, with

your shirt all tucked in

and everything."

I could feel my face turning red.

"Dora, fix this boy a plate."

They always fed me. I'd been coming over to their house ever since third grade.

Mr. and Mrs. Lohman never seemed to notice that something was wrong with me.

Emily didn't have any brothers or sisters.

Maybe that was why Mr. Lohman didn't have the same rules as Dad. And if you ever really could eat enough to explode and die, I would gladly do it on Mrs. Lohman's pancakes. So by the time Emily came down from her room and sat next to me at the table, I already had syrup all over my face.

She was not like the other girls in eighth grade. Boys in eighth grade could be rough. But the girls could be viciously cruel. Maybe that was why Emily didn't have many girl friends.

The other girls were mean to Emily sometimes. They teased her for being stuck up and not playing the other girl games, or because her dad owned the little store by the pier; because she took care of cows. No other girls at school did those things.

And no girls at school ever talked to me.

I asked her one time why she was friends with me.

She just smiled and shrugged. "Who else would I be friends with?"

I didn't know who else.

I was afraid sometimes that Emily felt all alone.

Even if we never said it, I think we needed each other.

"Hi, Em," I said with my mouth full.

"Hi." I watched as she smeared soft margarine across the

top of her one and only pancake. She said, "What do you want to do today?"

"I don't know. What do *you* want to do?"

We would usually ask this back and forth at least twenty times.

Especially on Saturday mornings.

"How was the basketball game?" Emily asked it like she could see there was a story on my face under all that pancake syrup.

Mrs. Lohman put a glass of milk on the table next to my plate and sat down beside me. She fixed the collar on my shirt and I felt the back of her fingers on my neck.

"I swear, you are getting so big," she said. "Do you want some more?"

"No, thank you," I said. I took a drink of milk and looked at Emily.

She was sitting on my left side. Like she always does.

"Me and Bosten got thrown out of the basketball game. Bosten got into a fight."

Mrs. Lohman leaned around the table so she could look at my face. She'd known Bosten for just as many years as she knew me.

And Emily said, "With who?"

"He beat up Ricky Dostal in the boys' bathroom."

Mrs. Lohman frowned, but Emily's father nodded, like it was fine with him that my brother messed up Ricky Dostal.

"Ricky Dostal had to have been asking for it," he said. "What did he do this time?"

I thought about it for a second. I felt bad when I lied and said, "I don't know. I didn't see it."

But I didn't want to tell them what Ricky Dostal did. I drew a circle with fork tines in the syrup that was left on my plate. "Ricky had to go to the hospital. To get stitches."

I finished my milk. "And now Bosten's going to get in trouble at school on Monday, and he's already being punished at home."

Emily put her fork down across her plate with a *clink!*

"Want to do something?" I asked.

Mrs. Lohman let Emily know it was okay for her to leave. "I'll clear the dishes, sweetie."

Then Emily said, "Sure. What do *you* want to do?"

She smiled at me.

We both pushed our chairs back and stood.

And Mr. Lohman flipped the front page of the paper over, so I could see it. He laughed. "Just don't let the aliens get you."

There it was, on the front page of *The Kingston Register*: a grainy picture of our bomb.

The handpop flare.

It was so beautiful and frightening.

Below it, the headline asked: UFO OR HOAX?

I leaned over the paper, and Mr. Lohman gave it a push around so it was right side up for me.

"That . . ." I looked straight at Mr. Lohman's eyes. "That is so cool! Do you think I could have that story, please, Mr. Lohman?"

He chuckled warmly. "Boys like that kind of stuff, don't they? Sure, Stick. Take it."

I began to carefully tear my way around the article, and Mrs. Lohman handed me some scissors from a kitchen drawer. I held the clipping in my hand and stared in awe at the photograph, thinking how Bosten was going to love this.

"You think that's really a spaceship?" Mr. Lohman asked.

I grinned.

"Yeah."

I folded the paper twice and tucked it into the front pocket of my shirt.

It's a rare March day in Washington when the sky is so clear and blue as it was on that Saturday morning. We went into the woods and followed the trail Emily walked every day to the school bus stop.

Here, at the north edge of the Lohmans' property, the trees were dark and smelled of dew.

"Okay, out with it," she said.

"What?"

"Tell me what *really* happened with Ricky."

"Oh." I stopped. There was a big black slug as long as my middle finger on the narrow trail, right in front of my left foot. "He tried messing with me in the bathroom. He threw my hat in the piss drain. Bosten saw it, so he socked him. One time. Busted Ricky's face open and knocked him out cold."

"*You* should have been the one who punched him," Emily said.

I was embarrassed.

"I thought about it. I just couldn't." I pointed at my zipper. "I was peeing."

"Guys like him are never going to leave you alone if you don't fight back."

I started walking again. "I'm pretty sure Ricky's going to leave me alone."

"Sure. If you say so."

"Anyway, after the game me and Bosten and Paul Buckley went to Pilot Point, and we shot off a flare from the army. That's what that UFO picture is on the paper. We did it."

"Nuh-uh," she teased.

"It really was us," I said. "Then Bosten and Paul lit off a green smoke bomb in the field by the pool at Wilson."

"You guys are dumb," she said.

"I know. They made me drive the car home."

"Maybe next time, I'll go with you," Emily decided.

We stopped where the creek cut across the trail. Sometimes, we'd come to this spot to catch tree frogs.

"Paul and Bosten do bad stuff," I said. Then I whispered, as if someone might actually hear me confess it, "They smoke pot."

"No wonder they make you drive. You don't smoke pot, do you?"

"No way. You should see how stupid they act when they get high."

Emily moved ahead of me. She stepped from rock to rock and crossed to the other side of the creek.

"You know what I want to try?" she asked.

"What?" I followed her across.

"Let's try riding our cows."

I laughed. "That sounds dumb."

"Want to?"

"Okay."

I followed her along the path toward the edge of their pasture.

"I want to ask you something, Em."

"What?"

She turned and came back to my left side.

"Yesterday." I swallowed the lump that was in my throat. "Why did you touch me?"

"I don't know." She said it so casually. How could I not believe everything she said? "I just wanted to, I guess. Why?"

"No one ever touches me there. Except maybe Bosten when we wrestle and stuff. That's why."

"Well, I'm sorry. I just wanted to see what it felt like. I won't do it again if it bothers you."

"It's okay," I said. "It's just . . . well, it's ugly."

She shrugged. "I don't think so. I think it's cool. Everyone else is so . . . the same. You know?"

Emily got closer to me. I'm not nervous around her, or embarrassed, ever, but it kind of scared me. I could feel my heart beating really hard, and the sound

bounced around

inside my head.

I didn't want that heartbeat sound to find its way out.

She said, "Watch my face if you don't believe me. Then you'll see."

"See what?"

Then she reached up, lightly, slowly. It was like watching that missile drifting in the sky. She took Bosten's cap away from me and put her left hand flat on the side of my head. Emily's fingers curled softly into my little hair. I watched her eyes.

I believed I would see her repulsion.

But she was so soft and perfect.

She lowered her hand and said, "See?"

But I couldn't answer.

She trapped my heart inside my head.

Everything was changing.

Except that quiet half of my head.

We decided we were going to ride those cows and play like we were jousting.

Cows don't listen very good.

Emily's cow ran toward the woods as soon as she got on it, and I had a hard time getting my cow to put up with me. I ended up flopped over its back, and when it started trotting, before I could straddle it, I was on my elbows and butt in the wet grass, watching it poop, eat, and run away from me, all at the same time.

"Stupid cow," I said.

Emily laughed.

I watched her run across the field to where I was sitting.

The cows disappeared. I guess they didn't think jousting was so fun.

Neither did I, actually.

Emily pulled my hand so I could stand up. She was so much smaller than me, but for a girl, she was real strong.

These were our Saturdays.

We did nothing and everything at the same time.

We walked along the barbed wire toward the road that led down to the pier.

"Hey, Em."

"What?"

"You take baths, right?"

"Why? Do I smell bad?"

"No. I mean, would you ever take a bath with someone else?"

"That's a weird thing to ask, Stick."

I told her about what I saw in the *Penthouse* magazine.

"It looked kind of neat," I said. "Would you ever take a bath with someone?"

"Yes. I think I would."

"Oh. Okay."

"Well, later, when my parents go for groceries, we can take a bath together at my house if you want. We shouldn't do it if they're home. They might get mad. You want to?"

"For real?"

"Sure." She laughed. "It sounds like fun. It's just a bath, anyway. Why? Are you scared?"

I was scared. I never thought she would react like that, like it was completely no big deal at all for us to take a bath together. But that's how Emily was. She never read anything into anything.

Maybe that's why things like my ear didn't matter to her.

"Of course I'm not scared," I said. "I drive cars and blow things up at night."

I was really scared.

I left my shoes on the porch, my jacket and Bosten's cap on the coat tree, and followed Emily upstairs. She stopped at the cupboard in the hallway and pulled out two big green towels.

"Do you like bubbles or no bubbles?" she asked.

I had to take a deep breath. I felt dizzy.

"Bubbles," I squeaked.

She turned around and reached behind me. That was the door to the bathroom.

Emily said, "You wait out here. I'll tell you when to come in."

"Okay."

I stood there, leaning against the wall beside the door, listening to the sound

of the water

filling the tub.

My knees shook, and my stomach felt like a galloping horse. But for Emily, it was nothing. Just a bubble bath with a friend.

After what seemed like an hour, the water stopped.

"Okay. You can come in now."

I'd been in that bathroom at least a hundred times, but never with Emily sitting there, naked in a bathtub full of bubbles and steaming water. The room was all white, lacquered walls, white cool tiles beneath my socks, sunlight streaming in through gauze drapes, just the slightest fog on the mirror, our towels laid out on the floor, and there was Emily, the bubbles frothing up to her chin, with her hair clipped up on top of her head. I think that was the first time I ever noticed her neck, how perfect it was.

If I tried to talk, I know I would have gagged.

It was like being in heaven.

Or in a magazine.

Then I noticed her clothes had been folded, so neatly with her panties on top, and left on the counter beside the sink.

"You can turn on the radio if you want," she said.

My hand didn't work so good.

When the sound came on, the Kingston DJ was saying something about the UFO attack last night, and then he started laughing, playing "It Came Out of the Sky" by Creedence. I turned it down.

"Was that *really* you guys?"

I nodded.

She asked, "Do you want me to close my eyes?"

I shook my head.

"It's really nice and warm," she said. She didn't look away.

I took off my shirt and undershirt. I tried to fold them, but that wasn't working out. I put them down next to Emily's clothes. I took a quick breath and slid my jeans off. I just left them on the floor. Then my socks. They looked like dead white bunnies next to my jeans.

Practically everyone I knew from eighth grade had seen me naked. Well, boys, I mean. It's just how it was since we all took showers together in a really big, open locker room, every day after gym class. I had friends besides Emily, and they'd all seen me naked. So I just told myself it was no big deal, and this was just another friend.

I tried to calm myself down, inhaled, and finally, I pulled

down my underwear. I stepped my feet free of them and felt the coolness of the floor tiles under my naked toes. Then I just stood there, not really sure what I was supposed to do next.

It didn't feel sexy or nasty or anything else, because Emily was my friend, and that's all there was to it.

In fact, after I got out of my underwear, I felt totally comfortable and relaxed standing in front of her.

In front of Emily, I never felt ashamed about anything.

She watched me the whole time I undressed, and after that, too, when I just stood there like a dummy, wondering what to do.

And she said, "I've never seen a naked boy before."

I shrugged. "Most of us have hair here." I drew a circle in the air around my nuts. "I don't yet. Just some under my arms. See?"

I lifted my right arm and pulled a few strands of hair straight between my finger and thumb.

"Are you going to get in the water, or what?"

I took the two endless steps to the edge of the tub, and Emily scooted over for me. I got in the water and sat down beside her. Our feet touched. Our legs rubbed together. We couldn't help it, and when I leaned back to rest against the deep side of the tub, my back pressed softly against her shoulder.

And I felt the skin of her butt against mine.

I didn't know what to do with my hands, so I just kept them cupped on my knees.

"This is fun," she said.

"Yeah."

What else could I say? I couldn't even pay attention to the radio, my heart was beating so hard inside my skull.

Emily moved.

She began washing off my neck and shoulders with a wet cloth.

I never felt anything as good as that in my entire life.

"You have all this hair stuck to you," she said.

"I got a haircut today."

She kept washing me, squeezing out water that trickled down between my shoulder blades.

"You should always

take a bath

after a haircut."

"I am."

She laughed.

I said, "We are only allowed to take baths on Saturday and Sunday nights. That's the rules, since we have to take showers at school every day, anyhow."

"Oh."

She had a small plastic tub, one that used to hold soft margarine. She dipped it into the water in front of my chest. "Close your eyes."

She poured the water, slow and warm, over my head. Then I felt something cold running through my hair. I jerked.

"It's just shampoo," she said. "Relax."

It smelled like candy.

"We don't use shampoo," I said. "Us boys don't."

She began rubbing my head with her fingers. Both of her hands were on me, massaging.

"That feels . . . smells so good."

"Close your eyes, I'm going to rinse."

"Okay."

She kept pouring the water over me, combing it through my hair with her hands. Then she said, "This is conditioner."

And something else, cold and thick, oozed over my head.

"What's it for?"

"It makes your hair soft and smell good."

It felt like being a king in a palace.

"There," she said. "You look beautiful. Now, let's go have lunch."

Just like that.

That was Emily.

I stood up, wiped the bubbles from my skin, and stepped out of the tub, dripping on the tiles of the floor. I dried myself as quickly as I could while Emily sat in the bath and watched me struggle at getting all my clothes back on, my shirt tucked in.

I felt new.

I looked at my hair in the mirror.

It looked real nice.

"Sorry about the water on the floor," I said. "Uh . . . I'll wait for you outside."

"I'll clean it up," Emily said.

I opened the door, and she called out after me, "That was really cool, Stick. A great idea. We should do it again sometime."

I said, "Yeah. We should. Again."

I closed the door and waited for her in the hallway.

I was so confused.

I wanted to tell Bosten about what we did, but I thought that wouldn't be nice to Emily.

It wasn't anything like the stupid magazine, either.

It wasn't sexy at all.

At least, not magazine sexy.

It was something else that I never heard of before.

Mrs. Lohman always left a lunch prepared for us on Saturdays when they'd go to do their marketing in town. That Saturday, it was tuna sandwiches and apple pie.

Emily sat to my left at the kitchen table, like it was nothing at all that we had just taken a bath together.

I watched her as she bit into her sandwich. But I felt bad, like I had stolen something from Mrs. Lohman, and it didn't feel right for me to be sitting there, eating her food, so I left it on my plate and watched Emily.

"What's wrong?" she said.

"Nothing."

"Okay."

"Maybe I should go home."

I never left Emily's house this early on a Saturday.

"I don't know why you have to be so weirded out, Stick. We didn't do anything bad. It was really nice, in fact. You take showers with other kids every day, right?"

I nodded.

"Well?" she said.

"That was the coolest thing I ever did in my life, Emily," I admitted.

"See? Now eat your sandwich."

"Uh . . . thank you for washing my hair. And the conditioner stuff. Nobody's ever done that to me. Ever."

"You're welcome."

I picked up half of my sandwich. Mrs. Lohman always cut sandwiches diagonally. I liked that.

"Did you mean it, Em? About how you think we should do that again some time?"

"Not if you're going to get all weirded out about it, 'cause it's no big deal."

"I promise I will not get weirded out next time."

"Then eat your sandwich and let's walk down to the beach."

BOSTEN

The rule was I'd have to be home before the sun went behind the trees lining the western side of the gravel driveway that led to our house.

It was the best day of my life.

I ran my hand through my hair and sniffed it.

In the mudroom, I took off my shoes and jacket. I carried Bosten's cap in my hands and cautiously stepped into the living room. Everything inside smelled like cigarettes and salmon frying in the kitchen.

Dad fished every weekend.

He was watching television when I came in. He looked up at me, to make sure I didn't have a hat on my head, then he pulled another cigarette out from his pack and yelled toward the kitchen, "He's back."

I heard Mom cough or something, and Dad looked at me again, harder, and said, "What's the matter with *you?*"

"Huh? Oh. Nothing. Dad."

Sometimes, in our house, for me and Bosten, it was like being bugs in baby food jars.

And I'd tiptoe everywhere. I couldn't ever hear myself, but I wondered how noisy I made their world, them having two ears and all.

I slid around behind the television, still carrying Bosten's cap. I glanced down the hallway, quickly, hoping Dad wouldn't notice I was looking. The old key was sticking out beneath the knob on the door to the spare room.

That meant Bosten was still in there.

Just as I got to the top of the basement staircase, Dad said,

"Get Bosten some clothes and tell him to take his shower before dinner. He can come out now."

"Okay."

Bosten's room was the next door across the hallway from the spare room. Mom and Dad's bedroom was on the top floor. We never went up there. When I passed the door to the spare room, I tapped my finger on it twice so he'd know I was coming.

I left Bosten's cap on his bed and grabbed clean clothes and a towel for him.

I was happy for my brother. It seemed like years had passed since the game last night.

I put all the stuff I'd grabbed on the bottom stair at the end of the hall. I looked back only once to make sure nobody was watching me, and then I carefully went up to Mom's bathroom.

It wasn't anything like Emily's bathroom. Mom's smelled like cigarettes and the kind of flowery soap my English teacher used. There was a small blue jar of hand cream sitting beside the sink, with lots of other strange-looking women's things scattered around, too. I didn't have the first idea about what those things could be used for.

I thought those were the kinds of things they should show women using in magazines, because the sex stuff didn't teach me anything real at all.

I stole her jar of hand cream. I slipped it inside my shirt, then buttoned it up and went back downstairs to get my brother.

I turned the key and opened the door to the dark little room.

Bosten was lying on the cot, covered by a sheet. He was on his side with his back to me, so I couldn't tell if he was sleeping or not. The steel pail was on the floor at the foot of the bed.

I put Bosten's clothes and towel down next to his feet.

"Hey," I whispered. I kneeled down next to him. "Dad said

you can come out now, and for you to take a shower before dinner."

"Okay."

"I'll clean the room and take the pail out."

Bosten didn't say anything.

"Are you okay?"

"Yeah."

"Let me see. Okay?"

I pulled the sheet down, away from Bosten's shoulders, so I could see his back.

We'd both been beaten plenty of times before. This was one of the bad ones. It happened every so often.

"It's pretty bad," I said.

From the middle of his shoulder blades, past his butt and onto his thighs, Bosten was streaked with purple welts. Some of the marks that were raised had actually bled; all of them, angled up like slashes, like fractions with no numbers.

I whispered, lower, "Turn flat. I'm going to put something on it to make you feel better."

Bosten rolled flat onto his belly. He rested his chin on his forearm and stared at the wall at the head of the bed.

"I   hate them."

I saw a shadow from behind, in the doorway.

Dad heard what Bosten said.

I saw it in his eyes.

Dad didn't say anything. He pulled a drag from his cigarette and quietly walked back down the hall toward the living room.

"He heard you."

"I   don't   care."

I unbuttoned my shirt, remembered what I'd been carrying in my pocket all day.

I unfolded the newspaper clipping and held it in front of Bosten's face.

"Look at this," I said. "We have invaded. All Earthlings must surrender or die."

My brother looked at me and smiled.

I said, "You know. You really are my hero, Bosten."

"Shut up." Bosten turned his face back to the picture of our UFO, the story about the panicked farmer who snapped it with his Brownie camera. "But this is fucking cool, Sticker."

While Bosten read the clipping, I unscrewed the cap to Mom's hand cream. It was cold and felt like lard between my fingers.

"Does this hurt?" I began tracing the lines of Bosten's wounds with the cream.

"No. It feels good."

"I'm going to sneak it down to my room. I can put some more on after your shower."

"If Mom finds that, it's going to be you in here."

"Don't worry about that. I'm throwing it out in the incinerator tonight."

While Bosten showered, I cleaned the spare room.

Saint Fillan's room.

I had to replace the sheet and bedspread with clean ones, so that the room actually looked like a guest room—which it definitely was not—in case any visitors happened down that hallway. The door was only kept shut if someone was inside, and nobody ever stayed in that room in my entire life except for me or Bosten.

I thought, my parents are very unhappy, but me and Bosten aren't.

Not yet.

Sometimes I wondered about what made them that way, but Bosten told me that things don't make people the way they are. He said it's not like catching a cold or something.

You just *are*.

So Bosten said, "I did the math, Sticker." And he figured that *he* was the first mistake that ruined their lives.

"Look at me," I said. "I am number two."

Now *that's* math.

The pail always had to be emptied into the incinerator pit, then hosed clean with bleach and water. Then it had to be left, upside down, on the rocks beside our well house.

That was how we had to do it.

Then, after dinner, I'd have to go get the pail and put it back inside the empty closet in the dark spare room.

I threw Mom's hand cream in the incinerator, too.

PAUL

In the morning, Dad went fishing with Ian Buckley.

He left before we got out of bed.

Mom never cooked breakfast. Breakfast for Mom was a cigarette and two or three cups of coffee with sugar and half-and-half. Bosten and I ate toast with apple butter. Bosten couldn't sit with his back against the chair. The night before, Dad got mad at him for leaning forward at dinner, so Bosten had to sit back.

On Sunday afternoon, we were going over to the Buckleys'. When the dads got home from fishing, we would have dinner and then the grown-ups would drink and smoke and play cards until we had to go home.

Mr. Buckley smoked a pipe.

When I was small, even before I talked much at all, I thought Mr. Buckley's pipe was magic, because it always made smoke and never seemed to go out.

I liked those nights.

Nobody cared at all about what we boys did.

It was like the bugs had escaped from the bottle.

Mom made potato salad in the kitchen.

I stole into the living room and quietly dialed Emily's number on the telephone next to Dad's chair. On the seventh ring, her mother answered.

"Hello, this is the Lohman residence."

"Oh. Hello, Mrs. Lohman. It's Stark."

I felt guilty just talking to her. I felt myself going pale.

"Who are you talking to?"

Mom stood in the doorway. She held a knife in one hand and a cigarette in the other.

She didn't like me talking on the phone. She said it was a bad habit for boys my age to get into. I guess she probably believed that telephones were like gateway drugs to jacking off.

I could have set her straight on that.

For boys, oxygen is a gateway drug to jacking off.

"Um. It's Mrs. Lohman, Mom. I was calling to speak with Emily."

"Stick? Do you want to speak with Emily?"

"Yes, ma'am."

Mom shrugged and spun back into the kitchen, trailing smoke like our UFO behind her. "I want you off that phone in two minutes."

"Yes, ma'am."

Mrs. Lohman couldn't tell I was talking to Mom.

"Is everything all right, Stick?"

How could I have done that to her?

Mrs. Lohman was the nicest person in the world.

"Yes, ma'am. Everything is fine."

"Emily said you two had a great time together
yesterday."

I almost felt like I would throw up, thinking how much of a goddamned liar I was.

"We had fun."

"We love having you over, Stick.
I hope you know that.
Maybe for Easter vacation, you
can come over and
spend a couple of nights here at our house."

"That would be nice. Thank you, Mrs. Lohman."

"I'll talk to your parents about it. Ask them for you."

"Thank you."

"You hang on, sweetie, and I'll get her."

I chewed my lip. I think it started to bleed.

Finally, Emily came to the phone.

"Hey, Stick."

"Em."

"What's up?"

"Uh. I just wanted to say hi. 'Cause I can't come over today, since we're going to the Buckleys' house."

"You sound weird. Are you weirded out again?"

"No. Really. It's just I felt bad talking to your mom is all, and I felt bad about Bosten getting in trouble because of me. Dad whipped him pretty bad. And I mostly really wished we could hang out together today."

I could hear Emily cupping her hand around the mouthpiece of the phone. And she whispered,

"I bet I know why you wanted to hang out today."

I sighed. "That's not why."

"What time are you leaving?"

"Mom has to make potato salad. We're on potato salad time. I think that's probably an hour and a half."

"Good. We went to Poulsbo last night to see a movie, and I got something for you."

"You did?"

"I'm bringing it over."

I felt myself turning red. It was different for me. Emily never made me feel like this before. Maybe I was *weirded out*.

"Time to get off the phone," Mom called from the kitchen.

"Uh. I got to hang up now, Em."

"I'll be there in, like, ten minutes."

"Okay."

Bosten knew something was up when he saw me getting my shoes and jacket on in the mudroom.

"Can I wear your cap?" I asked.

"Where are you going?"

"Meeting Emily at the road."

"Can I come, too?"

"Uh. Yeah."

I didn't want him to. I felt like if he saw us together, he'd know we did something bad.

But what could I do? By the time I was out the door, he had already returned with his cap and started following after me down the gravel drive.

"Don't you want this?" Bosten trotted up behind me, waving his DWHS ball cap.

"Oh."

I brushed my hand over my hair; resisted the urge to sniff it and see if the smell of Emily's conditioner was still there. I knew it couldn't be, anyway. Everything in our house smelled like cigarettes.

"Thanks," I said.

"Is something wrong?" Bosten asked.

"No. Em said she got something for me."

Bosten said, "Oh."

But the way he said "oh" wasn't just an "oh." It was a whole soliloquy.

So I said, "Yeah."

We saw her coming through the gate by where the mailboxes sat, crooked on rotten posts. I noticed Bosten slowed down, dropped a few feet back, when we got closer.

She was holding something black in her hand.

I said, "Hi."

"Hey. Hey, Bosten."

I turned around and saw Bosten nodded at her.

"Well, here," she said. "I got this for you. I know you guys probably got to leave soon."

She held out her hand to me. She had a Pittsburgh Steelers wool beanie.

"I thought you would like this."

It was amazing.

"That's the coolest thing ever, Em. Thanks!"

Well, I thought, it wasn't the coolest thing, not compared to what we did the day before.

"I figured you'd need a new one."

"You heard about that?" Bosten said. He took his cap from my head and put it on.

"I would have paid to have been there and seen Ricky get punched for that."

I put the beanie on, pulled it down over my ears. It felt so good. "You couldn't have been there, Em. It happened in the boys' pisser."

Emily smiled.

"And we left him there, on the floor, laying in a puddle of piss and blood," Bosten said.

Emily looked at Bosten. "Why don't you teach him how to punch like that?"

"He knows how to punch," Bosten said. "Believe me."

"Well, it looks good on you, Stick," she said.

I felt myself going red again. I wanted to kick something for being so dumb. I looked back at my brother, and I could see he felt awkward being there, too, which made me feel even more flushed.

"Thanks, Em. I'll see you at the bus stop tomorrow."

"Okay," she said.

And as I turned around and started heading back up to the house, she called out, "And it does look good on you."

On the way back up the drive, Bosten walked right beside me. One time, he bumped his shoulder against mine and said, in that same tone that meant he knew everything without me or him saying it, "Oh."

And then he said, "Sorry for getting in the way with you and Em, Sticker."

But Bosten would never be in the way.

Mom and Dad gave me things on birthdays and Christmas.

But nobody ever gave me anything just to give me something before that day.

Mom sat up front, in the same spot where I'd gotten a boner two nights before looking at Dad's jack-off magazine. She held a big orange Tupperware bowl of potato salad hammocked between her spread thighs in the sling of her parrot dress.

Her dress was blue, and had orange and red parrots and bright green bamboo on it.

I wondered if parrots really lived in bamboo forests, or if, maybe, the artist in charge of Mom's dress just figured parrots plus bamboo equals fun.

She lit a cigarette with the same dashboard lighter that had last been used to burn Bosten and Paul's joints the night of the UFO invasion.

I swear the thing still smelled like pot when she pulled it out, but she didn't seem to notice.

Bosten was stiff and slow getting in behind the steering wheel.

He moaned when he sat down. I couldn't hear it, but I knew he did.

Mom couldn't drive a stick.

Especially with that bowl of potato salad sitting on the lap of her parrot dress.

I could see how much it hurt him to sit down like that. His eyes were wet.

"Are you going to be okay?" I asked. The car was already fogged with Mom's smoke.

Bosten started to say something, but it just came out as,

"Eh."

"I could drive."

Mom turned around, but she couldn't really look straight at me. I was sitting directly behind her. That was the only seat in the car where I could hear what was going on.

I could see Bosten's eyes in the rearview mirror. I knew what he was thinking.

"Well. I'm tall enough. I've seen Bosten do it enough times. I'm sure I could do it."

"You're crazy if you think I'm going to allow a

thirteen-year-old child to operate an automobile." And Mom turned around sharply, to accent her decision, but the bowl of potato salad nearly spilled onto Bosten.

"It's okay, Stick." I could tell Bosten was nervous.

"There's nothing wrong with you," Mom decided. "Stop being such a baby and drive."

Then she put her hand, softly, on Bosten's shoulder. I knew she was trying to be sympathetic and kind, but she just wasn't very good at it.

She said, "And what's that on your head, Stick?"

I felt myself shrinking down into the seat.

"Emily gave it to me."

"That was very nice of her."

Bosten glanced at me in the mirror.

He winked.

The Buckley house was huge, and the surrounding property had a long bank of shoreline with its own dock where Paul's father kept two boats—one for sailing, and the smaller one he and Dad took out that morning to fish on the Sound.

The three of us hung out in Paul's bedroom while our moms sat in the sunroom and smoked.

"How bitchin' is that?" Paul asked. He'd already pinned the clipping from the front page of the newspaper on the wall above his bed.

"We are taking over the planet," I said.

"Ha-ha. You're not taking over anything, Stick. You were sitting in the car looking at porn when me and Bosten lit that shit off."

I liked Paul, but sometimes when Bosten wasn't around, he could be mean to me. Once in a while, like today, he made it obvious that he wished I wasn't hanging around him and my older brother. And at times like those, Bosten kind of played along with it, too.

I understood. I thought I knew what a pain it might be, always having a little kid hanging around. Especially one like me.

"Lay off Stick," Bosten said. "If he wasn't with us, we probably would have gotten into a hell of a lot of trouble."

I gave Paul a dirty look. "And you need to give us that magazine back, by the way."

"Okay." Paul said, "Why don't I just give it to your mom right now, then?"

I sat down on Paul's bed like I didn't care about anything. I knew he was full of it. So I said, "Because you don't have the balls. That's why."

Paul got down onto his hands and knees and reached between my feet, digging around under his bed.

"Oh yeah? Just watch me."

Then Bosten said, "Real funny, Buck." He jumped onto Paul's back like he was wrestling an alligator or something and had his friend pinned, facedown into the carpet, in no more than three seconds.

Paul laughed. "Okay. Okay. I wasn't going to do it."

"Don't have the balls to," I said.

Bosten looked at me. He tried to sound serious, but his eyes told me it was a joke, "How much more shit are you going to cause for me this weekend, Stick?"

And I knew he was only joking, but it still made me feel bad.

Jokes do that, sometimes.

So I said, "Sorry, Buck."

"It's all fun. It's all fun," Paul grunted. "You mind getting off me now, Bosten?"

Then I heard Mom calling for me, shouting from down the

hallway, in the Buckleys' sunroom. That's how they did things. They never came and got us, never came to us at all, only yelled when they needed us to do something.

"Stick!"

I took a deep breath. "Be right back."

I slipped my new Steelers cap off my head and stuffed it into my back pocket as I headed down the hallway to where Mom and Mrs. Buckley were waiting for me.

The sunroom extended from the back of the house, surrounded by windows that faced out on the small harbor where the Buckleys' neighbors all kept boats. The polished wood floor was slick under my socks, and I had to resist the strong temptation to skate on it.

Mom and Mrs. Buckley sat beside each other on a short blue sofa. They drank coffee; and both of them had cigarettes, tilted and burning, resting in an ashtray. Mrs. Buckley looked so pretty that I actually was embarrassed and felt a lump in my throat when I saw her, thinking about how I got a boner when she put her hand on my knee at Paul's basketball game.

Something was happening to me.

All of a sudden.

Everything was changing.

I didn't think I liked it very much.

Then she said, "Stark, I can't believe how tall you've gotten! And to imagine all three of you boys will be in high school together next year. You should think about going out for the basketball team with Paul. Wouldn't that be nice?"

I *had* thought about it.

And I felt weak in my legs with Mrs. Buckley smiling, glowing, looking me up and down. I tried willing myself to not get an erection, but that kind of thinking always has a reverse-psychology effect on my penis.

"I'm not good enough to," I said.

"Oh, of course you are," she said, brushing my arm with her fingers.

Then Mom took a last drag from her cigarette, and every word came out in a haze of smoke. "Joy said that Bosten told her a different story than what Mr. Dostal said to us about the fight with Ricky."

Dad never
asked us what happened.
He never asked at all.
He was too busy
beating
the shit
out of my brother.
He didn't care what happened.
You held me there,
with your hands pulling my hair so I wouldn't look away.
You are
both so angry at us.
Why would you care
what we had to say?
As long as we'd
stand
still.

"Uh. I don't know what Mr. Dostal told you," I said.

Then Mrs. Buckley looked at me. Her eyes were so soft and blue. "Bosten said Ricky started the fight in the bathroom."

I shrugged. I thought, how long could these people live here and think Ricky Dostal *wasn't* the one who was always starting fights? "Well, Ricky did. Bosten would never start a fight with no one."

Then I kind of got mad, and looked directly at Mom and

said, "Dad never asked us what happened. Neither one of you did."

And Mom said, "Don't get that tone with me, young man."

I glanced at Mrs. Buckley. I could tell she felt uncomfortable, and I was certain I'd hear about my "tone" later, after we got home.

"I'm sorry, Mom."

She pressed her lips together and took in a breath through her nose.

"I left an extra pack of cigarettes in the glove box. Run out and get them for me."

And I was relieved to be out of the spotlight for the moment. I spun around on my socks.

"Yes, ma'am."

Paul and Bosten took the opportunity to play Ditch Stick while I was in the sunroom. When I got back to Paul's bedroom, they were gone.

They did that kind of stuff all the time, and Paul's property had so many hiding places I almost always lost the game.

"Screw you both," I said to the empty room. "Let's see who drives home next time you guys decide you want to get stoned."

And for just a moment, I thought about looking for Dad's magazine under the bed, but I was afraid of the disgusting stuff Paul Buckley was probably hiding under there, how I might touch it with my bare hands. So I snuck out through the side door and headed down toward the boat dock to look for my brother and him.

It was a false-spring day, the kind of day where boys in Washington would play outside shirtless, as though all that pale, winter-bleached skin could act as some kind of magic charm to turn the seasons. I even considered taking my own shirt off as I walked out onto the Buckleys' dock and checked around their sailboat for my brother and Paul. Out at the entrance to the harbor, I could see the small aluminum boat coming back in from the Sound, with Dad and Mr. Buckley riding in it, bouncing up and down on the troughs of the chop as they got nearer.

I turned and headed out along a deer trail that led into the woods.

I wandered around the property for about twenty minutes and was about to give up looking for Paul and Bosten, when I caught a glimpse of them through a break in the trees. I noticed them because they had their shirts off, and the whiteness of Paul's skin was like a spotlight shining in the woods.

Bosten was standing under a bare dogwood tree.

They were kissing each other.

Not just kissing—Paul and Bosten were *making out*. They had their mouths open and their jaws pumped, opening and closing like they were chewing on each other's tongues. It wasn't a trick or a game, either. I could tell it wasn't, by how lovingly Bosten stroked his hand through Paul's hair.

I'd heard about stuff like that. Boys constantly teased about it at school, but until that day, I never honestly thought it was real, or that I'd ever know any other boys who actually wanted to do things like that with each other.

I was scared and ashamed at the same time.

It was like watching my house catch fire, but I couldn't look away, because how many times do you ever get to see a house burn down?

Paul unbuckled Bosten's belt and slipped his hand down inside my brother's jeans. Paul started kissing my brother's chest and belly. Then he pulled Bosten's jeans and underwear all the way down to his feet.

Then, after that, I'm not going to say what happened. It's

because what happened next wasn't ever about me. It was about my brother and Paul.

I knew I had to get out of there and leave them alone and never talk about it to Bosten.

Let him and Paul do whatever they wanted to do. It wasn't my business, and I shouldn't have been there. I suddenly felt so sad for Bosten, like I was hurting him or I was doing something wrong. But I didn't even think Bosten was doing anything "wrong" with Paul. It was just surprising to me, I guess.

Just then, Bosten opened his eyes and looked right at me.

I turned and ran.

And I know Bosten yelled something. There was a kind of urgent and pleading sound behind me, but I couldn't hear anything anymore, except my feet crashing through the brush, slipping on slick spots of mud and leaves.

I just ran.

I was stupid to think I might outrun Paul Buckley.

When he caught up to me from behind—I couldn't hear him at all—he pushed me, square between my shoulder blades; and I fell, face-first, into a tangle of thorny blackberry vines.

It hurt.

My hands and wrists started bleeding, cut with little slashes from the thorns, and I was completely out of breath. I turned over and saw Paul standing behind me. He had a crazed look on his face. His cheeks were red, and his stomach and chest pumped nervously.

"What the fuck do you think you're doing?"

I didn't know what to say. I was so scared that Paul was going to do something crazy.

He took a step toward me. His neck was bulging. He looked like he could explode. Paul punched the air and kicked the brush next to my feet. He screamed,

"WHAT THE FUCK, STICK?"

I stared directly into Paul's eyes, but neither of us backed down and looked away.

I felt the tickle of blood running from my wrist down toward my hand.

"I . . . I'm sorry, Buck. It's . . . I didn't . . ."

Paul ranted, "What did you see? What did you see?"

I didn't want to answer him.

"If you say anything about this to anyone, I'll fucking . . ."

Then he took another step toward me, leaning heavily on one leg. He was going to kick me. But by that time, Bosten had caught up to us.

"Hey! Cool it!"

Paul glanced back, then he relaxed.

Bosten had gotten his clothes back on, but his shirt hung open, and his belt dangled, unbuckled and jangling. He carried Paul's basketball sweatshirt with him.

Bosten looked at me, but quickly turned his eyes back on Paul.

My brother looked sick, worn-out. Pale. He fired an angry look at Paul. "What did you do?"

Before Paul could say anything, I answered, "I tripped. Buck didn't do anything."

Paul looked down, and Bosten handed him his shirt. "Here," he said.

Paul slipped it on and turned around, making it obvious that he didn't want to look at either one of us.

It was so quiet.

The three of us seemed frozen in place.

"I'm sorry, Bosten."

My brother shrugged.

"For what?"

"If you guys would have told me to leave you alone, I would have left you alone."

"I know that."

Paul stood, facing away from us. He pulled his hood up over his head. He rubbed his eyes, then put his hands in his pockets.

Bosten reached out for me. "Come on. Get up."

"There's blood on my hands."

"Let me see."

He fumbled at buckling his belt, and gave me an embarrassed kind of smirk as he straightened his clothing. Then he kneeled down and began pulling the dried vines from around my ankles.

"It's not too bad," I said. I held my palms up in front of me, turned them over. The cuts stung, and the sleeves of my flannel had bloodstains around the cuffs.

"Here." Bosten grabbed my hand and grunted as he pulled me to my feet.

"They're ringing the bell," Paul said.

I couldn't hear it.

Mrs. Buckley had a big brass bell hanging outside the back of the house. She'd use it to get Paul back inside.

I followed them. Paul never once looked at me the whole way back to his house.

Not one of us said a word to one another.

Mom and Dad were sitting in the living room with Paul's father when we got to the house. Mrs. Buckley waited at the door, sweeping her arm down the hallway with instructions for us to clean up for dinner in Paul's bathroom.

She noticed the blood on my hands and sleeves and stopped me, alarmed and looking so soft and concerned.

"Stark! What happened to your arms?"

Paul and Bosten froze in the hallway.

"Oh. We were just playing around and I fell in some blackberries."

"It looks awful!" she said. "Paul, bring the Bactine out here."

She put her hand on my shoulder and pushed me inside the kitchen, toward the sink. She ran the water, testing it with the back of her arm. I watched as it ran over her peach-fuzz skin. Then she turned to me and began unbuttoning my shirt.

I thought I was going to pass out.

This was the most insane day I could ever imagine.

Actually, I don't think I ever could have imagined it.

"Let's get this off you, honey." Mrs. Buckley pulled my shirttails up out of my jeans. My dick was so hard, I thought she must have noticed, but I couldn't say or do anything. I felt like a fish, just lying there, yawning my useless gills.

She balled my shirt up and dropped it on the kitchen counter. Then she gently grabbed my arms and began bathing them under the warm flow of water, stroking my skin, cleaning away the dried blood and dirt.

Mrs. Buckley turned the water off.

"You stay there, Stark. I'm going to throw this shirt in the washer. I'll be right back."

I followed her out with my eyes.

Bosten and Paul stood behind me with the first-aid spray.

And Paul said, "Please don't say anything, Stick. I'm sorry I got mad."

He sounded weak.

I whispered, "Why would I say anything? Why would I do something like that to my own brother? You're my friend, too, Buck."

Bosten stared down at his feet and shook his head.

Mrs. Buckley came back in, carrying a towel and a clean

sweatshirt for me. It was one of Paul's basketball sweats. She toweled off my arms and sprayed my cuts with Bactine.

It stung and smelled good at the same time.

Then Mrs. Buckley handed me the sweatshirt. "I'm certain this will fit you. You're just as tall as Paul."

Paul and Bosten quietly stared at me while I put it on.

DAD AND MOM

Paul had his own color television set in his bedroom.

The Buckleys even had a special cable service that let him watch R-rated movies. I'd never heard cussing or seen naked breasts on television before I watched TV in Paul's room.

After dinner, our parents all played cards and drank. Dad and Mr. Buckley were already drunk when they came back from fishing, anyway. I was glad for that because I was still worried that Mom would say something after we got home about how disrespectful I was to her in front of Mrs. Buckley.

And that would most likely mean I'd spend the night in the spare room.

Sometimes, Mom and Dad forgot things when they'd had enough to drink.

So the three of us watched television with the lights off in Paul's room. It was hard for me to pay attention, though. My brain was too full of other stuff.

Mostly, I wanted to talk to my brother.

I sat on the floor, cross-legged, in front of the television. Paul and Bosten were up on the bed. Paul had his arm around

Bosten and leaned his head against Bosten's cheek. They rubbed their bare feet together. I heard him say,

"It doesn't matter what we do or say in front of him anymore."

And I tried not to listen.

One time, while we were watching a comedian, I heard Bosten say, "Don't!"

And then they both laughed and wrestled on the bed.

But I did not turn around to see what it was that he was telling Paul to not do.

I wished I could just disappear and leave them alone.

Mom and Dad took the Pontiac home that night.

Bosten and I drove back home together in the small car.

It started out awfully. Neither one of us knew what to say; and it had never been like that between us before. Never in my life.

Bosten didn't even look at me once.

Finally, when we got out onto Pilot Point Road, I said, "So. Are you gay or something?"

Then he looked at me. The reflection from the rearview mirror made a white band right across his eyes.

"Yeah."

"Oh."

I wondered if it mattered. What that meant to me.

"And Paul?"

Bosten laughed a little. "Duh. What do you think?"

"Well, I've seen him with so many girls all the time."

I was glad he smiled. Then he cleared his throat and said, "To be honest, I don't know about Buck. Maybe he just likes . . . well, doing it. I can't say for sure. We knew for such a long time that we wanted to, but we were scared.

It took me so long to talk him into trying anything with me in the first place."

"It looks like he's adjusted to it pretty good."

Bosten grinned and shoved my shoulder.

"How long have you guys been doing this?"

Bosten pulled the car over on the side of the road. He turned toward me and put his knee up in the space between our seats. For the first time in hours, he finally looked comfortable. Like my brother, Bosten. It made me feel so much better.

We could see the water.

"It started happening last summer."

"Oh."

"Is that all you want to know?"

I chewed on the inside of my lip. "It's kind of weird. I . . . uh. I don't think I'd like for it to happen to me."

Then Bosten laughed for real. "Ha-ha . . . you are such a dumbshit, Stick! It doesn't *happen* to you. It's just how I am. Believe me, I *know* you're not gay."

"I get a boner every time Buck's mom looks at me."

"Ha-ha! Everyone sees it."

I had to swallow. "They do?"

"Heh . . . I thought you were going to bust your zipper in the kitchen tonight."

I felt myself getting hot, turning red again.

"You don't have to worry. I mean, about me saying anything about you or Paul."

"I know that, Stick."

"And it doesn't matter to me about it. Just next time, tell me to leave you guys alone."

"Shut up."

"What's it feel like, being in love with someone?" I asked.

"It feels really good, Stick. Like how things are always supposed to be."

I wondered if I would ever feel that way.

If anyone might ever feel like that about me.

Bosten started the car. I rolled down my window. It was very cold now.

"Bosten?"

"What?"

"What if they find out?"

He knew what I meant. Mom and Dad.

"You know what Dad said to me yesterday morning? When I was in the room, he said, 'Sixteen is old enough that you can get out any time you don't want to put up with this house. And I won't chase after you.' But you know what? I think he would kill me, Stick. I almost thought he was going to kill me over Ricky."

"Are you scared?"

"Sometimes."

"I don't want nothing bad to happen to you. You have to be careful."

Bosten put his hand out, and I held it.

We didn't need to say anything after that.

It's just how things were.

Everything else could change and go crazy.

But not that.

Next time we went to the Buckleys' for dinner, I watched television in Paul's room by myself.

Mom didn't forget to tell Dad about me.

And he was mad because Bosten and I took so long coming home.

"Where do you get that mouth?" he said. "Where do

you get that goddamned mouth, talking to your mother like that in front of Joy Buckley?"

He pulled me by my neck. His fingers were claws into my flesh, and he threw me over his chair. But he didn't use his belt, only his hand, slapping, stinging like wasps, eating my flesh. He yanked Paul's sweatshirt entirely off me. I thought it would choke me, but it came free and Dad threw it across the floor.

I saw Bosten standing there, watching.

He had to.

That was the rule.

Then Dad pulled at my pants. And he beat my back and legs. He punched me, too, and his hand made a sound that was higher and meatier than the sound his belt would make.

I couldn't help but cry. I was not as tough as Bosten.

I could never be that strong.

My tears felt good and clean, like the water in Mrs. Buckley's sink, and they made a dark circle on Dad's chair. When he was finished, he pulled me up by the back of my arm and marched me down the hallway toward my Saint Fillan's room.

Dad didn't have to stop for me. I knew the rule. I won the race.

"Good night, Mom," I said.

And I added, "Good night, Bosten, I love you." And I almost choked on my words, I was crying so hard, but it felt like winning a game when Bosten said, "I love you, too, little brother."

Then I was pushed onto the cold cot in that dark room. Dad stripped the last of my clothes away. He locked the door.

And this was how everything in the world ever was.

Sometimes Bosten talked about running away.
He had a dream of California.
When we were small,

when Bosten still played,
we liked to play California,
and we would drive on freeways
smoking pretend cigarettes with our arms out the windows.
We believed
boys like us could make our own rules in California.
But I told him I could not run away with him.
I thought they'd put me in mentally retarded school
in California,
and I would miss Emily
too much.

When he was in grade nine, Bosten really did run away.
He was gone for four days.
I was terrified
he was dead.
The police came every day.
He'd gone to Seattle.
When they brought him home, two things happened:
I begged him to promise he would never leave me,
and Dad beat him to exhaustion
and locked him
in this same room.

It was so cold in there I could not sleep.

EMILY

Bosten went off to school. Paul Buckley came and gave him a ride in the morning when I was downstairs getting dressed. If I thought about them being alone together, I would imagine bad things, and I felt that wasn't fair for me to do. But I was jealous because I knew my brother was in love, and I was afraid that Paul was going to take him away from me.

And what else did I have without Bosten?

I didn't get a chance to take my regular Sunday night bath, but it didn't matter. They had to let me out of the room to go to school, and my hands still smelled like Mrs. Buckley's soap. As soon as Mom said I could come out, I ran to the bathroom. I didn't use that pail during the night, because I knew it would sit there the whole day while I was at school, and I'd have to clean it out when I got home.

So I held myself and ran, naked, down the stairs to the basement so I could piss in a toilet just as soon as I heard the key turn in the lock.

I almost didn't make it.

Things like that happened a lot at our house.

I wore my Steelers cap.

I carried a book bag with my things for school, a sack lunch, and my every-Monday-morning-laundered gym clothes, rolled up perfectly, the way Mr. Lloyd showed us he wanted them to be. On the outside, a T-shirt with S. MCCLELLAN (8) showing, written in black marker, wound tightly around the green shorts, white socks, and athletic supporter.

That was another thing they made us do: wear jocks. Mr.

Lloyd would check that off every day, too: which boys were wearing their jocks, and which boys weren't.

For Mr. Lloyd, gym grades depended on two simple things: wearing jocks and taking showers.

I realized, in eighth grade, that physical education was far less about fitness than it was about *fitting*. And how could a kid with only one ear ever be expected to fit in with everyone else, even if he did wear a jock and take his showers every day?

I never understood what jocks did for boys other than make us follow rules. They were supposed to protect our balls, Mr. Lloyd explained, but I'd seen at least a hundred guys who wore jocks and got hit in the balls, and it always seemed to hurt just as bad as if they had their balls hanging out and fully exposed. I mean, a shot to the balls is a shot to the balls, pretty much no matter what you're wearing.

Well, I guess an exception could be a suit of armor, but you can't shoot free throws in one.

Twice per year, the school would line up all the boys so they could weigh us and check our height. Mr. Lloyd would write that down, and the entire class period of boys' gym classes would have to wait in line, by last names, wearing only our jocks, for our turns to have this important information recorded in Mr. Lloyd's book.

To me, it felt like we were all in some kind of cruel Nazi science experiment, but we didn't question it. I realized that it's hard to question rules when you're standing in alphabetical order, waiting in line, freezing and scared, wearing nothing but a jockstrap.

The last time we had weight-check day was in January. Ricky Dostal and Corey Barr, who had gone through the line and been measured by Mr. Lloyd ahead of me, went and put their gym uniforms on and then pulled me out of my place between the other kids with Irish last names. I thought about fighting back, but it was only a thought.

Apparently, being dressed in only a jock makes you even more of a pacifist.

They forced me out of the boys' showers, and pinned me up to the outside wall, facing the tennis courts, with my bare ass cheeks pressed against the icy and damp bricks of the locker room, while the girls' classes all came out from the other side of the building and stared at my freezing, pale near-nakedness. Ricky and Corey announced it was to show all the girls what a retarded one-eared stick looks like wearing nothing but a jock.

Later that day, and for a few more days after that, about half of the girls who'd seen me asked why do boys wear jocks, and I felt like I was lying when I said, "Because they keep our balls safe."

My jock never kept anything safe on me.

Thinking about it that day, as I dutifully carried with me my cleanly laundered jock, perfectly rolled up inside my gym clothes, I thought Corey and Ricky must have been two of the "key guys" who Emily thought I should grow some balls and punch.

I had balls.

But I wasn't sure how punching someone would make me feel like having balls made a difference.

It was St. Patrick's Day.

Emily waited for me by the mailboxes.

She had a green scarf slung around her neck. I noticed her so much more now.

All of a sudden.

And I wore a green flannel shirt, buttoned, tucked into my jeans, of course, with a white undershirt beneath it. She smiled as I walked toward the mailboxes. It was a smile that said she approved of my green.

I am Irish, after all.

"Neither one of us gets pinched," she said.

"The crab kids will have to leave us alone."

Once, while we walked in the quiet woods last summer, I told her the story of my name.

"Sometimes," I said, "names make you the opposite of what they say."

"Oh."

"It's supposed to be strong and unyielding," I explained. "Stark. It couldn't be farther from the truth if it meant 'boy with two ears.' "

"I don't like that," she said.

"What? My name? Neither do I."

"No. I like your name. Stark."

That was the first time I can remember Emily saying it, and she made it sound almost musical.

"But I don't like it when you make fun of yourself."

"Oh. Okay."

"So you're not allowed to do it in front of me anymore."

"Okay."

"Because it's nice to have a friend like you."

"No girls would probably catch crabs with you. Or hang out at our fort."

She nodded. "But when you make fun of yourself, it's like saying anyone who really likes you is a loser or something."

She made everything sound easy.

"The other name, McClellan, has a story."

We'd stopped next to a fallen tree. It was stair-stepped with white mushrooms, jutting out from its mossy trunk, and stacked in layers like trophied ghostly ears. In the dark gap ahead, between the trees, was our plywood fort.

"It means 'son of the servant of Saint Fillan.' That name, I think, says who we are."

"Who is Saint Fillan?" Emily poked a stick into the narrow cleft between the mushrooms.

"He was the patron saint for the insane. His left arm glowed, so he could see in the dark. And the mentally retarded people would take a bath in Saint Fillan's pool. Then they would be chained to a cot all night. And, in the mornings, if the chains were loose, it meant they were cured. Just like that. So, me and Bosten, we are the sons of the servant of Saint Fillan."

"Do you believe in that?" Emily had a look of wonder.

I said, "Yes. You can't make stuff like that up."

"Well, someone does."

We were the only two kids who ever waited at that bus stop.

And I wasn't what Emily would call "weirded out" over anything specific on that Monday morning. It was just that the entire weekend—beginning with Emily softly touching my ear (and I couldn't get the sensation of her fingers out of my thoughts) and Friday night's UFO invasion, to winding up in punishment last night and everything in between—ricocheted around in my head and made me feel like I was choking back an explosion.

Everything was changing.

I felt sick, and Emily could see it.

"Are you all right?"

"I think maybe I'm getting sick."

"You should stay home from school."

"I'd rather drink poison."

"I would ditch school with you if you wanted to," she said.

"Could we take a bath?" I teased.

"No. My mom's home. She wouldn't understand." Emily's matter-of-factness, again, told me she didn't think there was anything more complex to our bath-taking than the simple sharing of some time together.

Like catching crabs on the beach.

Emily.

"Yeah," I said glumly. "So's mine."

"I guess we might as well go to school then."

That was Emily.

Perfect.

There was a special bench in the gym for kids who couldn't do PE.

Ricky Dostal, his face zippered shut with a picket line of black stitches under his left eye, sat on it, watching me watching him.

And two rows up in the stands, sitting in almost the exact spot where I'd gotten a hard-on when Paul Buckley's mom put her hand on my leg, Mr. Lloyd sat, making pencil marks in his blue book of records.

Mr. Lloyd always wore dark glasses. Even indoors, like in the shower room. I don't think I'd ever seen his eyes. Maybe he was missing one. Or maybe he was blind from jacking off too much when he was a boy.

Every so often, guys would brush over to Ricky. I could tell they were talking about his stitches and Bosten McClellan and me. And, once in a while, Ricky would erect a stiff middle finger at me, holding it close in front of his waist, penis-like, so Mr. Lloyd couldn't see.

The gym steamed with our sweat. Mr. Lloyd's class had three basketball games going on simultaneously—half-court five-on-five, shirts against skins, at the main baskets on either end of the floor, and one more game being played on a backboard that could be lowered electronically where the visitors-side stands had been rolled away. And, as things worked out, in my game, Ricky's best friend, Corey Barr, assigned himself the spot of covering me. So every time my team got the ball, Corey would press up into me. Sometimes it felt like he was trying to hump me, rubbing my back with his sweaty chest, leaning over me with his chin in my spine and his hips pushing against my butt, even when we were away from the play.

When our teammates were playing in the key and he caught me outside, he'd grab my shirt and pull me around, calling me a pussy and saying how I couldn't cry to my big brother now. I tried to ignore him, but he kept after me through the game. I finally told him to fuck off.

Corey was close-guarding me from behind then, and he tried to lean over my shoulder, but he was too short, so he put his forehead into my back, and he said, "You're a faggot, Stick. I'm going to beat the shit out of you."

Next thing I knew, the ball was passed to me. Corey reached around my hips and slap-grabbed me, hard, right up into my nuts.

It hurt so bad I almost fell down. I thought about Bosten—what he would do. And I thought about Emily, too. And even though I didn't really want to do it, I spun around, already feeling sick and dizzy from Corey clawing my balls, and made a fist, shut my eyes; and then I punched Corey Barr squarely in the nose.

It hurt my hand.

Corey was stunned. He tumbled back onto his elbows, hitting the wood floor with his butt. He sprang to his feet, swinging wildly, and we were instantly surrounded by every other boy in the gym. I could hear Mr. Lloyd stomping his way down the bleachers, yelling, "Hey! Hey! You dipshits, cut that out! Cut it out, NOW!"

Corey hit me at once in the ribs, but I couldn't feel it. I was already in too much pain from his hand on my balls. In fact, I probably would have fallen onto all fours, but I was afraid Corey would try to kick me in the face. Before I could throw any more punches, Mr. Lloyd squeezed between us, pushing us apart with the flat of his hand pressed into Corey's sweaty, bare chest, and his other hand twisted into my own damp T-shirt, right where my name was written.

Corey's nose bled.

I made him cry.

It felt horrible, and I was honestly ashamed for what I'd done. I know this was stupid, considering what he did to me, but I had an urge to hug Corey and tell him I was sorry. The boys in our gym class stood around, invigorated, thrilled, some of them teasing Corey for getting punched by the retard and especially for crying about it.

And Corey left a trail of dark maroon blood-dots leading all the way across the floor from where our fight started to the doors through which Mr. Lloyd angrily escorted us to the principal's office.

When we got out of the gym, into the freeze of the morning, I shivered, partly from cold, some from the pain in my balls, but mostly because of what I'd done to Corey Barr. Mr. Lloyd leaned over to my left ear and whispered, "It's about fucking time you did that, McClellan. Nice job."

To add to our shame, the principal was busy, so we had to wait in the front of the office, sitting on the same bench in our sweaty gym clothes while everyone who came and went just stared at us. At least I had a shirt on. And wasn't bloody. Or crying.

The crying was the worst part, because everyone who looked at us seemed to immediately assume an expression like they'd figured everything out, and that *everything* meant that I was the bad guy, since I wasn't bloody, bare-chested, and in tears.

I felt like telling Corey to shut up.

I dreaded the thought of what Mom and Dad would do if I got kicked out of school for this. So I found myself wishing I'd gone ahead and agreed to ditch school with Em when she offered it, bath or no.

In the end, Corey and I were escorted back to the locker room where we had to be watched while we showered and changed into our school clothes, so we wouldn't fight again.

Neither of us got suspended. They tended to be more lenient about boys fighting in junior high than at Bosten's school, and I think Mr. Lloyd said something to them about how Corey started it. We did have to spend the entire day together in detention hall, though.

But a phone call home had been made, and I knew what that would mean.

By the time school let out, everyone in eighth grade apparently had been talking about how I'd beaten the shit out of Corey Barr and made him cry, too.

Every day I'd ride home on the bus and sit next to Emily, so that day, as she made her way back toward my seat, I could tell by the look on her face she'd heard about what happened in Mr. Lloyd's gym class, too.

She smiled and her eyes gleamed, and when she threw herself down beside me she actually hugged me, tightly. I could feel the side of her face against my neck, and how her tight breasts pushed into my arm. It was the first time she'd ever hugged me like that. I thought it was way sexier than us being naked together in the bathtub. I tried thinking about poor Corey Barr's nose, just so I wouldn't get a boner, but it didn't work.

It was too late now.

Everything had changed.

Everything.

"I am so proud of you, Stick."

And that was the first time anyone ever said that to me.

I got so choked up. I thought we were going to kiss or something, but in junior high, making out on the bus will get you into much deeper trouble than popping some asshole in the nose.

Still, I couldn't help thinking about putting my tongue in her mouth, the way I'd seen Bosten doing, and I wondered what that would feel like. And that wondering mixed with my heated embarrassment over getting a boner with Emily sitting next to me, and the frustration I felt about not knowing how to really sort out in my mind what I'd done to Corey. So I just sat there, dumbly, moping.

But we did actually hold hands the entire way home.

And she said, "I knew you could do it! What did it feel like? Corey Barr is just as big a jerk as Ricky Dostal.

"With both those guys laid out, you're exactly like Julius Caesar now, or something."

How could I even say anything to that? I was so confused and flustered, I didn't know what she wanted to hear from me.

"Well. I felt bad about making Corey Barr cry."

Emily laughed and squeezed my hand tight. "You really felt bad?"

"I think I could get over it, though."

When I came home, Bosten was already there. I knew he'd be suspended that day because of what happened at the basketball game on Friday night. Dad had to go down to Wilson, sign his forms with the dean of students, and take Bosten out of school for three days.

That was the usual high school punishment for boys who got into fights.

Bosten didn't mind, I guess, but Mom made him stay inside the spare room all day until I got home. I think Mom had come to expect that she'd never have to see or deal with us during school hours.

I wondered how she was going to manage our being home for two weeks with Easter vacation coming up. So I hoped Mrs. Lohman was really going to make that call, like she said she would, and suggest I go sleep over at Emily's house for a while.

If I could last until then.

So Bosten came out, and I went into my Saint Fillan's room.

Mom didn't touch me.

She stood back in the hall and said, "Your father will decide what to do about this when he gets home."

And Bosten said, "What happened now?"

"I punched Corey Barr in gym class."

Bosten smiled approvingly.

That was all.

Then I got locked inside.

One of these times they will let me out and I will be cured.

BOSTEN

Dad came home late.

He was drunk, and I had fallen to sleep on the cot without eating anything for dinner. I heard Bosten arguing with Mom about it, but nothing happened.

It was ten o'clock.

The key turned.

Dad came into the room. When I opened my eyes, he looked like a shadow puppet with a Cyclops red eye where he sucked air through the cigarette he pinched in his lips. I had all my clothes on. This wasn't a regular trip to the spare room; today, it was more of a holding cell. The flannel shirt I had on was damp from my sleeping sweat, and I felt a chill when I pushed the thin sheet off from me.

"Bosten," he slurred, and swiped a hand over my head in the air.

I ducked. "No. It's me."

"Bos—"

Dad grabbed me by my shirt, began pulling it up out of my pants.

"No!" I said. "It's Stick!"

He fell onto his knees at the side of the bed. He smelled terrible, like vomit and gasoline. His cigarette tumbled out of his mouth and onto the floor.

Dad's touches were suddenly all over me—not hitting—he began grabbing, pulling at my clothes, tugging at me, slipping his cold hands up inside my undershirt, rubbing my skin.

I pushed him away.

"Stop it!"

I'd never said anything like that to my father in my life. It startled him. His gray eyes clouded angrily at me in the numb light from the hallway. He looked surprised, like he didn't understand what was happening. Then he collapsed weakly across the cot.

I got away from him and went to the door.

Dad was already asleep.

I looked back and saw the cigarette, still burning on the floor at the edge of the bedsheet.

I thought about leaving it there.

But I picked it up.

The rest of the house was dark and dead.

I went down to my basement.

Lying in bed, I pressed my ear against the pipe and stared up at the little window.

I couldn't see anything, but outside was lighter than in here.

No sounds came through the pipe.

Sleeping in the basement, I'd usually leave my door open.

But not tonight. Dad scared me.

Sometimes, not hearing things was good.

Other times, it was terrifying.

My bedroom door swung open.

"Shhhh . . . Stick. It's me," Bosten whispered. His voice made me jump, anyway.

I propped myself up, and Bosten came over, tiptoeing, and sat down on the bed with me.

"You scared the crap out of me."

"Sorry, Sticker. I wanted to see if you're okay."

"I'm okay. Dad's asleep in the spare room."

"I saw him."

"He thought I was you."

Bosten only said, "Oh."

And the way he said *oh* made me feel a little sick.

"He's drunk. I can smell it."

I said, "Oh."

Like that explained everything.

We sat there for a while. Neither of us moved, or said anything. I could feel the warmth radiating from Bosten's body.

"What about Mom?" I said.

"She went upstairs a long time ago. She's mad."

"At me?"

Bosten shook his head. "I bet you're hungry."

"I am."

"Want to go to Crazy Eric's?"

"Right now?"

"Yes, dumbshit. Right now."

I was out of bed in less than a second, scrambling around to put my pants on.

"They're going to be closed."

I was so hungry.

"Then we'll go somewhere else."

"Where?"

"California. It doesn't fucking matter, does it?"

I shrugged. Then Bosten said, "And if you tuck your shirt in, I'm kicking your ass."

I'd started slipping my arms into the sleeves of my flannel, but then just let it drop limply onto the floor at my feet.

"Screw it," I said. "I won't even wear a shirt."

"Punch your first asshole, and you're ready to break every rule in the goddamned house."

"Heck yeah."

I loved my brother so much.

We knew what to do.

Bosten and I unlocked the storm doors and stole out through our secret way into the night. It was cold, and I shivered, but I wasn't about to admit to my brother that I should have put on more than just my Steelers beanie and a thin T-shirt.

We made no sound. We even held the doors of the Toyota open, just a crack, knowing the clicking of their latch mechanisms could be just enough sound to alert Mom and Dad; and Bosten pressed the clutch in, so we could coast backwards all the way down to the drive by the mailboxes before he even started the motor.

"What about the odometer?" I said.

"Fuck it. He doesn't even know what's going on. And maybe we're not coming back."

"You're just kidding, right?"

Bosten smiled.

We headed south on the road, away from the Point, and I said, "Do you want to sneak over and see if Buck wants to come?"

"No. It's just me and my little brother tonight."

That made me feel good.

The hamburger place called Crazy Eric's was closed. I knew it would be.

We were both hungry for something else; something other than food.

Bosten drove.

In Bremerton, we found a diner called Nico's that stayed open all night.

"I only have three dollars," Bosten said when we sat down.

"I have two."

So much for running away, I thought.

We ordered hamburgers and Cokes.

It was one of the best nights ever.

It felt so free to be out of the house with Bosten, like we were hiding in a place where nobody could find us. Bosten fed a quarter into the diner's jukebox. We weren't the only ones there. A group of sailors sat and smoked in their white bell-bottoms, drinking Olympia beer, eyeing us with stubbled faces masked by glazed expressions.

The music blared.

David Essex sang, "Rock On," and as Bosten came back to our booth, he lipped the lyrics and popped his hips side to side. He sat right beside me.

"You know the only reason why I don't leave?" Bosten said,

"You know, like Dad told me to the other day?"

Of course I knew why.

But I didn't answer him. I didn't want to say it.

So he did.

"The only reason I don't leave is because I'm afraid of what he'd do to you."

"Let's not talk about this," I said.

Bosten had this look in his eyes. It said he wanted to tell me things. But I already learned them. My brother didn't need to make those words take up space in the air between us.

Not tonight.

Bosten shrugged and sang, *"Still lookin' for that blue jean baby queen . . ."*

Then he casually squeezed out a circle of ketchup onto the wax paper at the bottom of our basket of fries.

"Okay," he said.

"Okay." I slurped at my Coke. Mom and Dad would never let us have Coke after ten o'clock at night. "Bosten?"

"What?"

"Um. Nothing."

He watched me, then took a bite of a french fry. "I always knew you were stronger than me, Stick."

"You're crazy."

"Okay. If you say so."

I liked that song, too.

"So."

Bosten smiled and winked at me.

At midnight, we were on the road, heading north, back toward the Point.

"I'm not tired," I said.

"Good. Let's go to the beach, then."

"Okay."

Bosten pulled the car into the same spot where we'd parked the night Paul lit off the UFO flare.

"And anyway," I said, "you'd miss Paul Buckley too much."

"What?"

"I mean, if you ran away from home."

"I'd take him with me."

"But don't go, okay?"

Bosten opened his door and stepped out of the car. I followed him, and we both walked along the beach, right where the water lapped up onto the shore.

"I'm not going to go anywhere, Stick. Not yet."

"Good."

When we were under the pier, Bosten said, "Show me how you punched that dickwad Corey Barr."

NEXT:

california

Everything changed.

But, somehow, things managed to quiet down at our house after that weekend.

And Bosten and I avoided the Saint Fillan room for the next seven days, which was a rare long stretch of calm.

Bosten went back to school, and we visited the Buckleys the following Sunday, like we always did, except this time I let Bosten and Paul go off by themselves, without me tagging along.

It felt lonely.

But I could see in Bosten's eyes how much he loved Paul.

Mom smoked more. Dad spoke less.

Both of us pretended like we didn't remember or believe what he did in that room.

At night with my ear against the pipe, I imagined ways to kill him if he ever hurt Bosten again.

Beginning with the last week of March, Bosten and I were free of school for our two-week Easter vacation. Mrs. Lohman had followed through with her promise to ask if I could stay at Emily's house for a few days that first week; and Bosten was supposed to sleep over at Paul's. The thought of Bosten staying with him made me a little nervous that they'd end up getting into trouble.

I began worrying about everything.

Bosten followed the Pontiac. We drove home together from our visit with the Buckleys. Paul and Bosten acted different at dinner. I noticed they avoided looking at one another. There was no joking around, no talk at all, except from the grown-ups, who didn't appear to think anything was out of the ordinary with the boys.

But I could tell.

I watched his hands, how they wrung forward and back around the grip of the Toyota's steering wheel, while Bosten kept his eyes fixed ahead, motionless, as though we were being invisibly towed behind Mom and Dad's car.

"Something's wrong, isn't it?" I said.

"Don't worry about it."

"With you and Buck?"

"Yeah."

He still wouldn't look at me.

"You know, I like Buck, even if he doesn't talk to me anymore," I said. "I hope things are okay with you and him."

Bosten rubbed his eyes.

I could see Mom smoking in the car ahead of us.

"You're still going to stay with him tomorrow, right?"

Bosten nodded.

"I can't wait to go to Emily's, too."

I wanted him to ask me about her.

I wanted to tell him about what we did. I knew it wouldn't matter now, because Bosten and I had to make a kind of shell around us that would keep things in, and keep things out, too. But he didn't ask.

"But I'll miss you this week."

Bosten said, "I'll miss you, too, Sticker. Maybe you could just come and stay over at Buckley's house with me."

I smiled. "I don't think you want me there."

"Shut up." Bosten wrung his hands on the wheel again. He inhaled. "Paul told me he has a girlfriend. He said he isn't really—that he can't be anything but just my friend anymore."

"Oh."

Bosten bit the inside of his bottom lip.

I guess there was nobody else in the world he could say things like this to.

I felt bad. Not just for Bosten, but I felt bad because I wanted it to happen.

It was like I had been hoping, or believing, that Bosten would somehow snap out of it and *get better,* and stop being the way he was. But that was stupid. I knew it. So thinking about it made me feel guilty.

"But you're still going to go there?" I said.

He nodded. It was careful, measured. "If I stay home this week, I'm going to kill myself."

What could I say to that?

"Kill me first, okay?"

"Shut up."

"Bosten?"

"What?"

"Sorry. About you. And Buck."

When we got home, Bosten and I said our dutiful good-nights, but Mom held us up in the living room, saying she and Dad had something they wanted to tell us.

In our house, surprises were never what they were in other homes.

But Mom had been especially energized that day. She seemed relieved about something, but I didn't have any idea what could give her a feeling like that. I knew something was up, or that maybe she'd drunk as much as Dad. Her cheeks had color in them, like she was breathing fresh air. She stood in the center of the floor, alternating her gaze from me to Bosten; both of us with our backs turned to our respective routes of escape.

Dad sat quietly in his chair. Staring at us. Expressionless.

Mom exhaled smoke. "Your aunt Dahlia called this morning. She is bringing you both to California this week."

I looked at my brother, horrified. It was like Corey Barr slapped my nuts again. I didn't even know Aunt Dahlia outside the fact that she was my grandmother's sister; and we were being sent to her like five-cent postcards you mail to people you don't really like, just so they can dislike you even more.

Bosten swallowed. "Why?"

Mom's smile melted. "What do you mean, *why*? She's your great-aunt and she wants you both to visit. That's *why*. She's paying for your plane tickets and everything. She lives in *California*."

"So what? Lots of people live in California. I don't even know who Aunt Dahlia is," Bosten argued.

Dad leaned forward in his chair.

I thought there was going to be a fight, for sure.

And, somehow, I couldn't stop my mouth. "I'm supposed to stay over at the Lohmans' tomorrow. And Bosten's going to Buck's house. I don't fucking want to go to California."

I never cussed around my parents. I rarely cussed at all. So I knew what to expect, even though I just couldn't keep the word inside my head.

Dad's hand grabbed my shoulder.

I didn't want him to touch me. I twisted away. This time, he didn't fight me. He didn't do anything. It was like he was afraid of me, or something.

Then Mom slapped me so hard spit came out of my mouth.

"It's not open to discussion," Dad said. "You can march your goddamned ass down to bed. Now."

I put my hand on my face.

Bosten was smart. He knew when to quit. He said good night again and disappeared down his hallway.

I went down to the basement.

And I hardly had the chance to explain things to Emily, that at least we'd be back for the second week of vacation and, please, could I stay over at her house then; because by Tuesday afternoon, Bosten and I were at Aunt Dahlia's house, a thousand miles away on a wide sandy beach, in a place called Oxnard.

AUNT DAHLIA

We didn't even know who we were supposed to be looking for when we got off our plane in Los Angeles, but Aunt Dahlia apparently knew us.

I wondered how.

When I looked at her long enough, though, she looked like an older, happier version of Mom. One who didn't smoke.

She came right up to us and hugged Bosten first. Then she hugged me. And, as I expected and dreaded, she held me back at arm's length and said, "What happened there?"

Just like Emily would say, if she was about eighty years older and had never seen me before.

Dahlia, not the least bit timid or reserved, lifted up my beanie and turned me so she could look at—no, *examine*—the right side of my head. All at once, I felt myself going pale.

I believed Dahlia was probably a woman who'd taken plenty of baths with boys in her life.

I saw Bosten beginning to tense up, look defensive. Neither one of us was happy to be there, anyway.

As I swiped at my hat to pull it back down, Dahlia said, "Did you get into a fight with a grizzly bear or something?"

She smiled at me, and her fingers stroked the side of my head like there was nothing at all wrong with her doing that.

Finally, I squirmed myself away from Aunt Dahlia's grasp.

"I was born that way."

I felt dirty and embarrassed.

Ugly.

I pulled the hat back down as low as it could go, so it completely covered my ear.

"I never knew that," she said, and her voice was filled with a kind of joy and wonder. I looked at my brother. I was mad enough to walk back to Washington, and I wanted to leave right then.

"He doesn't like for people to touch him," Bosten said.

Aunt Dahlia looked hurt. "I apologize, Stark. That was rude of me. Can you hear all right?"

She craned her head around to my normal side. I wanted to die.

"I can hear things," I said. "And they call me Stick, by the way."

"Oh."

I wanted to let her know, clearly, that I was not planning on making anything easy for her after the greeting she'd just given me.

I wished I were back at Point No Point, at Emily's house.

Aunt Dahlia put her hand on my shoulder, soothingly. "There's so many things I didn't know."

"We're all real good at keeping secrets," I said.

She drove us, in a 1968 Dodge Dart, north to her home on the beach. Bosten and I both wanted to sit in the backseat, but Dahlia said she thought that was creepy, and made us stay up front, next to her. I sat in the middle, so I knew I wouldn't be able to hear Bosten very well.

I had the feeling he wasn't in a talkative mood, anyway. He'd hardly said anything at all to me on the flight down, and I knew he was still hurting and worried about Paul Buckley.

"Do you know," she said, "that I met your brother when he

was, oh, two years old, I think? But I've only ever seen you in a photograph, Stark."

"Stick."

"Do you mind if I call you Stark? It's a handsome name. There is something cruel, I think, in calling you the other one."

I rolled my eyes. "I don't care what you call me."

"Good then!" Dahlia slapped my knee playfully. "Stark it shall be!"

Dahlia's house was a white and green, flat-roofed bungalow built right on the sand, with single-sided walls and no attic. It looked like it could blow away in a storm, and I wondered how she ever kept warm in it during wintertime.

We dropped our bags inside the door, and Dahlia pointed to a room at the back of the house. "That's you boys' bedroom. Here. Let me show you the place."

There were only two bedrooms with a single bathroom between them; a living room with windows that faced out onto the ocean and a rock jetty in front of the house; and a long, wide kitchen with a clay-tiled floor in the back. Her property was fenced, all the way around, with rotten, gapped cedar that tilted and leaned in the wind, and the yards were nothing more than sand hills and tufts of native grasses.

It was the exact opposite of Washington.

We put our stuff into our room. It was sunny and light, and I realized that every window in the house was wide-open, still the place wasn't cold at all.

Dahlia stood behind us, watching.

There was only one queen-size bed in our room.

Bosten still hadn't said anything.

"If it bothers you to share a bed, one of you can

sleep on the couch in the living room," Dahlia said. "The place is small, as you can see."

"I don't care," I said.

Dahlia sighed. I knew I wasn't being very nice to her.

Bosten sat on the bed.

"Do you have any trunks?" she asked. "Boys in California don't dress all tucked-in and buttoned-up like you boys do."

"It's how we dress at our house," Bosten said.

"Well. Then I have an idea. Let's go to Ventura and pick you out some beach clothes, so you look like you belong here."

I looked at Bosten.

He shrugged.

I guessed it was okay.

And, on the way out the door, Dahlia said, "And you really should take off that wool cap, Stark. This is the beach, after all."

Something about her made me begin to feel it was okay.

I left my Steelers cap sitting on the bed, and Aunt Dahlia drove us up the beach to a city called Ventura.

She bought us some new clothes and took Bosten and me out to a place called Sal's for Mexican food, which neither of us had ever tasted before. It was really good. And I didn't want to, but by the time we came back to her house that evening, I was starting to like Aunt Dahlia.

Bosten was, too.

We'd stuffed our Washington clothes into shopping bags and wore our new stuff—baggy shorts, Adidas sneakers, and colored T-shirts (actually colored, and *not white,* which we could wear without putting on anything else over them or under them)—for the rest of the day. And I felt particularly tough because Aunt Dahlia insisted on buying me a "Mr. Zogs Sex Wax" tee, explaining that all the boys on the beach wore them.

It was like an unofficial uniform for teenage boys in the State of California, she said.

I didn't know what Sex Wax was, so I felt extremely uncomfortable when Dahlia waved the shirt like a flag in front of my eyes, in public, in a store where people could see us.

Dahlia explained that Sex Wax was used to keep you from slipping off a surf board.

So when she paid for the clothes, the guy at the counter of the surf shop gave me a plastic-wrapped chunk of Sex Wax for free, since I didn't know what it was. I felt myself turning completely red, but that stuff smelled better, I think, than anything I'd ever smelled before in my life.

So I didn't really get the *Sex* part of the name, but I realized there wasn't very much about sex I understood in the first place.

No matter what, I knew I'd never be able to wear the shirt around my parents' house, and that made it even more attractive to me. And if I brought the Sex Wax home and attempted to hide it in my room, it was a sure thing Mom would find it and throw a fit about me jacking off or something. So I was just a little bit sad thinking that my new favorite shirt, along with that amazing-smelling Sex Wax, would probably both have to be left in Aunt Dahlia's care when Bosten and I went back home to Washington.

She didn't make us get out of bed, either.

The only reason I woke up the next morning was because I had to pee.

And when I came out of the bathroom, Aunt Dahlia and the smell of bacon stopped me, and she took me by the hand and made me sit down at the kitchen table—barefoot and in my underwear—so I could eat breakfast while she cooked and talked to me.

It really was as opposite to Washington as I could ever dream.

Maybe things were supposed to be this way.

"Do you like coffee?" she asked.

"Uh. No, thank you."

"I guess it probably is bad for you, at your age, anyway." Dahlia opened a fresh carton of milk and poured a glass. Then she put a full plate of bacon, eggs, and toast down on the table in front of me.

"Thank you, Aunt Dahlia."

She scooted out a chair and sat beside me. "Oh, don't be so formal, Stark. Just call me Dahlia. Everyone does."

"Okay."

She smiled. She looked so happy, just sitting there, watching me eat.

I decided that being in California wasn't so bad, after all.

"What do you like to do?" Dahlia asked.

"Huh?" I took a bite of toast.

Dahlia frowned a bit, then stood up and moved around so she could sit next to me on my left side. She put her hand on my bare thigh. It felt almost funny, like being tickled. I thought it was maybe something real moms probably did all the time in California.

"I heard you okay," I said. I thought about it. I decided it probably wasn't a good idea to tell her that I liked taking baths with Emily Lohman. I'd save that for another time when I didn't have something to say. Because I got the idea Aunt Dahlia would probably be completely okay with me taking baths with a girl. "Uh. I don't know what I like to do."

"Well. It's a glorious day. I think after your brother has breakfast, we should all go out and explore the beach."

"We never get to stay in bed at our house. We might not see Bosten till tomorrow."

"Ha!" Dahlia laughed. A genuine, warm laugh.

How could I not smile back at her?

"There's someone you might like to meet. Evan and Kim, the twins. I told them about you. They live two houses down. It's important to make friends with people your own age, after all. You don't want to be hanging around with me all the time."

"It's not so bad," I said.

Just then, Bosten came into the kitchen, fully dressed, with a tucked and buttoned shirt.

Dahlia hitchhiked a thumb at him and rolled her eyes for me, smiling.

And Bosten said, "Stick, do you realize you're sitting at the table in just your underwear?"

Dahlia laughed, and I said, "I know. Pretty cool, huh?"

Bosten looked at us both like we were crazy.

I chewed a piece of toast. "I told Dahlia that in the State of Washington, thirteen-year-old boys make the rules in houses. I proclaim no pants at breakfast. Ever."

Aunt Dahlia nodded.

And my brother dropped his pants and kicked them out into the living room. Then he sat down like that's how you do things.

I tapped his hand with my finger. I pointed at his shirt collar and shook my head disapprovingly. He grinned, made a ball with his flannel Washington-State collared shirt, and threw it out the kitchen door.

Then I announced, "Now you may eat."

Bosten was the best person in the world at playing California.

EVAN AND KIM

We went through the gate in Dahlia's fence and walked barefoot, out across the sand toward the jetty.

"That's Evan and Kim." Dahlia pointed at two black figures bobbing like seals in the waves near the end of the rock breakwater. "I'm going back to clean up our breakfast. You two just sit and wait for them. I told them you'd be here. They'll come in when they see you."

Bosten sat down next to me in the sand. It was so warm, we took our shirts off.

"They surf here," Bosten said.

Behind the two kids on surfboards, miles out in the water, I could see the hazy outline of islands.

I kicked my brother's foot softly. "This is about the most bitchin' place in the world."

"Stick?"

"What?"

"Do you ever wonder what—"

Bosten began to ask something, but I cut him off. "No. Never."

Because I knew what he was going to say, and I wondered it all the time—what it would be like to live away from Mom and Dad. He knew it, too. He didn't have to say it out loud.

A swell came in. The deep green water rose up beyond the top of the jetty's point, spitting white blobs in the air over the toothy rocks. I watched as the kids in the water both flattened out on top of their boards and began paddling diagonally toward the peak of the wave.

I wondered if they used Sex Wax.

One of the black figures nosed the surfboard back and

spun out of the wave at its top, while the other pressed up, back bent, with straight arms, kicked into a squatting position, and, just like that, glided down the churning face of the wave, turning at the bottom, cutting back up, and then down again, until vanishing, completely swallowed in a tumbling froth of foam.

Moments later, they both appeared, standing up in knee-deep water, walking out onto the beach toward me and Bosten with their boards, dangling cords that attached to their ankles, tucked under their arms.

They nudged each other and nodded their chins at us. They looked like frogmen or something, wearing those black wetsuits, with just their tanned feet, hands, and faces sticking out from them.

"Are you guys Dahlia's nephews?" Evan asked.

I looked at Bosten. He said, "Yeah. Hi."

"Hi." Evan dropped his board on the sand in front of us, then bent down and unfastened the leash from his ankle. His sister unwrapped her leash from her foot, too. Drops of water from the girl's board flicked onto my legs.

Evan and Kim Hansen were fifteen. They looked like pictures of California kids you'd see in a magazine: bronze-skinned and lean, with long hair streaked golden from all the hours they obviously spent in the ocean. It took me a while to realize that my mouth kind of hung open when I looked at the girl. In fact, I wouldn't have been surprised if I actually drooled. There was something about how that tight wetsuit clung to her body and made her look naked. I couldn't help staring at the shape of her breasts, wondering what the salt water on her skin might taste like if I could lick her neck.

I tried to think about *anything* else, but I couldn't. All I could do was hope that proper etiquette would not require me to stand up any time soon. So I was happy when the twins sat down in the sand, cross-legged, in front of me and my brother.

We introduced ourselves and reached across the gap between us to shake hands. Their palms felt cold and wet, and I could smell the ocean on them.

Kim looked from me to Bosten.

I think, at that precise moment, I became fully aware of how much things had changed inside me since the day Emily and I had taken that walk together, catching crabs on the beach back home, just a couple weeks earlier. Kim was the most attractive girl I'd ever seen in my life, I decided. Even sexier than Paul Buckley's mom, and for me, that was admitting an enormous truth.

"You have interesting names," she said.

"Everyone calls me Stick," I said. I thought Bosten didn't feel like talking, anyway, and I wanted Kim to look at me. I even stretched my foot out in the sand until my toes got daringly close to hers.

"Why?" Kim asked.

"Because of how tall he is," Bosten explained.

That totally ruined the moment.

I felt myself stupidly getting jealous of my homosexual brother for talking to a girl who seemed like she wanted to flirt with him. And I knew, in horror, what was going to come next . . .

"How tall are you?" Kim asked. "Stand up, Stick."

I felt like I was going to throw up. I tried thinking of any medical affliction—like a seizure or something—I could fake, just so I wouldn't have to stand up in front of her and contend with the unforgiving boner that sprang up inside my shorts as soon as I saw Kim get out of the water, all glistening and smooth.

That was the only time in my life that I was thankful for my missing, ugly ear.

Because Evan leaned around to that side of me and said, "Cool," when he noticed it, like it was a biker tattoo or something.

I looked down at the sand between my feet. "I was born that way."

I didn't want Kim to look at me anymore.

But she laughed lightly, and said, "That's nothing. Evan was born with three nipples."

I lifted my face. "Oh."

"Yeah," she said. "Show them, Ev."

Evan smiled and shrugged. "Whatever."

He snaked his arm behind his back and unzipped his wetsuit. I noticed he was a little embarrassed, and I kind of felt bad for him, too. I mean, I knew what it was like to have people look at you because you were born with something different about your body. But I was so relieved that the suggestion of having me stand up in front of Kim had been forgotten; and Evan seemed to tolerate our watching him as he peeled away the top half of his suit and kneeled before us in the sand, stretching the skin on his left chest tight with the fingers of one hand, and pointing out the extra nipple with his other.

"See?" he said.

"That's kind of cool," I said. "I think it's a lot better to be born with spare parts than missing ones."

They both laughed about that.

"Maybe we're aliens," Evan said. "From another planet or something." He sat back, relaxed, with his knees bent and his arms propped on his surfboard.

"Yeah." I smiled at him, and then at Bosten. I felt like being here was okay, that Evan and Kim had instantly decided that we weren't freaks or something, and I knew we would be friends. "A couple weeks ago, Bosten and me made people think there was a UFO attack."

• • •

We sat there on the beach with them, telling our stories about Washington and listening to theirs about California, too. And both of them habitually kept looking out at the ocean, studying the waves.

Finally, Kim said, "Do you guys ever surf up there?"

"I don't think so," I said. I sounded really stupid and decided I'd better shut up.

"If you want to try and learn how, we got lots of extra stuff you could use," Evan offered.

"That would be really cool," Bosten said. I looked at him, and thought he was finally beginning to snap out of his gloomy mood.

"Bitchin'," Evan said, and pushed himself to his feet. His butt was powdered white where the sand glued on to his wetsuit. The upper half of his suit hung down in front of him, a lifeless, headless, spineless, flopping extra black torso. "Let's go to our house and get you some boards and wetsuits."

We started walking across the beach, following Evan and Kim. They left their boards, upside down so the wax wouldn't melt, lying in the sand.

And Kim asked, "Are you goofy or regular?"

I was horrified.

I glanced at Bosten, wondering what he was going to say to that. I was convinced that Kim's question was just the slang, surfer way that California kids asked other kids if they were gay or not gay—since California kids were obviously so comfortable and open with things like extra nipples and Sex Wax and, I guess, being gay, too.

Thank God Bosten was so cool about stuff like that.

He said, "I don't know what that even means."

Kim laughed and brushed her hand on his bare shoulder. I

hated myself for feeling like Bosten and I would end up being in some kind of competition with each other. I never competed against Bosten for anything, and the thought made me mad.

She said, "It means left- or right-handed."

At least that was a relief.

"Whichever one's left is me," I said.

"Goofy," Evan said. "Like me."

"Oh. Yeah. I'm goofy. That makes Bosten regular."

"If you need to pee, just do it in your wetsuit. It makes you warmer," Evan explained.

The four of us had paddled out beyond the shorebreak, near the end of the jetty.

"Boys are so gross," Kim said.

"You're a liar if you expect anyone to believe you don't do it, too, Kimmy," Evan said.

"Well, I don't."

"Are you really supposed to do that? Just pee in your suit?" I asked.

"I do it all the time," Evan said.

That kind of made me feel a little bit weirded out, as Emily would say, since Bosten and I were both wearing wetsuits that belonged to Evan. And, before we put them on, Evan explained to us that we were supposed to be *completely naked* underneath them, too, which made me feel especially exposed, and peed on at the same time, in front of his sister.

Good thing the water was so cold.

After he told us that, I actually did consider peeing, just to see if it would warm the inside of the suit up a bit, but I was too nervous to get anything out.

I'd never been in water like this before. It felt dangerous and thrilling at the same time, kind of like I was flying.

They used Sex Wax, too. I took particular pleasure in smearing that wonderful-smelling, gooey stuff on the flat deck of my board before following Evan and Kim out into the surf.

Evan showed us how to sit on our boards, straddling them with our feet below us. Bosten was good at it, but balance was always a tricky thing for me. And after we had squeezed our naked selves into those skintight suits at the twins' house, Evan and Kim taught us how to get up onto our feet. They laid our boards across Evan's bed, so we could practice snapping our legs up quickly beneath our chests.

It seemed easy enough.

I was goofy-foot. My left foot always wanted to be in back, just like Evan told me it would—just like Evan's was. They showed us how to look out at the humpback lines of swells stacking up on the horizon of the sea, how to find a peak and paddle with it.

But sitting out on the surfboard made the waves look monstrously bigger than they'd appeared from the warmth and safety of the sand.

"This is how you do it."

Evan caught the first wave. I watched him stand and drop down, entirely vanishing in front of the wall of roiling water, riding it backside, goofy-foot, as the wave broke down the shore away from the jetty. And I saw him come back up to the top of the wave, the nose of his board breaking up into the air like the fin on a shark, spraying an arc of water droplets, as Evan held his arms out and twisted his hips sharply, to ride his board back down the face.

It was beautiful and terrifying.

I didn't know whether I'd have the guts to try it myself. I was content with just sitting out there and watching everyone else, but then Bosten paddled into the next wave that came. It carried him away, so fast, and I saw him push up to his feet for no more than a second before wiping out, face-first, into the whitewater.

He howled with joy, a sound I'd never heard coming from my brother before.

It was pure.

Real.

I was alone out there with Kim.

"He's really cute," she said.

"Yeah."

I mean, what was I going to say to that? *No, he's ugly. And he's gay, besides.*

I loved Bosten too much to screw with him like that.

"Does he have a girlfriend in Washington?"

She put me in a terrible spot. There was no chance of doing a good thing for either one of them, no matter how I answered her. I saw Bosten and Evan in the wash near shore, struggling to paddle back to our spot against the stacked waves.

"Yeah. He does," I lied. Well, it was a 50-percent lie, if there is such a thing. And then I winked at her and added, "But it's always worth a try, Kim. You never know with my brother."

Then she put her hand on mine and smiled. "Thanks, Stick. I think you're cute, too."

I am ugly.

We stayed out in the water until the sun went down.

Bosten caught on fast to the technique of surfing. He looked like he'd been doing it all his life. And after many attempts, I finally managed to stand up twice before the day was over. It was a rush; it was terrifying, and I think I swallowed ten gallons of the Pacific Ocean. But at the end of it all, it was one of the best days I ever had.

Carrying our boards, wiping forearms across noses that

leaked a continuous stream of seawater, we walked, the four of us—wet, barefoot, and sandy—down Ocean Avenue, the street that ran parallel to the beach.

It felt like my brother and I belonged there.

And Bosten, Evan, and I all had our wetsuits unzipped, tops peeled down to our waists so they flopped in front of our knees. But I had to hold on to mine with my left hand to keep it from falling past my hips. I was skinnier than Evan, so every few steps I took Evan's wetsuit would slip down and show my scrawny, white, Pacific Northwest butt to anyone following behind, which happened to be Kim.

"Maybe tomorrow we could go to C Street," Kim said.

I didn't care if C Street was a leper colony where they tortured you, if Kim wanted to go there, she could count me in.

"What's that?" Bosten asked.

"California Street. By the fairgrounds, in Ventura," Evan said. "It has a really easy break. You can ride the waves there forever. It's the best place around to learn."

"Sure we want to go," I said.

"Let's go early, though," Evan said. "Do you think Dahlia will let you drive her car?"

Bosten nodded. "Yeah. I think she will."

Comparing experiences, I think I felt just about as clean, as whole—completely, physically, well—after a hot shower and putting on my dry clothes (including, of course, my Sex Wax T-shirt) that evening at the twins' house as I did after taking a bath with Emily Lohman.

Bosten and I promised we'd come back in the morning; and then we headed up Ocean Avenue, toward Dahlia's house, in the dark.

It was quiet and peaceful there, and we could hear the crashing roars of the waves in the night.

Or maybe that day the sound of the ocean had been trapped inside my head.

"Have you ever had more fun than that, Sticker?"

"If I did, I'm not telling."

Bosten laughed. "Yeah. Me neither."

Dahlia was so happy to see us when we got to her house. Her eyes shined and her cheeks blushed when Bosten and I thanked her for asking Evan and Kim to hang out with us.

Her home smelled delicious, and we were starving.

Everything here was different, and it made me wonder.

So, after dinner, when we finished the chocolate cake she'd made for us, Bosten and I were both wiped out and ready for bed.

Bosten yawned. "Dahlia, do you think it would be all right if I borrowed your car in the morning to drive Sticker and the twins up to C—"

She cut him off. "You can use the car any time you want, honey."

"I'm a good driver," Bosten said.

"I don't care if you rob banks with it and park it upside down. I said you can use it. And the keys are hanging by the door. After breakfast, I'll give you some money so you can put gas in it and maybe buy yourselves some lunch. If you're going to be gone all day, like you were today."

"Thank you, Dahlia," he said.

I opened the door to our bedroom. "Thank you, Dahlia. Good night."

"Can I ask you boys to sit down and talk to me for just one minute before you go to bed?"

"Oh. Sure."

"Here." Aunt Dahlia waved us over to her couch.

She sat down between us, then put her arm around my shoulders and squeezed.

People never touch me.

Bosten sat down at the end, away from us, and Dahlia said, "Come on over here, Bosten."

She lifted up her arm so he could scoot in beside her, too.

Then she just sat there, holding us.

It was weird, and it was nice, too.

I didn't know if I was supposed to say something else.

And Dahlia did two things that I don't think anyone had ever done to me and Bosten. She leaned over and kissed us both on our cheeks, and then she said, "I just want you boys to know that I love you, and I would do anything for you."

It was confusing.

I knew Bosten was confused, too.

Because, what do you say to something like that?

Then Dahlia put her hands on each of our knees, looked from me to Bosten, and said, "I just wanted you to know that. And I need to tell you I spoke with your mother today."

She shifted a bit. "Things are going to be different when you go back home next week."

Different from what? I wondered.

"Your mother and father. They're going to be living separate for a while now."

Then she didn't say anything. We just sat there for the longest time. A million thoughts bounced around in my head, and none of them was very nice.

"Is that why they sent us here?" I said.

She just patted our knees. She didn't have to answer.

And Bosten, surgical, asked, "Who's staying, and which one's leaving?"

She said, "Your mother thinks it's best for boys to stay with their father."

Aunt Dahlia cried for us when we told her good night.

She didn't need to do that.

I wanted to sleep, but I couldn't.

I just stared up at a spot in the dark where my little window would be and imagined I heard the sound of waves on the beach.

But it was Bosten's breathing, and it scared me that my brother was crying.

"It doesn't matter, Bosten. It's going to be okay."

"I know."

"Then don't cry."

"I want to go home. I want to see Paul."

"Oh. You want to know something funny? Today, Kim told me she thinks you're cute. And she asked me if you have a girlfriend."

Bosten rolled over in bed so he could see me.

"What did you say?"

"I told her you have a girlfriend, but she shouldn't give up trying for you, 'cause that's how my brother is."

Bosten sniffed, wiped his nose, and laughed just a little.

"You're dumb, Stick."

He pushed me with his foot.

"*You're* dumb, Bosten."

I pushed him back.

I loved my brother.

"Okay." And then he said, "I wish I wasn't like this."

"You're the luckiest and best person in the world, Bosten."

"Stick?"

"What?"

"I can't live with Dad anymore."

"I know."

AUNT DAHLIA

Dahlia cooked French toast and bacon for breakfast.

Bosten and I sat there in the kitchen, in our underwear, with our elbows on the table, puffy-eyed and pale, eating quietly while the sky grew lighter outside.

Everything was different.

Dahlia sat down and watched us.

She drank coffee.

I didn't want her to be sad about things.

"You could come surfing with us, Dahlia," I said.

She put her hand over mine and smiled. "You're so sweet. I think it would scare me too much, seeing you boys out there in that water."

I wondered what she would think if she ever saw us at home.

Dahlia scooted her chair out and went into the living room. When she came back, she put her car keys and a twenty-dollar bill down on the table next to Bosten's hand.

"I want you boys to have a good time," she said.

Bosten looked at her and nodded his thanks. Then he looked down and smiled. "I don't have any pockets to put that in at the moment."

I nudged him under the table with my toes and laughed. "You're dumb."

"So?"

I carried my plate over to the sink, and then I went up to Dahlia and kissed her.

I'd never kissed anyone before in my life. I felt myself turning red.

"Thank you, Dahlia. Come on, let's go, Bosten."

• • •

She didn't even watch us drive away or anything. I think Dahlia wanted to show Bosten how much she trusted him, and how much she really didn't care about things like cars when there were other things like people in the world.

I never knew about that stuff before.

Sometimes I wondered why she treated us that way, why she accepted us the way she did. It wasn't a sterile kind of tolerance, like kids could expect from PE coaches and nurses who gave you tetanus shots; it was something else.

One time, she told me about how her husband died when she was only twenty-five years old. I said he must have been a real nice man, but I couldn't look at her when I said that. It made me sadder than just about anything. It was hard to understand how things that make some people mean and cruel don't work on everyone.

She was a wondrous person, I thought.

And my head was so full of wonder after a couple days at Aunt Dahlia's house that I didn't know if I'd be able to shake it all out and put up with Washington ever again.

As we drove down Ocean to the twins' house, I started doing the math, like Bosten would do, calculating the days until we had to go back home; and it made me feel dark inside.

Five more days.

Monday.

The day after Easter.

We had to go back home.

"What are you all   quiet   for?" Bosten said.

"Nothing." I pointed. Evan and Kim were already outside waiting for us. "Park there."

At C Street, we pulled the car into the unmarked dirt lot on the ocean side of the county fairgrounds. We stood behind the open doors of the Dodge and stripped out of our clothes and slid into our wetsuits. Everyone at C Street did that. It wasn't a big deal at all.

Some of the cars that were there played music with their doors and windows open.

We'd parked next to a pickup that was backwards with its tailgate down. Two guys who looked a little older than Bosten sat there, watching the waves. They were wet and had their suits half-stripped down to their waists. They said hi to Evan.

Evan went over to them. "Hey, Mark. Dave."

They were smoking a joint. Lots of guys were getting high in the lot. It smelled like weed everywhere. A couple guys were even drinking beers, and nobody there could have been more than eighteen years old. The youngest kids were maybe seven or eight, wearing wetsuits or Sex Wax shirts just like the older guys. But everywhere around us, kids were laughing, talking loud, goofing around. It was only about nine in the morning, too.

A teenager standing next to a van behind us had a big cut over his eyebrow. Blood ran down his face and onto his chest, but I could hear him laughing, bragging to his friends about how he was going back out in the water.

It was like that.

Mark handed the joint to Evan, and he took a long, deep hit from it and held in the smoke for what seemed like easily more than a minute. I watched him. He was way better at smoking pot than Bosten or Paul. I could tell he had practice.

Evan said, "These are my friends from Washington. Bosten and his brother, Stick."

Mark and Dave nodded at us. The one named Mark said, "Hey, Washington."

Dave pointed the joint toward the Dodge. "You want some?"

I looked at Kim. I said, "No, thanks."

But Bosten was already over there, smoking with the other boys.

Kim whispered, "I don't smoke, either. They know that."

"I think it stinks," I said. "And just wait till you see how stupid Bosten gets when he's stoned. Just watch. He's going to make *me* drive now."

She smiled at me, and twitched her head so her perfect hair flicked back over her shoulder. "You drive?"

I liked her. A lot.

I tried to make my chest look hard, make the muscles in my arms show through Evan's wetsuit for her.

No success.

"I drive at night. I blow things up."

Kim laughed. "That's sexy."

"I know it is."

We had to climb down the rocks at the edge of the dirt lot; and when we got to the bottom, the only way into the ocean was to wait for the perfect moment between sets of waves, throw our boards in without the leashes attached, and then jump into the water and swim for them before getting crushed by the surf back into the rocks.

I thought that was pretty insane.

But everyone did it.

Bosten and Evan howled and laughed.

So I went last, after watching Evan, Bosten, then Kim go. And they had to shout for me to do it, because I wasn't really sure I had the guts.

Kim sat up on her board and yelled, "Come on! You drive at night and blow things up, right?"

She could ask me to jump face-first into the rocks and I'd do it.

So I decided I wasn't going to just stand there like an idiot in a borrowed wetsuit all day and watch. I finally took a deep breath, thought for a flashing moment about dying, and took the leap.

We surfed to the point of exhaustion that day.

Evan was right about the break at C Street. It was so much easier than catching the fast and slippery waves at the Strand in front of Dahlia's house. And if I paddled far enough out, Evan brought me to a spot where the waves broke left, so we could both ride them front-side. For some reason, too, the water was warmer there than it was at the Strand. It was murky and pale, and there was so much seaweed beneath the surface that every time I slipped off my board it felt like I was being attacked by sea monsters.

I didn't like the seaweed part, but I tried to act tough.

After all, Kim said I was sexy.

Kind of.

I got up on the board so many times that I actually began to feel confident, which was a strange and new thing for me. Bosten and I laughed and whooped and howled, and thought about nothing else besides just being there, on the water together, with our new friends. It was like we had completely abandoned the land and everything on it.

One time, we all floated together, holding on to one another, so we made this private island out beyond the breakers.

"This is the best day ever," Bosten said.

Kim held my hand on one side, and Bosten's on the other, and Evan had a hold on his sister's leash.

"I'm glad you guys came," Kim said.

I felt myself getting hot in the face when she looked at me, because I was peeing in Evan's wetsuit.

He was right about that, too.

When we decided we'd had enough, we all caught waves that took us halfway down to the pier, where we could walk out of the water onto the sandy beach. We found a warm spot in the sand, dropped our boards, and collapsed there, motionless, like basking seals, letting the afternoon heat from the ground slowly percolate up through our wetsuits.

I would have easily fallen to sleep, but after about twenty minutes of lying there, Evan sat up and announced, "I'm starving."

And Bosten moaned, rolling over onto his back, his face covered with sand and salt. "Me, too."

So we got up and trudged back to the dirt lot and the Dodge, tied the trunk lid down with our four boards sticking out, peeled our shrunken and pale bodies out of our wetsuits, and got dressed. I tried to casually watch Kim while she got undressed on the opposite side of the car from us, but she had this perfect way of changing clothes with a towel wrapped under her arms, so nothing showed. That's also when I learned that sand inside your underwear, plus a boner, can almost make you cry.

Evan and Bosten sat down on the rocks in front of the car and started smoking pot. Evan had a big bag of weed with him, and he sure knew how to roll joints. He'd probably kick Bosten out of California if he saw the crippled excuses for joints he and his boyfriend produced. And the pot Evan had was really green and smelled a lot different from the Mexican weed Paul's brother brought from Texas.

Stinkier, if it was possible.

I sat down beside Bosten and bumped his knee with mine.

"Give me the keys." I held my hand out in front of him.

Bosten dug around in his pocket and dropped Dahlia's keys into my palm. He put his arm around me and squeezed, then he bumped Evan's shoulder. "I have the coolest little brother in the fucking world."

They laughed.

I kept my hand out. "And your wallet."

I wasn't about to get caught without a driver's license in a different state, and I looked enough like Bosten from the front that nobody would question it. Good thing they didn't have a check-box for NUMBER OF EARS on Washington State licenses.

Bosten said, "Sticker, if you're looking for a rubber, I used my last one a month ago."

Evan and Bosten almost fell off the rocks laughing.

I rolled my eyes. "You are so dumb."

And as I stood up, I whispered to them, "But the deal is, you two have to sit in back and Kim sits up front with me."

Evan put out his hand, and I slapped it.

He said, "Fair enough."

I tucked Bosten's wallet down the front of my shorts and jangled the keys in my hand as I walked back to the car. Kim stood by the grille, watching me.

"See how dumb he is?" I said.

Trying to drive that big car through Ventura and Oxnard with a stoned fifteen-year-old kid in the backseat giving me directions was probably the same thing as being stoned myself. Bosten just kept giggling, especially when I forgot the Dodge was automatic and mistook the brake pedal for the clutch.

Yeah, that didn't win me any points with Kim. She almost put her forehead into the dashboard.

Evan attempted to navigate us to Sal's Mexican Inn, the place where Bosten and I had eaten on our first evening in California.

"Everyone from the Strand eats at Sal's," Evan said. "We've even been there with Dahlia."

"Okay. You said that a million times. Which way am I supposed to go?" I said.

I saw Evan kind of snap up in the rearview mirror. Then he looked around and said, "What are we doing in fucking El Rio?"

Bosten exploded in laughter. "Sticker! What are you taking us to fucking El Rio for?"

If I was a better driver, I probably would have seriously thought about reaching back and slapping Evan and Bosten. They were laughing so hard, I could see tears coming out of Evan's eyes, and they both kept chanting, over and over,

"Fucking El Rio.
Fucking El Rio.
Fucking El Rio."

I mean, I knew the place didn't look right. It was nothing but farmland, orange groves, and little shacks with chickens running around the yards and Mexican kids playing in the dirt on the side of the road. I pulled the Dodge over and parked it beneath a dusty avocado tree.

I sighed. "You are both so fucking dumb."

Then Kim started laughing. She slid her hand across the white vinyl seat and she grabbed my hand.

I looked at her. I wanted to be sure it wasn't the kind of hand-grab where she was just trying to calm a little kid down, or get my attention so she could tell me to grow up. It was an honest-to-God, actual holding of my hand.

It felt as good as Emily washing my hair.

Maybe better.

I had to look away from her instantly.

What was she doing?

She was so beautiful, and can't she see how goddamned ugly I am?

People don't touch me.

I felt sick, like I was going to pass out. There were little prickles under my hair. I squeezed her hand back. I was acutely aware of every needle-sharp grain of sand inside my underwear.

Kim said, "I know   how to get to Sal's."

"Why didn't you tell me?" If my voice was an eggshell, it had a million cracks in it at that moment.

"I thought   driving   around with you   was fun."

"Oh."

It turned out that Sal's was only about five minutes from fucking El Rio.

I wished it were farther, because I was getting pretty good at driving one-handed.

Kim Hansen was the first girl who ever kissed me. She did it when Bosten and Evan carried their surfboards around the twins' house to hang them up on the back patio. Right there in the shade on the side of her house, she just grabbed me by my neck and pulled my face right down into hers.

I didn't know anything about kissing, but I could tell that Kim was probably as practiced at it as her brother was at rolling joints. I never knew that tongues could be so useful, or the inside of someone else's mouth could taste so good. And Kim kind of made squeaking, satisfied noises while we made out.

She even slid her hand up beneath my Sex Wax shirt and rubbed my bare back.

But I was so scared, I couldn't talk after that kiss. And I felt terribly guilty and ashamed, too, because somewhere, in the back of my mind, I had this idea that if I wasn't ever going to have a "first kiss" with Paul Buckley's mom, it was for sure going to be with Emily Lohman. And now I was horrified, because what would Emily do when I kissed her all like I knew what I was doing and stuff? She'd have to know I'd done it before.

With someone else.

And that made me feel really bad.

"Okay," Kim said. "Sorry. I just had to see what you kissed like."

And then she just flipped her hair around and went back to where Bosten and Evan were.

Just like that.

But before Bosten and I went home to Aunt Dahlia's, I followed Kim inside the house and stopped her on her way to take a shower.

"That's not fair," I whispered. "You just can't do stuff like that and walk away."

"Why not? I was dying to know."

"Well? I nev— What *do* I kiss like, anyway?"

"Very, very sweet."

"Thank you."

"You're welcome. Now you can tell people you drive at night, oh . . . with just one hand, blow things up, and French-kiss older girls when nobody's watching."

I thought about slipping in something like *and I take baths completely naked with Emily Lohman.*

"Nobody has mottos that long."

I drove the car back to Dahlia's. It was still light outside, and we were happy to be home.

And satisfied.

Everything changed when we spent those days with Aunt Dahlia. We couldn't help it.

It was like the tide.

I never lied to Aunt Dahlia. It was one thing keeping secrets about other people—Bosten, Emily, Mom, and Dad—but I couldn't stand keeping secrets about me from her. So I told her that I'd driven her car home that day. I didn't say why, but maybe she already knew anyway. Maybe she could keep secrets about Bosten, too.

"I drive a lot of times," I said.

Her eyes smiled at me, like it was no big surprise. And she said, "When I was your age, there was no such thing as not old enough. You could either do something, or you couldn't."

"Well. I can drive."

"You're bigger than both of us," she said.

"If you're hiding something from me, don't put it on top of the refrigerator."

Dahlia laughed. "One day, I'll have you take me for a drive, Stark."

I nodded.

When Bosten and I were in bed, the phone rang. I sat up and saw the pass of Dahlia's shadow in the crack of light beneath our door.

Nothing good ever comes out of a telephone at night.

"I bet that's them," Bosten said.

"You want to get up and talk to them?"

"No."

There came a very soft knocking on our door.

Everything Dahlia ever did was soft.

She peeked in on us. "Your mother is on the phone," she whispered.

Bosten didn't move. It was like he was talking to the ceiling when he said, "Please tell her we're asleep, or we're out with our friends on the beach. Tell her anything you think of."

Dahlia just nodded and shut the door without making a sound.

"Bosten?"

"What?"

"Are you asleep?"

"Dumbshit."

"You know what?"

"What?"

"I made out with Kim today. She put her tongue in my mouth."

"Shut up."

"Swear to God."

"Why?"

"She told me she wanted to. Just like that. And I thought it was sexy."

"Did you like it?"

"Yeah."

"See? I told you."

"What?"

"You *are* what you *are,* Stick. Nobody and nothing is going to make you change."

My brother knew the truth about everything.

Easter was laundry day.

We had to get ready to go home.

I'd never been to a funeral, but I couldn't imagine anything could have made Bosten and me feel gloomier than thinking about leaving Dahlia and California.

And in those last few days on the Strand, we surfed from morning to evening.

Kim didn't make out with me again, but I so desperately wanted to. Neither of us said a word about it. Sometimes she'd hold my hand, or put her arm across my back out in the water, but she did that kind of stuff to Bosten and her brother, too. It was like nothing ever happened, which made it all seem even more like a dream to me, even if I couldn't get the taste of Kim Hansen out of my mouth.

The only good part about going back—if there was one—was that Mrs. Buckley and Paul were going to pick Bosten and me up at the airport in Seattle. They were going to take me to the Lohmans' house, and Bosten was supposed to stay with Paul until the weekend before school started again. So that meant I'd get to keep my Sex Wax shirt and actually wear it for Emily in Washington.

And, probably, with Mom out of the house, nobody would ever find it, anyway.

I was barefoot, wearing only my Washington jeans and nothing else, carrying every last article of clothing Bosten and I owned in a bundle through Aunt Dahlia's kitchen.

"Can you show me how to work your washer?" I said.

"Oh, sweetie, you just leave those here on the table and I'll take care of you boys' washing."

"Really?" I hesitated to put our stuff down on top of her table.

"Really. Don't be silly, now."

I put down the bundle of laundry. Socks and everything. "Me and Bosten always have to do our own stuff at home. Mom says boys' things are dirty."

"What kind of crazy notion is that?"

I didn't know what kind of crazy notion it was.

Bosten was dressed the same as me—jeans and nothing else—and he came scooting out of the bedroom when Evan and Kim knocked on Dahlia's front door. It was going to be our last day surfing together.

The twins already had their wetsuits on.

They smelled like Sex Wax.

I know I will never get that particular smell out of my head, no matter how long I live or don't live. The four surfboards leaned against Dahlia's rickety fence, and Evan carried the extra two suits he'd been loaning us all week, flopped over his shoulder like dead animal hides.

All of us could see the gloom in one another's eyes. In some ways, I guess, that was a good thing, because it meant that we really were friends, and that, maybe, Bosten and I did find a place where we could fit in. And it was a place that had only one rule, as far as I could tell, and it was an easy rule to follow: Love each other.

Evan plopped the wetsuits down on Dahlia's living room floor. "You guys can have these. Take them back to Washington with you."

"Really?" I said.

"Really. I get a new suit every few months, anyway."

Bosten said, "I don't think any guys surf in Washington."

"Then hold on to them until you come back," Evan said. I could tell it was kind of hard for him to say that. He shrugged, and added, "Besides, you peed in them."

"Ha!" I laughed. "Only about a million times! Thanks, Evan."

Bosten picked up his suit and started back toward our bedroom so he could put it on. I noticed Kim, standing behind her brother on the cracked walkway leading to Dahlia's door.

She said, "You know you guys have eggs out here?"

"What?" I said.

"Eggs. Colored eggs. All over in the sand."

Dahlia came out of the kitchen. She laughed. "You can't go anywhere till you do the egg hunt." Then she added, apologetically, "They don't

hide too well

in sand, I guess."

I went out onto the walk. Dahlia's yard was littered, everywhere, with colored eggs.

It was beautiful in the morning light.

"This is the coolest and most amazing Easter egg hunt ever," I said. Then I said something that just kind of fell out of my mouth: "I love you, Dahlia."

Bosten and I hurriedly changed into our wetsuits, then we went out into the yard with the twins and Aunt Dahlia to look for eggs.

And sometimes
we pretended
that we couldn't see them,
just to make Dahlia
stay out there longer with us.

Dahlia let us phone Washington that evening. Not to talk to Mom and Dad. I wanted to talk to Emily, and Bosten wanted to hear Paul's voice. I think he wanted to test things and see how Buck was feeling about him, now that they'd been apart for a week.

I went first.

As usual, Mrs. Lohman answered the phone.

I could tell right away from the heaviness in her voice that she knew about my parents splitting up. But she didn't really know how things were. Mom and Dad always seemed so perfect.

Everything always seemed so perfect.

"Oh my God, Stick! Are you okay?"

"Uh. I'm fine, Mrs. Lohman. And I'm really looking forward to visiting with you tomorrow."

"Oh, Stick."

She sounded like she was about to cry.

"I hope you know that if there's anything you need—"

"Um. May I please speak with Emily?"

"Sure, baby. We'll see you tomorrow."

"I'll see you tomorrow, Mrs. Lohman."

Dahlia sat at the table. She was listening, but I didn't care. There was nothing I had to hide from her, and she made me feel almost normal most of the times.

"Stick?"

"Hi, Em."

"How's California?"

At least she knew how to talk to me and not make me feel like I was in a hospital bed, dying.

"Oh my God, Em, it is so incredible here. Bosten and I learned how to surf. And we're pretty good at it. Well, Bosten's better than me."

"Does your *aunt surf?*"

I laughed.

It was like that. And Aunt Dahlia never once made me feel like my time was limited, or that telephones were not healthy things for boys. But I didn't want her to have to pay too much for long distance, either, and I knew Bosten was patiently waiting to give Paul Buckley a call. So I talked to Emily for about five minutes; and, in that time, I realized how much I missed her and needed to see her. And for the first time in my life, I honestly thought about kissing her. Not just thought about it, I wanted to.

On the mouth.

Like Kim taught me.

When I hung up, I noticed that Bosten had been standing in the doorway between the kitchen and living room. I winked at him, then took Dahlia by the hand and said, "Hey, Dahlia. Do you want to go for a walk with me?"

And Dahlia's eyes lit up like I was giving her a present or something. She stood right up and said, "Should we wait for your brother?"

I said, "No. It's just me and you."

"Is Emily your special friend?"

We walked out toward the jetty. The sun had gone down, but the sky was pale on the horizon, and everything seemed so clear.

"Yes. She's my best friend. Well, besides Bosten. Or you."

"It's better, I think, to have a 'best friend' than a girlfriend," Dahlia said. "Girlfriends are your friends because they're girls. But best friends are people you can share everything with and not be afraid they'll leave you with less."

"That's how it is," I said. "Exactly."

It was almost like she knew about me making out with Kim.

"Dahlia? There's something I need to tell you. I want to say that I am very sorry for how mean I was to you that first day. I didn't know. And I didn't think you, or anybody else in the world, wanted me and Bosten around them, anyway. So. Uh. I am sorry."

Then Dahlia hugged me so hard and just squeezed me. And nobody had ever really held me like that before in my life. She stroked my hair and said,

"What am I going to do
without you boys around?
What am I going to do?"

Kim kissed Bosten and me at the airport, but it wasn't a kiss like I got from her the afternoon we went to C Street. It was a sad kiss, because it said good-bye, the same way Evan's hand did in mine when we shook.

She and Evan rode with us in Dahlia's car. I was glad for that, not just for me and Bosten, but because I didn't want Aunt Dahlia to be lonely after we left.

I squeezed Dahlia so hard when we had to leave, and then me and Bosten just ran down the boarding gate without looking back. I didn't want to look at her again because I was starting to cry—we all were—and I felt like something inside me was getting killed.

Nothing would ever be the same again.

EMILY

It wasn't a long enough flight from Los Angeles to Seattle to make the sadness leave my head, or to stop thinking about all the *nevers* that seemed to pile up: never, on never, on never, like mountains in front of me.

Just before the plane landed, Bosten punched my shoulder and said,

"Snap out of it."

I punched him back. "*You* snap out of it."

"I know."

"What did Paul say last night?"

I already knew the answer, could tell by how relieved my brother seemed to be acting when Dahlia and I came back from our walk.

"Eh. He said he broke up with his brand-new girlfriend."

"That experiment didn't last long, did it?"

Bosten smiled and shook his head. "Nope."

"Oh good God! Look at you two!" Mrs. Buckley was practically in tears when she saw us at the airport. I fired a quick glance at Paul and could see in his eyes how much he wanted to hold my brother.

And I thought, why doesn't he? That's so dumb.

"You are so dark! You boys look completely new!" she said. "Look at your hair!"

I guess we didn't realize how much being out on the water all day had changed our appearances. We were tan and healthy-looking; and until Mrs. Buckley had said it, I didn't really notice how much lighter Bosten's hair had gotten.

And now we were back home in cave-salamander land.

Where Mom and Dad lived.

Besides giving me a boner every time I saw her, Mrs. Buckley drove just about the coolest car imaginable: a brand-new white and blue Trans Am, complete with air-intake, and a big bird-thing painted across the hood.

Bosten and I stuffed our bags in the trunk, and then Paul said, "I'll let Stick sit up front. He's tallest, anyway."

I didn't think I was the tallest, but I wasn't going to plead to squeeze into the backseat, either. And, anyway, there was always the chance that his mom would brush my leg with her fingers when shifting gears.

When we got to the other side of the Puget Sound, Mrs. Buckley asked if we needed to stop by our house and pick up any clothes or things, and Bosten and I both said no at the same time.

I turned around and looked through the gap between the bucket seats.

Paul had his hand on Bosten's knee; and my brother's arm was stretched across the top of the seat so his fingers touched the back of Paul's neck It was innocent enough, I guess, and there was no way Mrs. Buckley could tell what was going on, anyway.

They seemed really happy, and I was glad for that. But maybe I stared at them a little too long, because Paul fired a vicious dirty look that turned me around.

Everyone got out of the car when we arrived at the Lohman house. It was so close to our home, I could practically smell the cigarette smoke drifting over from Dad's chair, on the other side of the highway.

Mrs. Lohman threw open the door to the mudroom and stood on the porch. Then Emily squeezed her way around her mother and waved at me.

I was so glad to see her, so relieved to stop moving, being shuffled from one place to another, and sitting down for that entire day. I put my face inside my Sex Wax T-shirt and smelled.

"What the hell are you doing?" Bosten said.

"I still smell like the Strand. Like Dahlia's house."

Bosten put his nose into my neck. "You do."

I wanted it that way.

I purposely didn't take a shower after the last time we surfed together. There was still sand in my hair, too.

Mrs. Lohman said, "Stick! And just in time for dinner, too!"

"I'll be right there, Mrs. Lohman!"

Bosten came around and lifted my suitcase from the trunk of the car. He put it down next to my feet.

He looked sad. Paul looked anxious. And Mrs. Buckley looked like she always did.

Perfect.

I hugged my brother. Except for that time when he was in ninth grade and ran away from home for four days, we had never stayed in separate houses for more than just single-night sleepovers, and, in our family, those were rare occurrences.

"I love you, Bosten."

"Love you, Sticker. I'll see you Saturday."

"Yeah. See you."

"Hey," he said as I started to turn away. "That was the best."

"Sure was."

My suitcase felt especially heavy as I walked up the steps toward Mrs. Lohman and Emily. Bosten climbed in the back, and Paul got in the front seat next to his mom. In an instant, that fancy sports car roared away up the road toward Pilot Point.

Just about the first thing I had to do when I got inside the house, after taking off my new shoes, was explain to Emily and her parents what the Sex Wax shirt was all about. Mr. and Mrs. Lohman didn't approve of it at first, but when I told them everything I could about surfing, they seemed to accept it more easily.

"I wouldn't recommend you try wearing that around school, Stick," Mr. Lohman said.

"Or my dad." I tried to smile. It was a grim smile, a bad news smile.

I didn't really want to think of school or Dad at the moment.

And anyway, I didn't get what the hang-up was on a *word*.

Evan told me that one time he'd worn his Sex Wax shirt to Disneyland, and they wouldn't let him in unless he turned it inside out, so nobody could read the word "Sex." They said it was offensive. Bosten and I had never been to Disneyland, but after hearing that from Evan, I thought that maybe they had rules about the color of your underwear, too—just like Dad.

But before we sat down to dinner, I opened my suitcase on the floor of the Lohmans' mudroom and pulled out the hockey puck-shaped pack of Sex Wax I had, just so they could smell it, and see what surf wax was used for.

I showed them my wetsuit, too. But I didn't tell them about peeing in it.

I felt like an explorer, coming back from Africa with rare and exotic trophies.

Mr. Lohman said Sex Wax smelled so good he wanted to take a bite out of it for dessert.

He laughed when I told him how I'd tried that one time, but I almost threw up, and then it took about half a day to get the wax off the back of my teeth.

In all the years I'd known the Lohmans, it never came up about how the boys of the McClellan family didn't sleep in pajamas. Well, it didn't, that is, until Mrs. Lohman and Emily walked into the guest bedroom to tell me good night. Emily's mom carried a glass of milk and some cookies for me.

That's when they found out about the "no pajamas" thing, I guess. Because I was standing there, wearing absolutely nothing more than a pair of white (of course) briefs, about to climb into my own, private guest bed that smelled so nice, just like the conditioner Emily had used on my hair that day we took a bath together.

And Mrs. Lohman looked like she suddenly discovered a school of live electric eels in her panties. She said, "Oh my gosh!"

She then immediately dropped the cookies and the glass of milk all over the floor, while her arms became frantically occupied, flailing like she was drowning or something, pushing Emily behind her so she wouldn't be able to look at me.

My feet were soaked from the milk. There was broken glass and soggy cookies all over the floor, and Mrs. Lohman turned so red, holding Emily behind her with both her hands like she was protecting her daughter from a vampire.

"Stick! I am so sorry!"

Horrified, trying to keep her eyes averted, she began backing out through the doorway.

"It's no big deal, Mrs. Lohman," I said.

I bent down and started picking up pieces of cookie, glass, and plate.

It really was no big deal, but I wasn't about to tell Mrs. Lohman that her daughter and I had seen each other completely naked before.

Like Emily said, her mom probably wouldn't understand.

Emily giggled.

Her mom got mad. "Close your eyes, Emily!"

Yeah. Telling Mrs. Lohman about our bath was entirely out of the question.

Like, forever.

I didn't really have any option but to just stand there. I was barefoot, and there was milk and shards of glass everywhere around me.

"I guess I should have told you that me and Bosten aren't allowed to wear pajamas. At Aunt Dahlia's, she even let us eat breakfast in our underwear. It's no big deal at all."

That's what Emily would have said, too, if she wasn't laughing so hard.

"Stick! Don't you move, sweetie. I don't want you to cut your feet. Now, you stop trying to pick up that mess. I'll be right back."

She spun around and pushed Emily out into the hallway, but I could see Em poke her head around her mother's hip and smile at me once before she was completely protected from my inappropriateness and ushered away to her own room.

From somewhere down the hall, I heard my best friend's voice calling out, "Good night, Stark McClellan. I'm glad you're back home."

I kind of liked the way Emily said my name.

Mrs. Lohman came back, out of breath and flushed; and as she had ordered me to, I hadn't moved one inch away from my spot on the floor, standing with my feet in the middle of a slick of milk that I would much rather have drank than worn.

"Here, baby, sit. Oh! I am so sorry!"

She really was kind of going overboard.

I sat on the edge of the bed, and Mrs. Lohman carefully, gently, toweled off my feet. And, yes, I felt bad about thinking how her doing that to me felt really, really good.

"Too bad about those cookies," I said. "You make the best cookies in the world."

She looked up at me.

I thought she was going to cry.

She even dried in between my toes.

Definitely overboard.

"Oh. I just don't know what to do. I never knew the first thing about having a *boy* in the house. Please, forgive me, Stick."

The way she said "boy" sounded like some kind of disease.

"It's no. Big. Deal."

Mrs. Lohman pulled the covers down from the bed, then she scooped up my scrawny legs in the crook of her arm and slid them between the coolness of her wonderful-smelling sheets. She lifted my head, fluffed two pillows behind my shoulders, tucked the sheets down between the mattresses as tight as any mummy or papoose was ever wrapped, and then gave me a kiss, right on top of my head.

"I am so sorry."

Overboard.

And drowning.

Then she said, "I'll bring you some fresh cookies and a glass of milk. Just don't go anywhere."

Apparently, she believed *boys* could just vanish at will or something.

And why would I want to, anyway, if Mrs. Lohman was bringing back some of her cookies?

I couldn't sleep.

And I couldn't make my head be quiet.

So I rolled onto my left side. I trapped it all in.

Tried to starve those animals.

Mom and Dad
never wanted us.

Me.
Bosten.
Especially me.
I was the reminder
of everything
that was
wrong.

But Bosten came first
and paid the most.

He did the math.

Things don't change you.
And it doesn't just happen.

I felt stupid for crying.
I could have cried a thousand times before then.
But I felt so small and alone,
and I wanted to steal down the hall
so I could put my hand on Emily's face
or rest my head in her mother's lap.
I wanted to have Aunt Dahlia hold me so tight
and so relaxed
like there was nothing at all between our hearts.

I wanted
I wanted
mother.

I dreamed of climbing
through the window
of Saint Fillan's room
carrying a flame.

In the morning
my chains had not come loose.

I think Mrs. Lohman half expected me to show up at her breakfast table in my underwear. She was still nervous and embarrassed about what had happened in my room the night before. I could tell by the way she kept her eyes down, like she had to concentrate on counting the exact number of times she whipped frantic clockwise circles with the wire whisk in a bowl of pancake batter.

So I let her off the hook. I wore the shorts Aunt Dahlia had bought for me, and some clean socks, with a plain, white T-shirt, so she wouldn't have to stare at that word that got people so weirded out. And when she finally braved a cautious glance at me from her mixing duties and saw how I looked, I could almost feel the wave of relief, just like a big, fat swell past the craggy point of the jetty, lifting me up and making me forget about the terrible night I had just spent, not sleeping in that bed upstairs.

"Emily!" She bellowed out to the space that was her house. "Your friend's ready for his breakfast!"

And something about the way Mrs. Lohman said that made me feel a lump in my throat.

I wanted to hug her.

But I didn't.

Emily came downstairs, wearing slippers and yellow pajamas that had rabbits on them. She looked so soft and warm. I wondered what it would be like to sleep with her. And I mean just *sleep*, too, not anything else. But just thinking about that made me wonder what other things might be like, too.

I looked down at my hands on the table.

I didn't feel very good.

Everything was different.

Before I knew it, Emily came over to where I was sitting and put her hands on both sides of my face and lifted it.

People don't touch me.

But I could put up with Emily doing it.

"You look terrible," she said. "Like a raccoon. Look at your eyes!"

I wondered how anyone could look at his own eyes.

"Let me see," Mrs. Lohman said.

Emily's dad put his newspaper down and leaned over so he was practically chin to chin with me. "You do look a little dead from the neck up, son."

"I didn't sleep much last night," I said.

Then Mrs. Lohman grabbed my head and looked me square in the eyes. She laid her palm across my forehead. Her eyes filled with worry.

"You poor baby."

And the way she said it wasn't just, like, "Oh, I'm concerned you might not be feeling well."

It was more like, "Your parents are splitting up. You don't have a family. You were born wrong. There's something missing. And, by the way, you might have a cold, too."

"You're burning up," she said. "You poor baby."

I had pretty much had enough of being pouted over and touched at that point.

I sighed.

I wished I could be back at Aunt Dahlia's on the Strand.

"We need to get you back to bed."

I smelled pancakes burning.

I wished it was my house instead.

Mrs. Lohman put her hand on my shoulder and scooted my chair out so I could stand up. I guess I did feel a little dizzy and cold, but I hadn't slept, either, and my head was still full of that awful noise.

"Aw, I'm sorry, Stick," Mr. Lohman said. "I was going to take you and Emily down to the pier to do some fishing today."

He sounded sincerely disappointed.

It was weird. I mean, people caring about how I felt.

Mr. Lohman owned a little store by the pier that sold tackle and snacks, and he liked to take us fishing off the float.

"Maybe you'll feel up to it tomorrow," he said.

I nodded, and Mrs. Lohman began leading me out of the kitchen, toward the stairs.

"Fred, shut that off," she said, pointing Mr. Lohman toward her griddle.

Emily swooped in ahead of us as we went up the stairs. She opened the door to my room. I had already made the bed, and when her mother saw it, she groaned a little disappointed moan in the back of her throat.

But that was also a rule in my house. We couldn't come out of our rooms in the morning without making our beds first. And tucking our shirts in.

Emily peeled the covers down off the bed and stood there, watching as her mother led me across the perfectly clean floor where she had dropped the milk the night before.

"You step out of the room while this boy gets into bed," Mrs. Lohman instructed.

And as she went out into the hallway, before turning her back to the door, Emily gave me a wry look that said nothing really mattered, anyway.

Emily.

I slipped my shorts off and nearly collapsed onto the sheets. Then Mrs. Lohman carefully pulled the socks from my feet and tucked the covers over me. She brushed her hand across my forehead again and gave a sympathetic and cooing "Awww, now . . ."

She snapped my shorts flat and smooth with a flick of her wrists and folded them around my socks. "We'll bring you up some breakfast, sweetie. Here. Why don't you take that shirt off? You're about to melt, I think."

I sat up in bed.

Emily came back into the room as I was slipping my T-shirt over my head.

Then Mrs. Lohman said, "I think I better call your—"

Who?

Who would she call?

My mother was gone, and Dad? Dad just wasn't the person to call in these kinds of situations.

"No!" I said. I let my shirt drop on the floor. It was already damp, and Mrs. Lohman, eyeing me with concern and hurt, picked it up instantly.

"I'll wash this."

"Please don't call anyone, Mrs. Lohman. Please. I'll be fine."

She pulled the covers up to my shoulders and I leaned back on the pillows.

"I'll bring you some breakfast, baby."

The way she looked at me made me feel horrible, like I wanted to cry or something. And as she left us there, Mrs. Lohman said, "I suppose we can wait and see how you're doing this afternoon."

"Thank you."

Emily slid a chair across the floor and sat down, right next to my face. So close, I could smell her hair.

"Don't you want to have your breakfast?" I said.

"I'll have it in here. With you."

"I'm sorry about this, Em."

"Don't be dumb."

"I wasn't sad until last night. I guess I am being dumb."

"Well. Stop it."

"Okay."

She brushed her hand through my hair. She never did that before, not like this. I closed my eyes.

"I wish I could make you feel better."

"You are."

"It's going to be okay."

"Em?"

"What?"

"Nothing."

"What were you going to say?"

"Uh. Are you going to the pier with your dad today?"

She laughed. "That wasn't what you were going to say, Stark McClellan."

"I like that now."

"What?"

"When you say my name."

"Well. That's your name. Your name has always been your name. And, no, I am going to stay here with you. I missed you."

"I missed you, too, Em."

Mrs. Lohman appeared in the doorway, carrying a tray with pancakes and juice and milk.

I said, "Don't drop it."

Mrs. Lohman smiled. But I could tell she kept worrying about me, and about my parents, too.

"I've never had breakfast in bed," I said.

"Well, I hope this makes you feel better, sweetie. You just tell Emily if there's anything you need."

Emily stood out of the way while Mrs. Lohman put the tray down across my legs. "I'll be right back, Stark McClellan. I'm bringing some for me."

Then she flew out of the room.

"Is that something new?" Mrs. Lohman said.

"Huh?"

"Calling you *Stark McClellan.*"

"Oh." I shrugged and took a mouthful of pancake. "She's just joking around."

. . .

I didn't get better.

Emily sat there with me all day, too, like she said she would.

I woke up in a sweat in the early afternoon, when Mrs. Lohman was downstairs talking to my father on the telephone.

I didn't care what they said, just knowing what was happening made me feel worse.

Emily wiped my forehead with a cool, wet washcloth. It felt like when we took our bath together.

"Are you feeling any better?" she whispered.

I shook my head.

I pushed the covers entirely off of me. I was soaked, but I immediately began shaking from the intensity of the sudden cold.

"What are you doing?" Emily sounded annoyed. She stood up and grabbed the covers, to pull them back across my shivering bones.

I grabbed her hand and held it steady. I flattened her palm on my chest and pinned it there, just watching her. I don't know for certain what I was thinking. I was so sick and feverish and I only wanted Emily's cool hand to touch me.

And I wanted all the noise in my head to go away.

Emily waited.

She didn't pull back. She kept her hand on my chest.

I felt my heart through her.

"My mom's coming."

She picked the sheet out from the folds and twists in the bedclothes and draped it over me.

"Okay?" she said.

I closed my eyes and nodded.

Mrs. Lohman came through the doorway.

"He woke up," Emily said. "He was too hot."

I could hear Emily's mom as she took a seat on the chair

next to me. Then she wiped my face and forehead with the cool cloth. I opened my eyes.

"Your father said I should call him back if I think you need to go to the doctor."

"Do you think I need to go to the doctor?"

"No, Stick."

I stayed that way until Thursday.

Then the fever broke.

Mrs. Lohman never called my father again.

But I had to go home on Saturday, and I was afraid.

I had been doing the math.

I stunk. I needed a bath.

"I would like to, but we can't," Emily whispered. "I want to wash your hair. But."

"I know. Tell your mom I feel like getting up now."

"No. I'll go start the water for you."

"Thanks."

She stayed in the bathroom and watched as I shakily lowered myself into the tub.

This time, I think we both felt like we were stealing something.

Mrs. Lohman was in the kitchen.

We didn't say anything.

Emily came over and sat down on the edge of the tub. She filled the little cup with warm water and poured it over my head. Emily rubbed her fingers around and around my scalp. Then the coolness of the shampoo, more water, the cloth she'd use to rub suds into the back of my neck, my shoulders, and my chest.

I could have gone to sleep.

Everything was so quiet, so perfect.

It was like not being alive, and not being dead, at the same time.

Then Emily leaned down and whispered, "I better go."

I nodded. I kept my eyes down, watching the swirls of foam twisting on the surface of the bathwater.

I wondered what the waves were like at the Strand.

She put her lips so close to my ear. "And, goof, you forgot to bring any clothes to put on. I'll go get some for you."

"Okay."

Then Emily did something.

That was a miracle.

She kissed me on the back of my neck.

It wasn't like the kiss Kim gave me.

It was something else; a pure thing that, at the same time, didn't matter at all, and also had more words in it than I could contain in my head.

I closed my eyes.

She said, "I want you to get better now."

Then I heard her go out the door.

We sat downstairs, playing Monopoly and drinking hot tea with lemon and honey, with Mrs. Lohman for the rest of the afternoon. I desperately wanted to go outside, but Emily's mom was stubborn in her insistence against it. I mostly wanted to be somewhere alone with Emily. But feeling better also brought my mind to thoughts of Aunt Dahlia and Bosten, to counting the time between my now and my then, my first and my next, and it made me feel so small, like a feather floating on the sea.

On Friday morning, after breakfast, Emily and I left the house and walked through the woods, along the bank of the Sound toward the pier. Mrs. Lohman had finally given me permission to go outside, but she instructed us both that she would call Emily's father at his store in an hour to make sure I was still alive.

It was a perfect spring day, cold and clear, and I could see the dark, flat expanse of the ocean through gaps in the pines and dogwoods. I thought if I could touch the water, I would feel some kind of connection with Evan and Kim, with Aunt Dahlia, too.

And I was finally alone with Emily.

When we came around a small point on the bank, I could just see the end of the pier, the people standing out against its rail, fishing, and their bright-colored windbreakers.

"Hey," I said.

Then I grabbed her hand.

"What?"

"Nothing. I just wanted to hold your hand."

"Oh. Okay."

"And tell you thank you, too."

Emily shrugged. She smiled. "You're welcome."

"I like you."

"Well, duh."

Emily. Why did she always have to be like that?

"But I don't think we should take a bath together anymore."

"Oh. Okay. Why?"

I swallowed. "Because everything's different."

"You mean, like, your mom and dad?"

"No. It doesn't have anything to do with them."

We stopped walking. I could see the roof of Mr. Lohman's store at the front of the pier.

"It's me," I said. "Everything's different, Em. I'm afraid things might happen."

"I hope you know that I don't understand you sometimes."

She let go of my hand and climbed down the rocks on the bank. It was low tide.

I stood up on the bank and watched her. "Why doesn't anything ever matter to you, Emily?"

She put her hand up across her brow so she could look at me. The sun was directly behind. "Why do *you* always have to make things into bigger deals than they really are, Stick?"

It made me mad. So mad, I didn't want to answer her. All the words got stuck in my head, anyway. I felt like I would explode.

I wanted to go home.

I turned around and walked away from her.

How could she say that?

Couldn't she see me?

Everything had changed.

Everything was a big deal.

Everything was ugly.

And I was just looking for something that mattered.

"Hey! Hey! Where do you think you're going? You can't just leave!"

"Why not?"

I didn't want to hear it anymore.

Emily scrambled up the bank after me, but I was already in the woods, walking fast. Walking away from her.

"Hey! I'm sorry if I said something wrong, Stick."

I kept going.

When she was close enough to touch me, she said, "Stark McClellan. You stop right now."

I turned around and faced her.

"I want to go home." My voice was choked with frustration. "I want Bosten."

"Oh."

That's exactly when I grabbed her and put my mouth on hers; and I kissed her perfectly, just the way I wanted to for so long.

At first, I think it surprised her. But I kissed her again and again, holding her perfect neck in my cupped palm, opening my mouth, tasting her breath as I slid my other hand up inside her sweater and pressed it against the smoothness of her back so our bodies were as close together as they could be.

And when I stopped and looked into her eyes, they were wide and open, and I could tell something had changed in her. She was suddenly so serious, like I scared her.

Emily said, "Oh."

"Yeah. Oh."

"I. Uh. Um. Stark."

"I know."

"You want to do that again?"

And I tried to sound as much like Emily as I could. "Maybe we can. Sometime."

Then I spun around and started heading back toward the water's bank and the pier.

Just like that.

"Are you kidding me?" Emily came running after me. "You're kidding, right? Are you?"

"Don't make such a big deal out of it."

She grabbed on to my shirt and turned me around. "Stark McClellan."

So I kissed her again.

And that was why we couldn't take another bath together.

At least, not for a while.

My mother phoned the Lohmans that night after dinner.

She wanted to talk to me.

I was afraid.

I held the phone for a moment and looked at Emily and her parents. I wanted them to leave, but if they did, I was afraid I'd just hang up and not even say hello.

It was like I could smell the cigarette smoke coming through the receiver.

"Stick?"

"Hello?"

"How are you, dear? Mrs. Lohman told me you've been ill."

"Uh. I'm okay, Mom."

"Well, you be sure that you're not biting your nails. You catch things biting your nails. From the dirt, you know."

"Oh. I'm not doing that, Mom."

"How did you enjoy California? Don't tell me you didn't. I've already spoken with Bosten."

"Oh. Mom?"

"What?"

"When are you coming back home?"

I looked at Mrs. Lohman when I said that. She looked like she would cry. I didn't mean to make her sad.

"I'm coming to take you shopping next Saturday. For your birthday."

I would be turning fourteen on Thursday. And I didn't care.

"Oh."

"Maybe the three of us can go. For Bosten's birthday, too."

Bosten's birthday wasn't for four more months.

"Oh."

"I'll pick you up about noon. We can go to Bremerton, if you want."

I couldn't sleep.

All I did was lie there, thinking about going back home in the morning. I imagined Bosten would come into my room at any moment and say, "Hey, Sticker, get your ass up and let's go blow something up."

But that didn't happen.

I was most afraid of seeing Dad again.

But that's just how things were going to be now.

It must have been midnight. The television downstairs had long since gone silent, and the house was completely dark. A finger tapped outside on my door.

I believed that somehow Emily knew what I was thinking.

She always did.

She came in and sat down on the chair next to me.

I think we just watched each other.

It seemed like all of forever, balled up inside just a minute.

Then she climbed onto my bed with me, squeezed herself inside the sheets next to me, and hugged me. It was tight and steady, and it made me believe there was nothing in the universe between me and Emily Lohman. My heart pounded as we held each other. I felt my penis pressing against her through the thin cotton of my briefs, and it scared and thrilled me at the same time.

Emily put her face next to mine on the pillow and whispered, so faintly, "I just want you to know how sad I am about all this, Stark. I just want you to know that I will always be here for you."

Then she got up and left.

Just like that.

DAD

Dad said, "I imagine you've got some laundry to take care of for when school starts back on Monday."

That was the first thing he said when Emily's father dropped me off.

Dad stayed outside and talked to Mr. Lohman while I carried my suitcase through the door and down the stairs to the basement. Emily waited in the car.

I tried not to make a big deal out of our quiet good-bye.

There were things I thought we needed to say, but we just didn't get around to them, and all those words were stuck inside my head, anyway.

We promised to meet each other tomorrow, the last day of our break from school.

Maybe I could tell her then, I thought.

It seemed like I had been gone for a long time, but as soon as I stepped through the door and smelled the air in my house, all the time and distance got smashed away like glass beneath a hammer blow. I looked to see if Bosten was home yet.

He wasn't.

As usual, he was smart, and did his math.

I tried to stay busy, to make myself invisible if I could. I'd unpacked my suitcase. The wetsuit Evan had given me was hanging up from the edge of my little window, so I could look at it. It still smelled like the sea.

And I hid my Sex Wax T-shirt at the bottom of my sock drawer. I don't think Dad had ever looked through my things one time in my life, but I could be wrong.

Everything was different now, anyway.

And the wax itself was stashed beneath my pillow, so I

could smell it when I went to sleep. It was like I had complete control of my world when I was inside my room.

But that was a dumb thing to believe.

Dad came downstairs while I was loading my laundry into the washer. He stood on the last step, smoking, watching me. I had to concentrate on what I was doing. He made me worry that I was going to do something wrong, and then he'd tell me how stupid I was.

"When your brother comes home, the three of us are going to sit down and have a talk."

"Oh. Okay."

"Things are different now. We have to make some new rules. You boys are going to have to start taking care of more duties."

"Yes, sir."

Dad watched me for a few more minutes. When his cigarette was smoked down to the filter, he went back upstairs.

In the early part of the evening, just before dark, Dad went out to the wellhouse, carrying his toolbox, cussing; the tip of his lit cigarette seesawing with every "goddamn" and "shit" that mumbled past his lips.

And I was so relieved when I saw Mrs. Buckley's Trans Am cutting up our drive from the highway. I slipped my shoes on and ran down the steps from the mudroom to meet them.

As soon as Bosten and Mrs. Buckley got out of the car, I could tell something was wrong. They both saw me—they had to—but neither one of them acknowledged it at all. And Paul wasn't with them; it was only the two of them.

"Hey!" I said, as I came up to the car.

Mrs. Buckley opened the trunk for Bosten, and he mournfully lifted his suitcase and began walking toward me.

Something was definitely wrong.

Bosten looked scared, sick.

"Hey, Stick," he said as he passed me, lugging his bag up the steps to the mudroom.

"What's—"

"Where's your father, Stark?" Mrs. Buckley didn't look like herself. It scared me a little.

"He's fixing the pump in the wellhouse. Is something wrong?"

She didn't answer. She turned and walked toward our well, down the little path on the hill. I thought I should go with her out of politeness, but I stopped after one step and chased Bosten inside the house.

He'd left his suitcase and shoes in the mudroom. I heard him going down the stairs to the basement. I kicked my shoes off and went after him.

"Bosten?"

He didn't say anything. He went into my room and sat heavily on my bed, staring down at the floor in the space between his knees.

"What's wrong?"

"I'm in trouble. Bad."

"What happened?"

Bosten looked at me. I knew what he was going to say. He took a breath. "She—"

"You and Buck?"

He nodded. "She flipped out. We thought no one was home. She caught us together."

"Oh."

"At first, nothing happened. Everything was so quiet and heavy, like after a bomb going off. We all just stayed there, stupid and embarrassed."

"What did she do?"

"She started screaming and crying then. She called Paul's dad at the golf course and made him come straight home. And she started hitting Paul and breaking things. She said she was going to call the police and have us arrested; that what she saw us doing was against the laws of the State of Washington and God, and we both deserved to be thrown in jail.

She flipped out.

Then she told me I needed to get the fuck out of their house."

"What are you going to do?"

"Dad's going to kill me."

"We need to leave, Bosten. Let's get out of here before he comes in."

"Where can we go?"

"I don't know. Let's go to the Lohmans. They'll know what to do. At least we should go there until things cool off."

That's when the front door slammed, and we could hear—feel—the vibrations of Dad, upstairs, storming through the house, knocking into things, screaming for my brother to come out.

"Bosten!"

"Let's go," I whispered.

But Bosten just sat there, frozen.

Dad was on the stairs, coming down.

"Bosten!"

Lights came on in the basement.

Then he was standing in my doorway, heaving with rage.

I was so scared, I felt my throat closing up. Dad came over to the bed and grabbed Bosten by the collar and flung him toward the door.

"I should have known about you. Get out of here! Get upstairs, you goddamned faggot."

He tried kicking him, but Bosten was too far away.

Then Dad went after him and grabbed the back of his shirt, but Bosten swiped Dad's hands away.

"Leave me alone! You're not going to touch me again!"

Bosten stumbled out of my room, and Dad was after him.

I got up, started after them, but Dad whirled around with his fist raised, and said, "You don't move. You come out of that room and I'll break your fucking neck."

He slammed my door shut when he left.

All I could do was sit there and listen to what went on upstairs.

I put things against the door.

I didn't want him coming for me.

What else could I do?

It was worse than anything I could ever imagine.

But that's how things were at our house.

They didn't just happen. They stayed that way.

I climbed onto my bed, wearing all my clothes, kept my light turned on.

I pressed my ear to the pipe.

The little golden rectangle was a black mirror to the outside night above me.

The first sounds
were things being broken.
Big things.
Things that nobody would ever fix.
It sounded
like the house itself was coming apart.
I heard some words.
Goddamn
Faggot
Queer

And after the words more things were broken.

But I was never so scared in my life as when everything went silent and stayed that way.

Perfectly.

Until morning gray showed on the other side of my little window.

I never stayed inside my room as late as ten in the morning before that day.

Sunday.

But I had to get out. I had to see if Bosten was going to be okay.

The night before, I had wedged a straight-backed chair below the knob on my door, and there was a dresser bracing it in place.

Dad never came down for me during the night.

Even after I had cleared the barricade away from my door, I waited with my ear pressed to the wood for several minutes.

I imagined being in one of those science fiction movies where the entire world has been destroyed, and I was the lone survivor who'd hidden away inside some lucky underground vault.

I checked for any sounds coming from the pipe. I even climbed up and looked through the window, across our lawn to the driveway and the little trail to the wellhouse where I last saw Mrs. Buckley the evening before.

Nothing.

I opened my door and crept upstairs to the house.

It was like everything had been turned upside down. Dad's chair was tipped backwards, as though someone would sit in it just to stare at the ceiling. And everything that had been hanging, framed, had been knocked down or broken. There were fist-size holes in the wall, like empty eye sockets; and I had to be careful, as I tiptoed around, of the shattered glass that was everywhere.

The only thing that hadn't been knocked over was the narrow table where Dad's ashtray still sat, perfectly centered, full.

But there were no sounds at all.

I walked lightly down the hallway toward the stairs that led up to Mom and Dad's room.

The Saint Fillan room stood open, empty. Untouched.

I stepped across to Bosten's room. His door was shut. I waited in the hallway for a while, but I couldn't hear anything inside, so I quietly opened the door to my brother's room.

It was empty, too.

Everything in it was perfect.

Finally, I worked up the nerve and floated, soundlessly, up the stairs to Mom and Dad's room. I kept my feet wedged against the side wall as I moved, so the planks on the staircase wouldn't creak.

The door was open.

I saw Dad inside, twisted up in the covers of his bed, sleeping.

He must have felt that I was looking at him. Dad rolled over and sat up straight. He still had all his clothes on. He just looked at me. Neither of us said anything for the longest time.

"What do you want?"

"Where's Bosten?"

Dad lay back down.

"He left. Who knows? Maybe he's off with his fag friend."

I went back down to my room.

I was alone in the house now.

Bosten was gone.

LAST:

bosten

EMILY

Both cars sat in the same worn spots they always occupied. Water dripped from the bumpers and wheel wells where the dew had collected and run down during the night.

Everything looked the same from the outside.

But things were different.

I tried to make a plan, but it was like standing in a road that didn't just fork—it writhed like the snakes on Medusa's head—and every one of those twisted choices in front of me was terrifying. No matter what Bosten believed, I knew I wasn't brave.

I felt like Dad was looking out from the upstairs window, so I never turned back one time. Not even a little. I followed the path down to the highway and crossed it. I ducked through the barbed wire that ringed the cow pasture on the Lohman property.

Once I had squeezed through the wires, I stood, watching for something—anything—across the highway, the tilted mailboxes, the driveway that led to my house that was now obscured behind a row of pines.

I screamed.

I screamed as loud as I could. It felt like the flesh in my throat would tear open. The same word, over and over, so that it went in there and stayed in my head forever.

Bosten
Bosten
Bosten

. . .

I didn't go to their house.

Emily came looking for me because I missed breakfast, and I'd promised to be there. It was nearly noon when she found me. I was still standing at the barbwire fence, looking out across the highway, waiting for my brother to come.

"Stark McClellan."

It was like she woke me up. Emily stood, her hands on her hips, in the pasture behind me. I guess she'd been watching me for a while.

"Something happened."

"What?"

"Bosten's gone."

"What do you mean, *gone*? Where?"

That was the first time I ever really thought about it. I mean, I couldn't get it out of my head that my brother was gone, but thinking about the *where* made everything that much more uncertain; and scarier, too.

I glanced out across the road. Emily came up and put her hand on my shoulder, but it was almost like I couldn't feel it anymore.

"You need to tell me what happened, Stick."

"I know."

I told Emily everything.

I tried to be brave.

I told her about Bosten and Paul Buckley first. I carefully watched her eyes to see if she'd show any sign that maybe she thought Bosten was sick, or bad or something—or maybe even if she'd look at me and wonder if I was gay, too. And maybe she did think that, anyway. After all, we'd taken baths together. She'd seen me naked more than once, and I know she felt how I pressed against her when we lay in bed holding on to each other; but I never tried anything beyond those couple French kisses we shared just two days before; and those kisses weren't about sex, anyway, they were about something else.

I know that now.

Then I told her about my dad, and how he'd beat us, usually every week or so. I told her about the Saint Fillan room. And I told her about the time Dad came home drunk and found me there; and how he'd thought I was Bosten and he started grabbing me.

Touching me.

Emily just watched me while I talked. She didn't say anything but kept her eyes on me, like she was letting me know it was okay for me to say whatever I needed to tell her. And it began to feel like I was letting all this poison out once and for all.

Like all the words could finally come out of my head.

"So, I don't know for certain, but I'm pretty sure my dad's been doing bad things to Bosten. Worse than just beating us up once in a while. Bosten started to tell me once, but I didn't want to hear it."

I thought about the night we stole away and drove to Bremerton and ate hamburgers at a diner called Nico's.

And I didn't even notice it until after I'd finally said that one telling thing about my dad and me and Bosten; but Emily was crying.

"Please don't cry, Em."

I put my hands up and wiped her face with my thumbs. Then we held on to each other and stood there by the fence.

Two cars drove by on the highway.

We didn't say anything.

We just held on.

"Um. I love you, Emily. Do you know that?" I wasn't ashamed or afraid to say it. "So please don't cry, okay?"

"Of course I know you love me. Do you think I'm dumb?"

"No. I don't."

"Well, I love you, Stark McClellan."

"I know."

And then I said, "You want to try to ride your stupid cows?"

And for some reason, Emily started crying really hard when I said that.

I didn't understand.

But just like that, everything became a big deal for her.

Just like that, I guess.

We walked through the woods toward the beach. Emily and I sat down on the bank, holding hands near the same spot where we'd shared our first kiss.

"If he doesn't come back, I'm going to have to do something," I said. "I can't live there alone."

"What are you going to do?"

"If Bosten doesn't come back home by Tuesday, I'm going to go look for him."

"Where would he go?"

"I think I know."

"Well, I'm going with you then."

"We'll both get in trouble. I don't want your mom and dad to get mad at me."

"Then I'll ask them to let me."

Emily was always like that.

"No. Don't say anything. Please?"

"Maybe you should try calling Paul Buckley from my house."

I thought about how Mrs. Buckley looked the last time I saw her; how Bosten told me she said for him to get the fuck out of their house.

"Maybe I could try that."

But I was already making my plan. I had to decide which snake to follow if Bosten didn't come home. I still had his wallet and driver's license, packed in the suitcase under my bed, from the time he made me drive for Mexican food with Evan and Kim. And we had long before paid Mr. Lohman the ninety-nine cents he charged us at his little store to grind a spare key for the Toyota. Bosten kept that key in his wallet, too.

Now it was mine.

I'd give him two more days. Then I'd have to do something.

So I needed to get ready, because, deep down, I knew Bosten was never coming back home again.

Emily took me back to her house, and eventually I worked up the nerve to dial Paul Buckley's phone number. And I knew it was bound to happen, that his mother would answer. I knew them well enough to expect that Paul would not be allowed anywhere near the telephone after what Mrs. Buckley caught him doing. She sounded cold, like a stranger to me, and simply told me that her son was "unavailable." It made me feel terrible, hearing that tone in her voice, so filled with hurt and anger.

"Mrs. Buckley? Did I do something wrong?"

I waited. And in that time, I thought I probably did do something wrong. Because I knew what had been going on between Bosten and Paul, but kept quiet about it. It wasn't something that needed to be told, anyway. For me, it was a no-win situation; but I still didn't ever believe there was anything wrong about what they did.

How could it be wrong to be in love with someone who is your equal; who you respect and trust?

I could almost feel Mrs. Buckley thinking about my simple question.

"No. You didn't do anything bad, Stark."

"Okay. I'm sorry if I did."

"Things will be all right."

"Mrs. Buckley? Bosten's gone. You don't know where he is, do you?"

"No."

"If you see him, will you tell him he needs to come home?"

"All right, Stark."

"And will you please tell Buck I said hi?"

Then she just hung up.

I wondered what she really thought about me.

Emily begged her mother to ask Dad if I could stay over for dinner. It wasn't difficult, because Mrs. Lohman knew there was urgency in Emily's request. I believed she most likely thought it had something to do with my parents' breakup.

It pretty much had nothing to do with that.

But she told Dad she'd drive me home by seven so I wouldn't have to cross the fields in the dark; and my dad didn't seem to care one way or the other, anyway.

When I got home, the house was completely dark. Dad's car was gone.

"Are you going to be okay, sweetie?" Mrs. Lohman put her fingers on my shoulder, stopping me for a moment as soon as I opened the car door to get out.

"I'll be okay, Mrs. Lohman. Thank you."

"Oh, Stick, I just feel terrible about all this."

I glanced back at Emily with a look on my face that I knew she'd understand: *Please don't say anything about Bosten.*

Emily nodded at me.

Then Mrs. Lohman hugged me and kissed the top of my head.

"See you at the bus stop, Em."

I got out of the car and walked into the mudroom. Alone.

• • •

It's hard to explain, but the house smelled like broken things. Maybe it was the dust from the fractured wallboards, the stillness of the air, the stale cigarette smoke, the kitchen garbage pail that had gone untended for days now. I don't know.

It just smelled *broken*.

I went downstairs, closed myself inside my room, and got my things ready for Monday morning school. I climbed into bed, and, lying there, looked up at my little window. I could see stars, and I pressed my ear to the pipe, but no sounds came at all.

I woke after two in the morning. Dad had come home. I could hear him moving around the house above me. I knew exactly what he was doing. He went into the two rooms in the hallway. Through the pipe, I heard him call my brother's name.

"Bosten?"

Nothing.

Then I heard slow and heavy footsteps, going up the stairs to Dad's room.

I made some toast and left for school before Dad woke up.

Emily could see by my expression that nothing had changed in the night. We met, like we always did, at the bus stop. I wore my Steelers cap for the first time since taking it off at Aunt Dahlia's house.

We hardly said anything to each other all morning. We held hands on the school bus, but I could sense her nervousness like electricity pulsing through her skin. It wasn't at all an Emily way of acting. I could tell she was doing the math; that she knew I meant what I'd said about going after Bosten if he didn't come home by Tuesday. And Tuesday was just hours away.

I had everything ready.

I even packed clothes for my brother. And our wetsuits, too.

Over the Easter break, Ricky Dostal had been liberated from his stitches; and he returned, whole but scarred, to Mr. Lloyd's gym class. In the boys' locker room, while we changed into our PE clothes, he and Corey Barr made it a point to talk crap about me, obviously thinking it would goad me into some kind of rematch with them. But I was too preoccupied with thinking about other things.

We were only allowed four minutes to get our uniforms on, anyway, so how much crap could they talk?

Well, a lot, as it turned out.

Living in Point No Point, it was impossible to have an entirely private life, even if Mom and Dad had always been pretty good at making the McClellans seem so perfect and normal. So, of course, everyone at school knew about my parents' splitting up. In Point No Point, divorces were as commonplace as waking up and finding a unicorn grazing in your yard.

And it bothered me a little that Ricky and Corey tried to pick on me about it. What annoyed me most was that they somehow had the idea that my parents' breakup mattered to me, when it didn't matter nearly as much as other things. I tried ignoring them, but as I pulled my ice-cold gym shorts up over my bare legs, I was already thinking about which one of them I'd punch first, if it came to that.

I guess everything *had* changed.

"Oh," Ricky said, "and everyone's saying how your faggot friend, Fuck Fuckley, tried to cut his own wrists or something. There were police and an ambulance at his house last night. Did you even know about that, retard? Fuckley's so fucking dumb, he used scissors to do it. I heard he almost fucking died."

That stopped me cold.

"What?"

"Ha-ha!" Ricky elbowed Corey. "You didn't know? Sorry to break it to you, retard. Your boyfriend's in the psycho ward. Hope you and your fuckface brother aren't too broke up about being the last dipshits on the planet to know."

Corey laughed.

At least they didn't know anything about Bosten vanishing. Yet.

And calling Paul a faggot? That was just what all boys in eighth grade called other boys, even ones they liked. As far as I could tell, nobody had any idea about Paul and Bosten being gay. I'm sure I would have heard all about it if they did. I was even more certain that Mr. and Mrs. Buckley would never tell anyone the truth about their son.

Ricky farted and slid his hand down inside his jock to adjust his balls.

I sat down on the bench in the middle of the aisle of lockers and pretended to tie my shoes while Mr. Lloyd stood at the open doors with his blue book of records, shouting, "Let's move it, girls!" and all the boys dutifully and uniformly filed out toward the gymnasium.

The day seemed to stretch and expand. Minutes passed by like wintry weeks. And I couldn't stop thinking about poor Paul Buckley, and how hopeless and impossible everything must have seemed for him to try killing himself. I wished I could say something to him, but I had the feeling that I'd never get to see Buck again. The more I thought about it, the angrier I got at Mrs. Buckley. There was nothing wrong with Paul. He was gay, not suicidal. At least, not until his mother flipped out about the whole thing, threatening to call the cops on her own son just for being in love with another boy.

And it scared me to think about what Bosten was doing, especially if, somehow, he'd heard about what happened to Paul. So I felt even more resolved about my decision to leave.

I tried to imagine what it would have been like, if I could have seen and heard what actually happened upstairs between my father and him, the night Bosten disappeared.

I could wish, fantasize, about my brother fighting back against Dad, just like he'd punched that asshole Ricky Dostal.

Emily sat on the aisle, and I leaned my chin toward the window. We held hands.

"Stark?" She put her face to my ear and whispered. Still, the bus was so noisy I could barely hear her.

"What?"

"I would like to kiss again when we get to our stop. Just like we did the other day."

"Okay. Um. Right there on the side of the road? In front of everyone on the bus?"

She pushed my hand. "Don't be dumb."

Emily laughed.

"Can you come over to my house for a little bit?"

"Is your mom home?"

"Yes."

"Then I guess we can't take a bath or lay down in bed together again."

I felt kind of guilty about how hard my dick was getting, thinking about doing those things; how close Emily's hand was to my fly.

"I bet my dad's not home. We could do it at my house if you want."

I honestly was hoping she'd say she wanted to.

"You know we better not do anything like that now."

"I know."

Of course, she was right.

Everything was different, and everything was a big deal now, for both of us.

We kissed in the woods beside Emily's house until the muscles in my jaw were sore and I was all-over sweaty and felt wet inside my underwear. Emily's face was red and she breathed in shallow hiccups and couldn't talk.

I took her hand. "Come on. Your mom's going to wonder where you are."

"I love you, Stark." She sounded sad. I knew what this was about.

"I love you, Emily."

And later, before I went home, she slipped her hand inside my pocket and tucked sixty dollars in there. Her fingertips found the tip of my penis, too, and it almost made me faint.

"You might need some money," she said.

"Um."

I didn't know what to say.

Emily pulled her hand out of my pocket. We stood on the porch, in the cold April wind that blew in from the west.

"And you better take care of yourself, Stark McClellan."

"Okay."

"And you better come back."

Dad wasn't home.

I loaded Bosten's and my stuff into the backseat of the Toyota.

And when I drove away, I thought,

I drive at night
I blow things up
I French-kiss older girls

when nobody's looking
I take baths
and go to bed
with Emily Lohman
because I love her
I love her
I love her
and I steal cars
two days before turning fourteen
so I can drive to California
and stop my brother
from falling
over the edge.

WILLIE

On my fourteenth birthday, I slept in the backseat of the car I stole, wrapped in a sleeping bag with my head resting on my brother's clothes that still smelled like cigarettes and Paul Buckley's deodorant.

I had parked in the muddy lot behind a gas station, waiting for someone to come and open the place for business. I knew I was somewhere north of Portland, and the Toyota had run out of gas.

Fearing the police, I kept off the main highways as much as I could, but I was almost certain I'd taken a wrong turn after crossing into Oregon and ended up going more toward Canada than California.

A map would probably have been a good idea.

I'd been too afraid to stop at a filling station. I never in my life put gas in a car all alone, and for the past two days I had convinced myself that everyone in the world would be on the lookout for a car thief who was missing his right ear.

So I never took off the Steelers cap that Emily had given me.

I spent most of the first day parked along the Cowlitz River, hungry, waiting for something that never happened.

I ran out of gas on Wednesday night at about ten o'clock. I had to put the car in neutral and push it by myself with the window down so I could steer, all the way into the station. And it rained on me while I did that, so I threw Emily's cap inside the car and just kept pushing, counting the cars that drove past me without so much as slowing down.

Eleven of them.

By the time I got to the station, I was soaked and shivering; and I stripped naked right there in the mud behind a goddamned gas station, outside a place called Scappoose, Oregon, in the dark and rain, so I could slip into some dry clothes and bundle up in my sleeping bag for the night.

I left all my wet things in the trunk.

I hadn't eaten since the day before.

That's how things were going to be, I decided.

After midnight, I sang "Happy Birthday to Me."

There were only three people in the world I missed: Bosten, Emily, and Aunt Dahlia. So I pretended like they were there, singing with me, even if it felt empty.

The rain sounded like a swarm of bugs trying to eat their way into the husk of my car.

I was scared.

Then I went to sleep.

• • •

Willie Purcell and a girl named April I just naturally assumed was Willie's wife or girlfriend found me there and woke me up by tapping on my window around nine the next morning.

The rain had stopped during the night. The sky was clear and blue.

"Are you okay? You okay, buddy?" Willie kept tapping on the glass, pinching a quarter between his thumb and index finger.

When I opened my eyes, I gave him a dirty look. What would anyone else do? It was just about the most annoying sound I had ever heard and I just wanted him to stop that damned tapping.

At least I had the sense to lock the car doors.

Maybe Willie and April thought I was dead or something.

"I'm okay," I said. "I ran out of gas."

I bent as far forward as I could, over the flipped-up front passenger seat where I'd stretched my legs, and popped open the door.

Willie swung it wide the rest of the way and looked in, half smiling at me: the way you'd look at a trout on the end of a fishing line.

"I guess you picked the best possible place in the world to run out of gas at," he said.

When I looked at Willie, I thought he looked sick. He was so pale, his skin was the color of plastic piano keys, and he had curly red hair that swirled around his ears, with just the thinnest trace of beard fuzz that had obviously never been shaved, beneath the hook of his jawbone. His face was splashed with freckles.

I unzipped my sleeping bag and jammed my feet into the shoes Aunt Dahlia had bought for me.

It was like they were waiting for me to do something, but

what I did was just sit there in the back of that stolen Toyota with my feet stretched out over the front seat, yawning. I realized that I had never, not one time in my life, woken up from a night's sleep without a boner, and that morning was no exception. So I didn't really want to fiddle with myself or try to conceal it while attempting to get out of the car in front of Willie and that girl.

Because she would have given me a boner, anyway, just from the way she was looking at me. And I could tell she didn't have a bra on. There was something I really liked about the way breasts moved beneath cotton, so subtly heavy.

I stared at her.

At her breasts, actually.

"He's just a kid," she said.

"What are you doing out here?" Willie sounded a little too enthusiastic for me.

"I was sleeping," I said. "I told you. I ran out of gas last night."

Willie obviously worked there. I wouldn't imagine anyone would just show up at a gas station in the morning dressed in a blue jumpsuit with an Exxon patch embroidered on his chest unless he was a pump jockey.

He reached his open hand inside the car for me. "Well, come on. Let's push her over to the pump and get you set."

I pulled my Steelers cap down square so it covered that mistake on my head.

I was ready to get out.

While he filled the gas tank, Willie introduced himself and the girl to me. I stumbled getting the words out smoothly but managed to tell them my name was Bosten McClellan. I tried not to look at them when I said it. I'm a horrible liar. Instead, I watched the number wheels as they spun around on the pump.

"Boston? You mean, like the place?" Willie said.

"No. It's with an *e*. It's my name."

Willie shrugged.

"I think that's a cool name," April said.

I looked at her breasts; realized I needed to pee.

"How old are you?" she asked.

"Um." I almost told them it was my birthday. I had to think about it. "I'm going to be seventeen in August."

And just talking about Bosten—pretending to be inside his life—made me miss him terribly.

Willie lifted the Toyota's hood and began checking around in the engine. I didn't know anything about that kind of stuff.

The pump shut off.

Willie said, "Where are you heading, anyway?"

He wiped the oil stick on a blue rag that hung from his back pocket.

I thought about lying again but figured it didn't matter. At least, not here, in a place called Scappoose.

"I'm going to stay with my aunt. In California."

April said, "Nice."

I thanked Willie and paid him for the gas; then I got in behind the wheel and started the car. The engine turned over and ran for about three seconds, then we all heard a sudden pop, and the car died silently.

I looked up at Willie.

He said, "Uh-oh," and lifted the hood again. "That's a fan belt."

"What?"

When I turned the key again, there was nothing more than a click and a buzz.

I got out and walked around to the front of the car. When I looked down, I saw a black snake of frayed rubber coiled on the ground beneath the motor.

"Yep." Willie looked at me, his eyes sincere and apologetic. "I bet you five dollars that alternator's done."

He might as well have been speaking Chinese.

"It is?"

"Done."

Counting Emily's money that I kept in my back pocket, in Bosten's wallet, along with ten more dollars I'd stashed away in my suitcase, I had a total of sixty-one dollars after paying for the gas. Whatever Willie was talking about didn't sound too good to me.

April squeezed up to the front bumper between me and Willie and looked into the engine compartment. I couldn't help but notice how her breasts hung down when she leaned forward, and I thought she must know more about cars than I ever did.

She had to have known I'd been looking at her, too.

I rubbed my eyes. "What's it going to cost to fix it?"

"I might be able to get you a rebuilt one installed for about thirty dollars," he said.

"Oh."

April glanced at me. There was something in her eyes that told me she cared. Maybe I was just hypnotized by her boobs.

"I think I might be able to afford that."

"Well, it's not happening today. I'll have to get my parts guy from Portland to drive it up here. Maybe get it in first thing in the morning," Willie said.

I sighed.

"Do you think it would be okay if I slept out back in my car again tonight? I don't want to pay for a place to stay. I'm afraid I might not have enough money to make it to my aunt's house at this rate."

Willie looked at April, then at me. "I'll tell you what. I have a houseboat on the river with an extra room I rent out. Nobody's staying in it right now. I could let you stay there tonight, I guess. Maybe tomorrow, if you need to."

"I don't mind sleeping in my car."

"Do whatever you want, kid. I'm not asking you to pay rent. You probably shouldn't be out here all alone, anyway. We do get the cops in here, pretty much every day, you know."

I watched Willie's eyes when he said that. He knew there was a lot more to what I'd been telling him. He wasn't stupid.

"It's a cool boat," April said.

"For nothing?" I asked.

Willie smiled. "Nothing, kid. I hope you make it to California. We'll get this car fixed by tomorrow, and I'll give you as much of a break as I can on the price. Just my cost. No labor."

"Why?"

Willie grinned. "I ran away from home more than a few times. But I never got anywhere doing it."

So we pushed the Toyota into the garage, and I hung out at the station for a few hours helping Willie pump gas and wash customers' windows. It was the least I could do, considering how he was willing to help me out.

For nothing.

April cut hair in town for a living. Maybe ten minutes after Willie and I pushed the Toyota into the service bay, she left in their truck; but she said she'd come back and pick me up after noon to take me to the boat.

I did feel a little uncomfortable about the whole arrangement, but this was how things were going to be. I was stuck, and there was no getting around it. It was like being adrift and alone on the sea. And all I could do to calm my mind was to keep thinking about how, some way, Bosten was going to make it to Aunt Dahlia's before me, and he would be there waiting, too, when I finally showed up.

But I did the math.

I still had a long way to go.

Both of us did.

I washed up in the dirty restroom around the side of the station. It had one of those towel dispensers that looped a length of filthy cotton from a slot on its underbelly. I didn't want to touch it.

When I came out, I had my flannel unbuttoned and I'd pulled my T-shirt up out of my jeans so I could dry off my face. I had the Steelers cap in my hand and wasn't really looking where I was going. I walked square into Willie's chest.

That's when he saw my ear.

"Whoa," he said. "Careful, there."

And he grabbed my shoulders with his oilblack hands and stood me back at arm's length. He had this look on his face like he was watching some horrible accident.

I am an accident.

Do you think I don't know that?

"Wow! What happened *to you?*"

I fumbled with my cap, pulled it tight over my head. "Nothing happened to me. I was born this way."

Willie could tell I was annoyed. He backed off, embarrassed. "I'm sorry, Bosten. I . . . um. Can you hear okay?"

I tucked my T-shirt in and began buttoning up my flannel. "I can hear fine. Look, if you think I'm a freak or something, you and April can just let me stay in my car, like I asked."

"Hey. Hey now," Willie said. "I didn't mean anything, kid. I bet you've gotten enough shit about that for two lifetimes. I'm sorry. Really."

"Fuck it." I was fed up. I'd had enough. I walked away from Willie.

I just kept going, following the highway in the direction of the little town I'd seen in the distance.

"Hey!" Willie shouted after me. But he didn't follow.

"Hey! Bosten!"

A car pulled into the station when I looked back. I spit at the ground in front of me and kept walking.

I don't know what I was thinking. It wasn't like I was about to walk all the way to California; and just about everything I owned in the world—a suitcase with a tag that was the only thing with my name on it and ten dollars of my money, too—was sitting in that broken-down, stolen car that was stuck at the gas station.

I was so mad, I wanted to howl and punch somebody.

Anybody.

That was my fourteenth birthday.

Just like that.

And I was sick of all these rages that had been surging through me, because I couldn't control them. I couldn't control anything about myself anymore.

Because everything had changed.

So I kept walking until a truck pulled up slowly alongside of me, then drifted over and stopped on the shoulder of the road, right in front of my path.

April sat behind the wheel. When she turned around and looked at me, I had this momentary fantasy of getting in the cab and sticking my tongue in her mouth. Then I started getting a boner, and that made me even more disgusted with myself. I pulled my flannel out so my shirttail would hang down and cover my crotch. I realized there was nothing nonchalant at all in my doing that, and I felt the skin on my face getting hot, because she watched me the whole time.

She opened the door and came around to the back of the truck when she saw I had stopped walking.

"Is everything okay, Bosten?"

I took a deep breath.

"Yeah."

"Want to get in the truck? I can take you to the boat now. If you want."

I couldn't stop thinking about making out with her.

I swallowed. "Maybe I should get my suitcase."

"Okay. Come on."

I climbed up into the cab and April flipped a U-turn across the highway.

"You're not mad, are you? Willie feels terrible. Sometimes he just doesn't know what to say about things. You know, he's . . . well, he's not very mature."

"It's okay," I said. "I'm just stressed out about things, I guess."

April put her hand on my thigh.

I desperately wanted to grab my dick. My hand gripped the armrest, and I pushed myself back in the seat, like I was being thrust forward on a roller coaster.

"You'll like the boat," she said. "It's a totally cool place to hang out."

Willie came up to me while I was digging my suitcase out from the backseat of the Toyota.

"Look, kid. You gotta believe I didn't mean anything bad. I hope you're not bent up about this."

He put his hand out to me, and we shook.

"Don't worry about your car, man. It's a piece of cake. As soon as I get that part for you, we'll have it running and you'll be in California before you even know it."

"Okay."

"April will show you around the boat. Make yourself at home. Watch TV. I'll be around in a few hours."

"Willie? Um. I'm sorry about how I acted."

"Forget it."

I could forget it. That was easy enough. But I couldn't help but feel that Willie and April had wished they'd never thought about offering help to someone like me.

By the afternoon on my fourteenth birthday, the sky striped flat in ribbons of chalk and slate clouds that hung so low I could almost feel the pressure and weight of them, like a ceiling of sodden sponges that I could press my hands to if I had the courage to raise my arms high enough.

Here, the Columbia River looked more like a flat, unmoving bay, dotted with small nubbed islands that bristled with combs of gray pines. April pulled the truck off the road, steered it so the tires fit perfectly into naked grooves of mud that had been carved between the amber-burnt grasses that still hadn't woken up from winter.

I wondered why anyone would ever think to put a house on water here.

"That's it," she said.

Willie's houseboat sprang up square from the blank gray mirror of the river. A white metal catwalk stretched from the grassy bank and bent down to the floating wooden dock surrounding the structure. And it looked just like a house that had been built on the water. It was two stories tall, white, with a blue roof, and a square garage door opening to a boathouse on the lower floor below a railed balcony and porch fronting the windowed living quarters above.

There were no other boats, no neighbors, nothing, as far as I could see, in every direction.

I lifted my suitcase from the bed of the truck and followed April down the creaking catwalk. It felt like I was going to jail or a hospital, or something.

Everything moved: the metal walkway, the dock, even the

house itself shifted as the weight of our bodies made ripples beneath our footfalls. It made me dizzy.

"Ever been on a houseboat before, Bosten?"

I didn't have to think about it. "No."

I followed her up the suspended gangway to the porch, and April unlocked the houseboat's front door.

We went inside.

I put my suitcase down on the shag-carpeted floor. The place was as un-boatlike as anyone could ever imagine. The front room, the living room, looked like something you'd see in a regular apartment, with deep green carpeting, a sofa and chair with a glass coffee table shaped almost like a surfboard. The room was wide and surrounded by windows that faced out at the river and the bank. It opened onto the kitchen, made separate by a counter and bar that served as a dinner table. At the back were three doors that stood open on the bedrooms and a small bathroom in the middle.

"Put your suitcase in that room." April pointed to the door on the left. "That's Willie's rental. Where you sleep tonight."

"Okay."

"It's better than a backseat, wouldn't you say?"

"Um. Yeah."

The room had a small cot that was covered with a red corduroy spread, and empty shelves that looked like pine wood were built into one of the walls. For some reason, I immediately got the feeling that there had been lots of tenants coming and going over the years.

Then April showed me around the place:

the bathroom

"There's enough hot water for

one shower,

so if you're going to take one,

you should do it now, before Willie comes home."
(I wondered what it would be like to
take a shower with April.
I thought it would be nice,
especially the way she said to take one now)
the living room
"The TV gets three Portland channels on VHF, but
you might have to fuck
around with the rabbit ears."
(something about how she said that made me realize
I had a boner)
and the kitchen
"You can drink the water from the sink,
and Willie won't mind if you find something in the
refrigerator you want. Just be
sure to leave him at least three beers.
Willie always drinks three beers when he comes home."

"I don't drink beer."

"Ever?"

The sound of her question made my mouth water. And I couldn't stop thinking about kissing her, tasting her tongue, putting my hands up inside her blouse.

"Yeah. Never."

I had to take a deep breath.

Again.

"You looked like a good kid when I first saw you."

I look like a monster.

Who are you kidding?

I took off my Steelers cap and watched April's eyes.

She didn't flinch, didn't flicker any doubtful look.

April smiled. "Who cuts your hair, anyway?"

I looked at the floor. "My mom was the last one. That was weeks ago."

She shrugged. "It's a mess. I could give you a trim if you want."

April raised her hand. I knew what she was going to do, but somehow I couldn't stop myself from leaning away when she combed the side of my hair with her fingertips.

Nobody touches me.

I knew she could see how embarrassed I became. "I kind of want it to grow long."

"I could trim the ends. So it looks good when it gets longer. It won't look shorter at all."

"Really?"

"Yeah. Go in the kitchen and sit on one of Willie's stools. I'll get the scissors."

The kitchen had an orange linoleum floor. I pulled out one of the stools from the counter and sat on it. April went into the bathroom. Then she called out, "And take your shirts off."

First I had to adjust my boner. It was killing me.

April was making me insane. I stripped out of my shirt and T-shirt and sat there on a waist-high stool, waiting for her.

I wondered what beer tasted like.

April came into the kitchen, carrying some scissors and a thin black comb.

I kept my eyes on her swaying breasts as she walked.

As soon as she touched me, I tensed up. She ran her hand flat over the top of my head, pulled my hair up through the comb, and made a few quick snips with the scissors. I felt goosebumps spread from my neck down to my nipples. And I felt stupid and childlike when April sighed and put her tools down on the counter, saying, "Relax, Bosten. You don't have to be afraid."

Then she began to rub the back of my neck and shoulders—so hard it almost hurt—until my muscles loosened up. It felt really good, but not sexy. It felt like someone being nice to me.

April went back to cutting my hair. It tickled as it rained down on my skin and made me sneeze once.

"Bless you."

"Thank you."

"There. Done." She swung around in front of me. "You are a very good-looking boy."

I am ugly.
Don't lie to me.
I am ugly.

I didn't want to move.

She brushed the hair away from my shoulders and chest with her fingers.

Goosebumps again.

"I can sweep it up. I always do at home," I said.

"Don't be silly. This is where I cut Willie's hair, too."

I looked down at the orange tiles on the floor. "I bet you don't even see his hair when it ends up down there."

She laughed. "You should go rinse yourself off."

"Emily says I should always take a bath after getting a haircut."

"Is Emily your girlfriend?"

"Yes. And we take baths together."

I went red again, could see myself blushing on the pale skin of my belly.

April's eyebrows arched. "You do? I guess you're not the good little boy I thought you were, after all."

I laughed.

"But you won't want to take a bath in there when you see how filthy Willie's tub is. You better stand up."

"Oh." And, me being completely dumb, I thought she wanted me to stand up *now*. So I did awkwardly, hoping April wouldn't notice how I had to adjust the stubborn stiffness between my legs, so it wouldn't stick out so much.

She didn't see. She was already pulling a broom and pan out from the corner beside the stove.

"So, it's okay if I take a shower?" I hadn't taken one since Monday after gym class.

I probably smelled like Paul Buckley on a bad day.

"Sure. Make yourself at home. I've got to get Willie's truck back, anyway."

April leaned the broom against the stove, then walked over to me and gave me a tight hug. Her breasts, heavy and full, pressed into my bare chest; and I'm sure she could feel the boner inside my jeans that pushed against the soft warmth of her belly, even if she politely pretended not to notice it.

"I'll probably see you tomorrow, Bosten."

"You're not coming back?"

She laughed. "I don't live here. Willie's my cousin. He's just letting me use his truck since I wrecked my car on the bridge a week ago."

"Oh."

"My husband and me live over in McNulty."

Then I really felt stupid.

And alone.

"Bye."

I watched her walk across to the door and leave.

"See you, April."

I went into the bathroom and took a standing-up shower in Willie's oily bathtub.

I fell into sleep watching television on Willie's couch.

The news broadcasts from Portland fascinated and terrified me. It was probably the first time I'd ever paid attention to news in my life, but I was somehow convinced that if I watched long enough, I'd see someone reporting a story about the missing teenage brothers from northwestern Washington.

When I woke up, the TV was still on, and it was nighttime. Willie was cooking something in the kitchen. His hair was dripping wet, and he was wearing nothing but polka-dot boxer shorts, standing barefoot, drinking a beer. The smell of steam and soap drifted out from the open bathroom. He had just gotten out of the shower, I figured.

I sat up, and Willie turned around when he noticed me.

"Hey. Your alternator came in tonight. I'll get it installed first thing tomorrow."

I rubbed my eyes. "Sorry. I didn't mean to fall asleep."

"No big deal. I'm making hot dogs. You like hot dogs?"

I was starving.

"Yeah."

"But I only have ketchup. I hate mustard."

"That's okay."

"You want a beer?"

"No thanks."

Willie shrugged like he couldn't figure me out. I guess teenager equaled beer drinker in Scappoose, Oregon.

When I slept that night
I had a dream
that Bosten was dead.

I didn't realize how much two nights spent sleeping in a Toyota had deprived me of rest, so when I woke up in Willie's rental room the next day, it was already nearly noon and I was all by myself in the houseboat again.

I didn't bother getting dressed, either. I figured Willie was the same as Aunt Dahlia as far as morning—or evening—standards of clothing were concerned. I went out into the living room. That's when I saw the note he'd left for me on the counter.

I always was a slow learner and had particular trouble, they said, with "language acquisition," but Willie's spelling made me feel like a college professor.

bostun,

I will fix youre car for you today. Sorry thiers not a phone, or I would call you when its done. I'll be back when I can get finished up at the station. Theirs instant coco in the kitchen if you drink that. If it takes to long or something comes up you can stay till tommorow. See you later.

willie

I had to wash out a pot with cold hot dogs in it, just so I could boil water for Willie's instant hot chocolate, but it was what I wanted, and it tasted good after the long night of sleep I'd had.

I started missing Emily so much it hurt.

And I didn't even want to think about Bosten.

But they were both trapped inside me.

It was deathly quiet on the river, and I wanted to leave. But I was stuck there, floating on the water, helpless, just like I'd imagined so many times before. I tried watching the news, convinced that I was ultimately going to hear about me and Bosten, but we either weren't important enough, or nobody even knew we were missing.

Kids disappeared all the time, I supposed, and Bosten was technically old enough to take care of himself, anyway. At least he was old enough according to Dad, and to the State of

Washington, even if the State of Washington had its own other set of special rules about boys like Bosten and Paul Buckley.

Nothing happened at all until Willie came home.

It was after dark.

Then more happened than I care to think about.

Through the living room windows, I saw the headlights on Willie's truck bouncing along the bank. And I heard him talking to someone when he walked over the catwalk down to the dock, but it was too dark to see, and I naturally assumed—in an excited kind of way—that April was with him.

She wasn't.

Something was different. I could see it right away.

Maybe the way I hear things, or how I *don't* hear things, makes me more sensitive to the expressions on people's faces, the way they tense certain muscles. It was like that time Mrs. Buckley drove Bosten home, and I could see, just by watching how they moved, that something wasn't right. But I was at the door as soon as Willie opened it, and I looked him square in the face. He seemed like a different person.

He walked past me, carrying a paper grocery sack that was obviously heavy. It was full of beer bottles. I heard them clink when he put the bag down on the kitchen bar.

There was an older man standing behind him in the dark on the porch. I put my hand up on my head. It was a habit of mine around strangers, especially when they surprised me. I wanted to be sure I had my Steelers cap on.

I smiled at Willie. I guess I was lonely, sitting there in that house by myself, all day long. "Hey, Willie. Is my car fixed?"

Willie looked serious, edgy. He held the Toyota's keys out and I grabbed them.

"It's running good, kid." Then he pulled out a carbon

receipt from the pocket on his jumpsuit and handed it to me. "It cost thirty. Like I said."

"Oh."

The man on the porch came into the living room and shut the door.

I fumbled in my back pocket for Bosten's wallet and handed Willie a twenty and two fives. "Thanks so much, Willie. I guess I should head out." I strained at doing the math, trying to figure out how much money I had left, and whether it would be enough to get me to Aunt Dahlia's.

The older guy carried a black canvas duffel bag. He dropped it on the floor and went over to Willie's couch, where I had been watching TV most of the day. He had wild gray hair that made him look as though he'd been electrocuted, and he wore a dark wool CPO-type jacket that gave off a damp, sweaty odor.

"Well," Willie said. "I'll take you back to the station in the morning. It's Friday, kid, and I feel like doing a little partying, if that's okay."

What could I say?

I tried to think about how far it was back to the gas station.

"Oh. Um. Sure thing."

Willie pulled two brown bottles from the sack. He had one of those bottle openers that had been bolted right into the kitchen wall. He let the caps fall and roll across the linoleum.

"Want one, kid?"

"No. No thanks, Willie."

I glanced at the man on the couch. He didn't say anything more than a grunted and unintelligible something when Willie handed a beer across the coffee table to him.

Then Willie put a full six-pack on the table and sat down, pulling the chair across the carpet so he was close enough to grab them.

"Oh," he said, "and this is my buddy, Brock."

The old man looked at me and nodded. His eyes were sunken and stained yellow.

"And the kid's name is Bosten," Willie added.

"Hi," I said.

"I been to Boston. Around twenty years ago, I think," Brock said.

I didn't care enough to correct him. I just stood there, wondering if I should sit or leave, thinking about how many times in his life Bosten had heard comments about baked beans and tea parties, or the Red Sox.

Willie emptied his beer and took out another bottle. He opened it on the edge of a key he wedged into his palm. He dropped the cap on the rug.

"And you'll need to get your shit out of the room. Brock's renting it tonight."

I didn't really understand what was going on.

I still don't know for sure exactly what happened that night.

The old man looked at me like he was waiting for me to say something.

"Okay." I started toward the room. "Maybe I can sleep on the couch."

"No," Willie said. "We're going to be partying. You can stay in my room."

"Oh."

Brock took off his coat and dropped it on the floor at the end of the couch as though marking a territory where he didn't want any kids hanging around.

His party territory, I guessed.

It wasn't like I had that much "shit" to clear out of the room, anyway. I un-carefully stuffed what I had out on the bed into my suitcase and carried it through the doorway into Willie's bedroom.

"Maybe I should just get out of your way. It's not that far of a walk back to my car."

"It's five miles," Willie said. "Relax."

Brock looked at me and then at Willie. I could tell he was quietly trying to make some kind of a decision about me, and I found out soon enough.

Willie said, "He's all right."

Brock tweezered two fingers into his shirt pocket and pulled out some little folded squares of white paper. He spread them out, like playing cards, in front of him on the glass tabletop.

Willie tapped my forearm with his beer bottle. "Hey, Bosten, will you do me a favor?"

I was already confused enough about what was going on. I imagined all the possible unreasonable things Willie was getting ready to ask me to do.

"Sure."

"Put some music on, will you? And then go over there to that first drawer by the sink and grab me a couple razor blades. They're right in front."

"Uh. Okay."

I turned Willie's stereo on. It sat on three overturned plastic milk crates beside the bar. Buffalo Springfield. A little old, but I liked them. I thought of all the times I'd watched Bosten sing and dance around to "Mr. Soul."

Is it strange I should change? I don't know, why don't you ask her?

The razor blades were each wrapped in thick paper. Single-edge utility blades, right where Willie said they'd be. I still didn't have any idea what he wanted them for.

As I picked them up, I thought about Paul Buckley. I wondered if he was okay.

Brock opened up one of his paper squares and dumped a

small pile of white powdery stuff out on the glass table. I gave Willie the blades and watched as he unwrapped one of them.

Brock caught me staring, my mouth hanging open.

"Haven't you ever seen coke before?" he said. "Where'd you grow up, anyway? In a monastery?"

Two things ran through my head: First, I didn't think Brock actually wanted to hear me answer those questions, and, no, I had never seen coke before. I knew what it was, though. Kind of.

I shook my head and swallowed.

Willie started chopping the coke, finer and finer, with his razor blade. It made an interesting sound, the crispness of the granules, the high-pitched whine of the blade against the glass as Willie scraped the powder into a perfect pile.

I sat down on the carpet with my hands behind me and my knees bent.

"You want to try some, kid?" Willie asked.

I felt my eyes get wide. I shook my head. I thought that stuff killed people, and here were these two grown men doing it right in front of me like they were sitting around a campfire roasting marshmallows or something.

"What's it do to you?"

Brock said, "It makes you feel new. Give it a shot, punk."

I didn't want to feel new.

At fourteen, I was tired of feeling new.

"No thanks. I really don't do anything."

"I bet you do a few things." Brock said, "Especially when no one's looking." Then he and Willie both laughed, like they knew something about me that I didn't. It made me feel a little creepy.

Willie ran the blade out across the glass and separated a wide white line of coke from the pile. Then he reached into his pocket and pulled out the twenty I'd just given him. He rolled the bill up into a tube and offered it to Brock.

I guess cocaine manners prescribed that Brock was obliged to say a silent "after you" to Willie, just by waving his hand graciously, almost with a religious weight to the motion. Willie didn't protest, anyway. I had never seen anything like it. It fascinated me and terrified me, all at the same time. But here I was, floating on the water.

Helpless.

So what else could I do?

I watched.

Willie put one end of my twenty into his nostril, plugged the other side with a straightened index finger, and snorted half the line right up into his nose. He closed his eyes, sniffed in again, and looked at me with a strange and pleased expression on his face. Then he finished it off through the other nostril.

They took turns.

Brock and Willie did the same thing, over and over, through two packets of Brock's coke. They kept staring at me, too, which made me feel like I was in the wrong place, because all I did was watch them as though it was some kind of movie.

By the time they had emptied the first six-pack of beer, Willie licked his finger and ran it over the surface of the table. He was sweating. So was Brock. I thought it was cold in the houseboat.

I got up and turned the record over.

I watched as Willie rubbed his finger all around on his gums, the way you'd brush your teeth if you didn't have a toothbrush.

I realized I didn't bring my toothbrush with me when I left home.

Willie made his fingertip white with the cocaine again. Just when I turned around from his record player, he stood up and came over to me. Willie put one hand behind my head, the way you'd hold a girl if you were going to make out with her, and before I could do anything about it, he began pushing his finger into my mouth.

Brock sat on the couch, laughing. "Oh yeah! Kid's first coke!"

I twisted away from Willie, but it was too late. His finger swiped all around inside my mouth. I thought about biting him, but I was too scared.

It tasted like poison.

It tasted like something you'd use to clean up spilled paint.

I shoved Willie back.

"What the fuck, Willie? What the fuck are you doing?"

And already my mouth felt like it was detaching from my face.

Willie laughed. "That's good shit, isn't it, kid?"

Brock laughed. "Make him do a line! Let's hold him down and make him do it!"

I didn't know what to do. My heart was racing, and I honestly thought I was going to die. But part of my head was telling me that I'd just watched these two idiots snort up a sandbox full of this stuff and they weren't dead yet.

"Leave me the fuck alone! Why the fuck did you do that?"

I spit on Willie's floor, tried to get all that crap out of my mouth, but it wasn't going anywhere.

As Willie and Brock laughed uncontrollably, I stormed past them into Willie's room and slammed the door behind me.

I heard them laughing at me in the other room.
I sat on the edge of Willie's bed
with my face in my hands.
My head was on fire with words.
I had to slow myself down.
I had to slow

myself
down.

They kept laughing.

Someone changed the music.
I heard Brock calling me a pussy faggot.
He told Willie
to make me come out there and suck their dicks.
Willie said no.
Brock said he was going to
come in the room then and force me to do it.
He said the kid should pay us for letting him stay here.
Willie said leave the kid alone, he's messed up.
Then there was pounding on the houseboat's door.
I heard more voices.
More men outside in Willie's living room.
This was Willie's party.
Laughing.
Music.
I just sat there.
My heart was beating so hard I thought it would
break my ribs.
I wanted to leave, but there was no way out.
I wanted to leave.
I didn't move.
The noise of the party grew and grew.
Maybe an hour later
maybe it was just a minute
a minute when my heart beat an hour of life away
they began fighting about something.
The old man opened my door.
Smoke followed him in.
Then he closed the door and it was dark.

He said, boy, take off your shirt.
I said no.
He said you got to pay for staying here.
I said Willie told me I didn't have to.
Brock said fuck Willie.
He grabbed me and threw me down on the floor.
He pulled Bosten's wallet out of my pocket.
He took everything I had in there.
The old man said one way or another you're paying.
I said I need that money to get to California.
He said when you run out of money
you can start giving five-dollar blowjobs, I guess.
Want to make some money, kid?
I was crying.
I said fuck you
and he left.
Not long after that, someone started shooting
in the living room.
There were five gunshots.
I did the math.
Then it was as quiet as death.

SUTTON

I had to leave.

I waited until I couldn't stand it anymore.

I was shaking so hard it made me sick.

And sometime during the wait, I desperately needed to

pee, so I just did it in the corner of Willie's bedroom. It made a thick sound in the carpet where it pooled up, and I could feel its warmth and smell it. It smelled like the locker room after Mr. Lloyd's gym class.

I took a deep breath and turned the doorknob. It didn't make a sound, but how would I know, anyway? My pulse was a roaring tornado trapped inside my head. I pulled open the door.

The first thing that hit me was the cold. The front door of the houseboat stood open.

The glass table where Willie and Brock had done their coke was broken at one end. It looked like crystal teeth. There was a bullet hole in the center of it, too. Willie's turntable spun around, but the arm had been flipped up. It pointed directly at the ceiling, like it was saying, "Look up there, kid."

And the room smelled like blood. Everyone knows what blood smells like; and when there's a lot of it, it kind of makes you want to throw up.

The old man who'd stolen my money was stretched out on the couch. It looked like he was sitting in a puddle of blood, and his eyes were frozen open, looking across the room, just watching the mute record that spun and spun on Willie's turntable. I couldn't see any mark on him, but there was this odd color under his skin; and even standing away, on the other side of the room where I was, I could almost feel how cold he was.

If he still had my money, it would be in his back pocket, down somewhere in that pool of blood on the sofa cushion. I didn't care how much money it was. I wasn't going to touch that old man again.

Willie was in the rental room, the one where I'd slept without paying the night before. I saw only his feet through the open doorway. He was facedown on the floor, missing a shoe, and had obviously stepped in blood with his white sock.

It didn't matter.

I could tell by how still he was that Willie wasn't going anywhere, either.

I picked up my suitcase and left.

Outside, the air was wet and inescapably cold.

Willie's truck was gone.

The houseboat and the river were perfectly quiet, perfectly dark.

I followed the mud tracks back toward the highway, careful to keep my feet in the grass. I didn't want to leave any footprints.

Whoever did that must not have known I was in Willie's room.

Or maybe they knew it was just a little kid in there.

That's the only way I could explain why I was still breathing.

Before I got to the highway, I hid beneath the pines and waited for a while. I thought, maybe the ones who did this were going to come back. As quietly as I could, I opened my suitcase. There was no way I'd be able to carry it all the way back to the gas station, but I knew there were ten dollars inside it. Ten dollars the old man didn't steal from me. I took the money out and shoved it down into my front pocket. It made me think about Emily.

I believed I would never be able to see her or Bosten again.

Still, I couldn't leave my suitcase behind. Someone would find it, and I'd get caught. I decided to carry it as far as I could, and then I'd come back for it after I got my Toyota from Willie's gas station.

I thought anyone in the world who knew I was staying there would think I had something to do with killing those men. Or Bosten did.

All I knew for sure was that I never wanted to set eyes on that houseboat again.

. . .

By the time the sun came up and I'd turned off the headlights, I was passing through a place called Sutherlin. I was too tired to keep driving, and too scared to sleep. I scripted out with certainty the nightmares I'd have, even if I knew I was making them worse in my own mind: Willie, Brock, waiting in that room after the gunshots went off—another Saint Fillan's room—and wondering if my brother was out here, anywhere; if he was even alive.

When I'd gotten behind the wheel of my stolen car and started the engine, that's when I felt like I was no longer Bosten. But I didn't know who I was anymore, because everything about Stark McClellan was changed now.

I reasoned that Willie saved my life. He may not have intended to, but if I hadn't gotten as mad at him as I did, and then slammed myself inside that room, I most likely would have been out there with them when the shooting started. I guess, sometimes, things that seem like such a big deal take on a whole new shape when you turn around and look at them from a couple hundred miles away.

Sutherlin was about a hundred and forty miles.

There was still gas in the car, and California was getting closer.

But I had to rest.

I stopped at a small grocery store and bought one loaf of white bread and a jar of peanut butter. That was all I could live on for now, I decided. I had to use every cent of what was left to buy gas. I knew the money would not get me anywhere near where I wanted to be.

Sitting in the parking lot, eating a sandwich the morning after I'd been on a boat where people were murdered, I tried to imagine where it was going to be that I would finally have to abandon the car and start walking.

I climbed into the back of the Toyota and kicked off my shoes. I stretched my legs out over the front passenger seat.

When I went to sleep, I didn't have any dreams at all.

It happened just south of Fresno, California, the following morning.

For maybe the last fifty miles, I kept my eyes more on the gas gauge than the road ahead of me. I knew it was coming.

I had one dime in my pocket. It was my last safety net, I figured. I knew the Lohmans or Aunt Dahlia would accept a collect phone call from me if I ever gave in and decided to let that dime drop.

But I was too scared to talk to them, too.

After running out of gas up in Scappoose, I knew what would happen once the motor started to hiccup. I pushed in the clutch and let the car coast as far as it could. It made it into a gravel parking lot at a roadside rest stop that was divided into separate areas: one for cars and, across a grass median with restrooms and some sick-looking trees, another for long-haul trucks.

That was it.

Just like that.

I can't say that I was too disappointed. In some ways, I was relieved. Since I left Point No Point, running out of gas was the first thing I truly *expected* to happen to me that actually *did* happen. And looking back at things now, I think I was numb, or maybe in shock, after what I'd seen two nights before on the river outside of Scappoose. Every time my mind flashed back on images of the old man and Willie, lying in their own blood, I would shake my head quickly. I had been doing that so much the last two days, I was beginning to think I was going to develop an involuntary twitch.

There was just one other car, parked nearer to the restrooms, with a family that stood outside and watched while their cocker spaniel made shit in the grass. Across the way was an idling black Kenworth eighteen-wheeler, hooked up to a trailer, painted all over with bouncing, smiling vegetables, that said TEIXIERA FARMS down the side.

By Washington standards, it was ungodly hot here. I rolled down both windows and sat in the car, just thinking about things, watching the little stub-tailed dog spin in a tight circle while he dropped off his turds.

Maybe five minutes later, the family packed up their cocker spaniel and pulled back out onto the highway. I watched them without making it look like I was watching them. Then I got out of the car and took my suitcase out from the trunk. I changed into the shorts and Sex Wax T-shirt Aunt Dahlia bought for me. I wore the cap Emily gave me. I emptied just about everything I had out of the suitcase, leaving only enough room to take one complete change of clothes for me, one for Bosten, my peanut butter and white bread, and our wetsuits.

I thought, maybe I was the only guy in the entire state of California who packed a wetsuit in his suitcase.

I put the case down next to the bumper, then I sat behind the wheel and penciled a note on the paper grocery sack my food came in.

> *To Whom It May Concern:*
>
> *My name is Stark McClellan. I am from Point No Point in Kitsap County, Washington. I have run away from home and am traveling using my brother's identification. His name is Bosten McClellan. Two days ago, I was in a houseboat on the bay in Scappoose, Oregon, when two men were murdered. One of them was named Willie Purcell, and the other I only knew by his first name, which was Brock. I was hiding in a room when it happened, and I did not see who did the shooting. But*

when I came out, Willie's truck had been stolen, too. My brother, Bosten, didn't have anything to do with it.

Stark McClellan

I folded the sack carefully and put it inside the glove box. Then I took a deep breath, pulled the note back out, balled it up, and walked over to a garbage can. I dropped the wadded sack into the trash.

I went back to the Toyota for the last time. I rolled up the windows and locked the doors. Then I grabbed my suitcase and started walking.

Everything seems bigger, farther away, slowed down, when you walk alongside a road. It felt like it took me fifteen minutes just to get halfway down the ramp onto the main highway. By then, the big truck was leaving the rest stop, too. It shuddered as it rolled over the gravel ramp.

The truck stopped. The driver dangled his arm from the window and leaned his face out.

"Is that your car back there?"

I looked up at him, squinting. He was black. There were only two black kids at my school in Washington. I don't think that I'd ever talked to a black grown-up in my life.

"Not anymore."

He hitched a thumb at my suitcase. "Plan on catching a bus or something?"

I didn't have a plan at all.

"I am out of gas and out of money."

"Not going to win any girlfriends like that," he said. The driver looked down the road, checked his mirrors. I watched him. He had perfectly rounded black hair and a mustache that curled down toward his chin. "So. Where are you going?"

"Cal—" I caught myself being stupid again. "I'm trying to get to a place called Oxnard."

"That's a good walk. I'm heading to Long Beach. If you want, you can ride with me to Los Angeles. It's maybe another four or five hours. Maybe your folks from Oxnard can come pick you up in L.A."

I looked down the road.

Then I glanced up at the driver one more time.

I walked around the nose of his truck and he pushed open the passenger-side door.

I had a hard time fitting my legs into the truck. The floor in front of the passenger seat was cluttered with cans of soda, some extra shoes, and sacks of food and magazines. I noticed there wasn't a *Penthouse*, though.

Well, at least not one I could see.

When I climbed up into the cab, the driver began grabbing what he could reach from where he sat, throwing it back into the small room behind the seats. There was a cot back there and even a television set strapped against the wall.

I had never seen the inside of a truck before. I thought you could probably live here forever if you needed to.

"Here." He grabbed my suitcase and slid it inside an open plastic locker in back of my seat.

I sat down.

The man revved the motor and slammed the gear shifter upward.

"You want a Coke or something? Just help yourself."

"Thanks."

I opened a can of Coke. It was warm, but I didn't mind at all. At least it didn't stick to the roof of my mouth, unlike the only other nourishment I'd had since the day before.

The truck driver's name was Sutton Broussard. He told me all about how he came west from Louisiana; and now he drove artichokes to Southern California for a living. I'd never seen an artichoke in my life, but I guessed by the size of Sutton's truck that people in Southern California liked them.

I told him my real name and how I'd just turned fourteen three days before; but not much beyond that. I didn't want to chance making any more trouble for Bosten by pretending to be him, and I wasn't going to be driving again, anyway. So it didn't matter.

"Fourteen and driving your own car?"

"I'm pretty tall."

"I can see that. I can see that," Sutton said. "And Washington tags on it, too. You got yourself a hell of a ways from home, I'd say."

Maybe, I thought, he'd been paying a little too much attention to things. Maybe everyone just naturally noticed things that I didn't think were obvious enough to care about.

"You're not going to do anything weird or anything, are you?"

Sutton's brow creased. "I was just about to ask you the same thing."

I took a gulp from the can, and Sutton said, "Why would you say something like that, anyway? Do you think a guy's going to do something weird just because he offered you help?"

He sounded a little defensive, maybe annoyed, too.

But, yes, I guess I did think that.

"I'm sorry."

We were on the highway now, moving fast. I felt like a giant. Sitting in the cab of that truck was like riding on the nose of a whale.

"Where do you live, anyway?"

"Nowhere. That car, until just now. But I'm on my way to my aunt's house."

"I see. Oxnard, right?"

"Do you live in this truck?"

Sutton laughed. He pointed to a pair of small, discolored photographs taped to the underside of the shelf above his head. "That's my wife and daughter. We have a house in Salinas."

I tried to think if I'd driven through Salinas.

I couldn't remember.

Sutton cleared his throat. "Can you get me a Coke, please?"

"Sure."

He popped the can open, still keeping his hands rocking on the wheel, and he said, "So, what happened up there?"

At first, it shocked me, like he knew something about Willie and Brock, but then I noticed he began drawing a circle in the air around his ear. I made sure my Steelers cap was still on my head.

"People usually don't notice when I have the hat on."

"I notice things," he said. "I knew something was wrong the minute I saw you pull into the rest stop. I saw how you watched those people with their dog. I could tell you were in some kind of trouble. Then, when I saw you start walking, I said to myself, 'Yep, that kid needs someone to give him a little help.' I notice things."

"Oh." I took off the cap. It was so hot, anyway, and the wind in my sweaty hair felt good. I ran my hand over my head, surprised at how I could actually pull hair.

Dad would never tolerate hair this long.

"I was born this way."

Sutton's head mechanically jerked, back and forth, from looking at me, to watching the road ahead.

"Well," he said. "I never seen anything like that before."

I am ugly.

"I bet."

"Can you hear nothing there?"

"Nothing's the only thing I hear there."

Sutton laughed. "That's fortunate, then. Must be nice to miss out on half the nonsense the rest of us have to endure listening to."

I had to think about that.

"I don't know."

"I believe so," he said. "But I'm not going to ask you one more thing. So you don't have to tell me nothing about that car back there, Stark, or where you came from. I don't want to know."

"I was robbed," I said. "An old man stole all my money, except for ten dollars I had hidden in my suitcase. That's why I was walking."

I pictured Brock, cold and stiff, lying on the same couch where I'd watched two days' worth of news broadcasts. They must have found the bodies by now. I tried to think if I'd left anything at all behind that might bear witness to my having been on the houseboat.

"Some people don't deserve to walk this earth," Sutton decided.

That made me feel sick.

"I don't hold grudges."

"Tell me how to do that, Stark. If I were you, I imagine I'd be pretty bitter."

"Not about the money. Or the old man, I'm not."

There were other things, though.

"Okay. Look, if you're tired, you can sleep on the bunk back there. You don't have to worry about nothing. But one thing . . ."

"What?"

"We'll be coming up around Bakersfield in an hour or so. I should tell you that we're going to go through a highway patrol check station."

The thought of police scared me. Maybe Sutton could see that, too.

"What for?"

"They check all the trucks, usually. I was thinking you probably might not want them to see you."

"Why do you think that?"

I shifted in my seat. My back was damp with sweat.

" 'Cause I think you probably ran off from your home in Washington. And that car you ran out of gas in was probably not willingly loaned to a fourteen-year-old with permission to drive it through three states."

"Yeah. Probably."

"They're probably about bound to wonder what some white kid's doing in a truck with me, too."

"You probably could say you're my dad."

Sutton laughed. "Shit."

"I'm not tired."

But I went to sleep, anyway, on the little bed in the back of the cab.

I woke in terror, smothered in red, as hot as hell, struggling to breathe.

I thought I was back on the houseboat. Somehow, I imagined I had just heard the crack of five gunshots, and I counted them: one two

three

four five.

Just like that.

And all I could see was red. The red corduroy spread on the little bed in the rental room that Willie said I didn't have to pay for. I heard men's voices. They sounded far away. I was being smothered. I needed air.

I thrashed my arms and sat up.

The truck.

I'd completely forgotten I was inside a truck, somewhere in California. It wasn't moving, and I could see a bar of flashing yellow lights ahead through the windshield. The cab was empty. The driver's door stood open. Sutton must have covered me up with the red nylon sleeping bag I was under.

To help me hide.

We were stopped at the checkpoint.

I inched higher and could see a row of parked highway patrol cruisers on the right shoulder of the highway in front of the truck.

I put my head back down and covered myself again.

I waited.

I tried listening to the faint voices coming from outside Sutton's open door.

Thanks, Mike.
kids
McClellan
north part of Washington
no one said
anything
if they're together
where
one of them
I never saw him
Oregon
murders
or
fucking bloodbath
something
Toyota

"I'll keep an eye out when I head back through Fresno."

"See you next time, Sut."

"Sure thing, Mike."

It was like being back in that room, waiting and waiting. I felt the shifting of the truck as Sutton climbed back up into his seat, could sense the change of the air inside the cab when his door whooshed shut, then the tingling vibration through the thin cushion on the cot as the motor revved up.

It was so hot under there.

We began moving.

I uncovered my face, breathed, and watched Sutton stow away some notebooks and papers on the shelf over his head.

"What did they tell you?"

Sutton visibly jumped when I spoke.

"Holy shit, kid! Don't just stick your face out and talk like that. I just about pissed my pants."

"Sorry."

The truck jerked forward, began rolling. Soon, we were back up to speed, away from the inspection area.

"You're okay. You can get up now."

I climbed up between the seats and let the air from the open window blow through my hair.

"What did they tell you?" I repeated.

Sutton glanced at me. "You got a brother?"

"Yeah."

"What's his name?"

"Bosten."

I watched Sutton. I could tell he was thinking about things. Doing the math.

"Where is he?"

"I'm trying to find him."

"I'm only going to ask this once."

"Okay."

"Are you telling the truth?"

"Yes. I pretended to be him. I have his license. So I could drive. What did they tell you?"

Sutton didn't say anything.

"Look. I have his license. I'll show you. You can see it doesn't really look like me at all."

I pulled the empty wallet from my back pocket, slid Bosten's license out, and offered it over to Sutton. He hardly glanced at it.

"Okay. Sorry. I believe you."

"I didn't do anything wrong. I'm just trying to find my brother."

"I know. Nobody thinks you did anything wrong. The cops. They think you're in trouble."

We began driving up into the mountains. The road was steep and the truck seemed to crawl along, shuddering. And I told Sutton the whole story. I didn't say why Bosten left home, but I did tell him about how Emily gave me sixty dollars, and then I stole my dad's car and ended up stuck in a place called Scappoose. And I told him everything about April and Willie, and what happened with Brock on the houseboat; and how scared I was that I was going to die, too.

Sutton just shook his head slowly. "Shit."

Then I didn't want to talk anymore.

At the top of the grade, Sutton pulled into a truck stop to gas his rig.

"They have pretty decent burgers in here," he said. "Let's get something to eat. Okay?"

"I only have one dime."

"I didn't ask you anything about how much money you had."

Sutton paid for my food. We ate quietly. The place was noisy enough, anyway, and my head was so full of words I couldn't straighten any of them out. I kept wondering why there are people in this world, like Sutton, who are willing to help other people just because they simply *can,* and why there are people like Brock and Willie, like Mrs. Buckley, or people like Emily and her mom; like my mom and dad.

But all my wondering always brought me back to thinking about Bosten and how he told me that things don't make people the way they are.

It doesn't just happen.

I had a vanilla milkshake.

There is something about vanilla milkshakes that makes everything seem okay. At least, a little bit better. And I wasn't wearing my cap. I was tired of wearing my cap.

Sutton only drank water. The kind they give you in truck stops like the one we sat in, served in grainy plastic cups with big, clear cubes of ice. But despite the ice and the plastic, it always tastes like tin.

He said, "I decided something."

"What?"

But I knew what he was going to say. I was ready for it a long time before Sutton said it. He was going to tell me that when he got up to go, he wanted me to just sit there; that I was on my own now. There was no reason for him not to say something like that to me.

I drive at night
I blow things up
I get people killed

"I'm probably going to get docked for being late. But up ahead a few miles, I can turn off and get on the one-twenty-six. It's maybe an hour and a half to Oxnard."

I studied him. I never met anyone like Sutton before. Well, maybe Mrs. Lohman, if she drove a truck.

He said, "You know how to get to your aunt's house?"

"I've driven there before."

Sutton laughed. "Shit. You are *not* driving my truck. I don't care how tough you are."

I never thought I was tough.

On the narrow stretch of highway that followed a shallow river basin cutting west toward Ventura, I slipped a sweating hand into my pocket and flipped that one dime around and around between my fingers. I tried imagining what things would be like when I showed up unannounced at Aunt Dahlia's door, but it scared me to do that. Although I had absolutely no doubt she would cry and make a fuss over me, and take me in without any questions or rules, I tried to search somewhere in my heart for any faint kind of vibration that the road was bringing me closer to Bosten.

But all I could feel was dark emptiness.

I started shaking my head again, without thinking, trying to clear the pictures from my mind.

Sutton asked, "What's wrong?"

I didn't want to tell him how I kept seeing that old man, dead on the couch, and Willie's bloody foot sticking out through the doorway of the room I'd slept in, on the cold and quiet houseboat on the Columbia River.

"Nothing."

The sun began to dip down behind the feathery tips of the picket lines of giant eucalyptus trees that had been planted in perfect lines to mark orchard boundaries and to keep the frost from settling on the endless rows of oranges and lemons. We drove across railroad tracks, through a tiny town named Fillmore, and then to another place called Santa Paula, where Mexicans sold produce or played music along the roadside.

"We'll have you home before sundown, Stark."

I said, "Thank you. But I just want to ask you one thing."

"Go ahead."

"Why would you do this for me?"

"Because I know what it's like."

I didn't think anyone knew what "it" was really like. Not to me.

"You do?"

"I do."

"Do you ever eat Mexican food?"

"Everyone eats Mexican food in California."

"One day, when you come back, all of us will go have Mexican food together."

Sutton said, "That's a deal. Don't forget. You owe me."

I wasn't going to forget.

I guess everyone thought it was some kind of mistake. I mean, it was probably the first time ever that an eighteen-wheeler filled with artichokes arrived on Ocean Avenue and stopped on the sand-covered asphalt directly in front of Aunt Dahlia's house.

It seemed like forever since I'd been there.

I didn't need to do the math.

The sun had dropped below the horizon out on the sea, and I realized that there was a certain unique color the light here would cast at precisely this hour. Down the street, I saw Evan and Kim and a few of the other kids who surfed on the Strand, walking barefoot, away from the beach with surfboards cradled under their arms. Evan looked back at the truck. I could tell he said something to the others—probably something like *what's that dumbshit doing down here?* Of course, he had no way of knowing I was the dumbshit sitting in the cab. I almost wanted to yell out at him and his sister, but I didn't want Sutton to think I'd just brush him off so easily and leave him there.

"Those kids down there are friends of mine," I said.

"Welcome home, Stark."

Aunt Dahlia's door swung inward, almost suspiciously. I remembered how thin the walls of her home were, so I could only imagine how the rumbling of the truck's diesel engine must have been shaking it.

When she peeked her face out at us, I threw open my door and said, over my shoulder to Sutton, "Don't leave!"

I ran down and hugged her. I made myself not cry. I willed myself to be tough, like Bosten was and like Sutton thought I was, too; and Aunt Dahlia squeezed me and kissed me and kept saying over and over, "Oh my God! Oh my God! Oh my God!"

AUNT DAHLIA

Aunt Dahlia tried to make Sutton come inside. She offered him some money, too. He wouldn't take it. I knew that without him saying the first word about it. Sutton explained how he'd probably be in a little bit of trouble for his lateness and had to get moving down the coast, so he apologized for not staying.

And the whole time I was lugging my suitcase down from the truck, and even while we stood there and waved at Sutton as he left, it seemed like Aunt Dahlia never took her hand off me for even a second.

It was almost as though she was afraid that I'd vanish again.

. . .

She had lots of questions for me. I had just as many for her.

But I knew right away, even before I got out of the truck, that Bosten wasn't there. I could feel it. And wondering about him weighed heavily on me, like it slowed my mind down from being able to clearly understand anything else that was going on.

It took Dahlia a good half hour to settle down. I told her I wasn't hungry, but she insisted on cooking bacon and eggs for me. While she rumbled about in the kitchen, cursing her toaster for burning one side of the bread, I brought my suitcase into the bedroom that Bosten and I had shared. I guess I stayed in there for a while, thinking about things: about Bosten, about how this suitcase was in the same house where people had been murdered; and then Aunt Dahlia appeared in the doorway, like she still couldn't believe it was really me, and she grabbed me by the hand and took me in to sit at her table.

"Now, Stark," she said, "you have to tell me what's going on."

Just like that, I could see in her face that she had some idea about things. But there could be no way she knew even half of the bad stuff that had happened to Bosten and me.

I sat down and began to eat, and Aunt Dahlia covered my left hand with hers.

"I don't know where to start, Dahlia."

"There were police here, two days in a row, looking for you and Bosten," she said. "Where is your brother?"

I put down my fork and looked directly at her. "I don't know. I thought he would be here. I hoped he would."

Aunt Dahlia's eyes were wet and heavy with concern. "The first day it was a detective from Oregon, asking only about Bosten. On the next day, when he came back, there was another detective from Washington. Then he started asking about you, too."

I didn't know what to tell her. I felt guilty, even though I didn't do anything wrong.

She said, "They told me that someone got killed. It scared me so bad I thought I was going to die. I thought it was you or Bosten."

I shook my head.

"They didn't tell you who it was?"

"No. They didn't say anything else, except there had been a killing in Oregon, and they needed to find you boys."

I pushed my plate away. I couldn't eat.

I must have sat there for five minutes, just looking at the food Dahlia had made for me.

It was so quiet.

"Some people got shot. It happened on a boat. I was hiding inside a room. I didn't see who did it or why they started shooting. When I came out, there were two people dead and whoever did it was gone."

I felt Dahlia's hand shaking on top of mine. Then she stood up and squeezed me and said, "Oh."

Aunt Dahlia stroked my hair and kissed me on the top of my head. I think she was crying.

"I need to tell you about me and Bosten. And why I'm here."

I suppose that in most ways memories are like the sounds that get trapped inside my head. They just swirl around at their own pace, making their own order, doing the math by themselves. Because as we sat there and I tried to tell Dahlia the whole story—everything—I would find myself at times backing up as something forgotten rose to the surface and became important.

And none of what happened to us would ever make sense if I didn't let the biggest monsters that swam in my head come up and reveal their teeth—*there is no love in our house, only rules.*

But there is this room.

I told her about our name and Saint Fillan and how I believed the story to be real and she said there is nothing wrong with you.

When she said it, it sounded true
it sounded like chains coming loose

my little window
and our secret way out
all Bosten and me ever had was just us

I told her about Ricky Dostal
I told her
every detail
about what happened to us in the Saint Fillan room
about our bucket
what Dad did
to Bosten
what Dad did to Bosten
what our goddamned father
did
how I dreamed one day
I would be brave enough to kill him
but Bosten was smarter and stronger than me
and he left

and then I told her what happened with Buck
I had to
I knew it wouldn't make a difference to her
but it sent Dad over the edge
Buck tried to kill himself with scissors
then they sent him away
so I took the car

to save myself

and save Bosten, too.

Dahlia patted my knee. She waited until she was certain I'd finished.

"Your brother told me about it. You remember that evening, you made me go outside for a walk with you?"

I nodded.

"That night, Bosten told me why you took me outside while he was on the phone. He told me about the boy back home in Washington. He said that's why he loves you so much, too, Stark. Because none of this other stuff ever came between you two. It doesn't make us change how we feel about each other."

"I need to find him."

"I know. We will."

On Monday, the Strand was deserted of all the kids I'd usually see out in the water.

Normal kids go to school.

I slept in too late to catch Evan and Kim before their school bus came; and I felt bad about that, but Dahlia told me she'd rather watch me sleep than wake me up.

As I sat there eating the breakfast she cooked before I opened my eyes, Dahlia said we had plans to take care of.

"It starts with a shower," I said. "I think I smell bad enough to curdle milk."

The last time I took a shower was after April cut my hair, on my birthday.

"And maybe when I'm in there, I could throw my stuff in your washer. I don't have anything to change into."

Dahlia looked surprised. "What's in your suitcase?"

"Our wetsuits, one set of clothes for Bosten, dirty socks, jeans, and underwear, and a newspaper clipping with a picture of a UFO."

She smiled and shook her head.

"What am I going to do with you, Stark?"

She took me to a Sears in Ventura and bought me all the clothes I'd need for a few days, even socks. And underwear and T-shirts that weren't all white. I changed in the men's room at the shopping center.

Then she drove me across Oxnard to Anacapa Junior High School, and parked her Dodge in a space in front of the office that said VISITORS.

"What do you think?" she said.

What was I *supposed* to think? I wondered.

"It doesn't have hallways."

That was the first thing that struck me about the school: All the classrooms had doors that opened onto the outside, and instead of hallways, there were sidewalks.

The second thing I wondered was if they were going to put me in the mentally retarded class.

I think Dahlia saw the nervousness that came over me as we sat there in front of the school. I was never a natural fit into any situations involving new kids; and I dreaded the thought that somewhere, on the other side of the stucco wall we were facing, was a PE coach who was ready to start recording as much as he could about my life, my measurements, what I wore, and whether or not I took a shower.

Aunt Dahlia put her hand on my arm. "Let's just see what the people inside are like. Then we'll talk about things. But, you know what, Stark? This means I intend that you're going to be staying here with me. I think they're going to have to put me in jail before I'll let them send you back up to Washington."

I never knew anyone who'd stick up for me like that, with the exception of Bosten, and Emily. So it made me feel safe and lonely at the same time. I didn't know what I would do if I couldn't see Emily Lohman again.

I felt small and so far away from her.

I gulped, and said, "Okay."

And I was terrified that they were going to take me directly from the office and deposit me in some hostile class—probably gym—right on the spot. But after we talked to the school registrar, she gave Aunt Dahlia an enrollment packet that listed all the things we needed to provide before they could do such things to me; and that meant I was off the hook, at least for a few days.

When we stepped outside, Aunt Dahlia said, "That was better than I thought it would be. I have a feeling things are going to work out just fine for us. Of course, this is all up to you, Stark. I just want you to be sure that you're safe here."

"I know that. Thank you, Dahlia."

The strange thing was how much it seemed to me like I was really home, maybe for the first time in my life.

After we left the school, we drove into Oxnard, to a grocery store. Aunt Dahlia said she didn't think she even had a stale cracker left in her house, and she was afraid I was going to start eating her furniture if she didn't stock up on provisions.

On the way there, I thumbed through my new school's registration packet and found the page I dreaded the most: "Boys' Physical Education Participation Requirements." It had all the same important words that the Mr. Lloyds in the world kept precise records on: "daily showers," "deodorant," "hygiene," "athletic supporter."

School.

I wondered how long it would be until I had to punch one of Anacapa's "key guys" in the face.

Because things were different now.

In the afternoon, Aunt Dahlia phoned my mother. I pretended to be sleeping in my room. I even got undressed and slid under the sheets. My new T-shirt and underwear had that chemical smell that I always liked. And anyway, I wasn't going to talk to Mom. I didn't believe she really wanted to hear anything from me, either.

They were making arrangements. Mom was going to send down the papers the school needed so I could start going to classes. I kept my eyes shut, but I could tell by the way the conversation went Mom didn't mind at all that Aunt Dahlia was planning on having me move in with her.

Mom was always doing the math, and I guess things were finally starting to equal out to zero for her.

Not more than twenty minutes after that phone call, as I was still lying quietly in my bed with my door open, four policemen came to Aunt Dahlia's front door, asking if I was here and could they come in.

The police probably had some special guidelines that required them to always arrive when the guy they were looking for was in bed, in his underwear. I mean, what are you going to do in that situation? The only worse possible time would be if you were at a urinal, holding your dick, like when Ricky Dostal started that shit that got me here in the first place. I honestly did think about running, even if I didn't really understand what I could possibly be running away from.

I sat up. I could see the door right from where I was in my bed.

Two of the cops had on uniforms, with shining badges and

guns; and the other two, the ones standing in front, wore suits, neckties, and expressionless, bored faces.

They were there for me.

Just like that.

So there I was, sitting at Dahlia's kitchen table, barefoot, in my new T-shirt and underwear, talking to Detectives Adam Berkowitz from Portland and Guy Sheehan from Seattle. I wondered why anyone would name a guy Guy, but that thought went right out of my head as soon as Berkowitz said my own name.

"So, you're Stark McClellan?"

It sounded like something a sheriff in a Western would say, just before he shot the guy he knew he was going to shoot even if he didn't ask his name, anyway. It was part of the plan.

"Um. Yeah."

The two uniformed cops—from the Oxnard Police Department—waited outside with their car, in front of Dahlia's house. I guess they knew the stories about how the surfers on the Strand did things like leave dead rats under the windshield wipers of unattended patrol cars. At least, that's what Evan told me, and I believed him.

Detective Berkowitz sat right in front of me, so close that he actually had to spread his knees apart so we wouldn't knock legs—kind of like he was getting ready to apply a scissors-takedown if the wanted guy facing him made the slightest wrong move. Aunt Dahlia sat on the other side of the table, looking alternately at me, and then at each of the detectives, with an expression on her face that plainly said she was ready to kill either one of them if they had any ideas about taking me away from her.

"A lot of people have been looking for you." Berkowitz's voice sounded grim.

"Oh."

I swallowed spit.

I looked at Aunt Dahlia. She wasn't budging.

Then Guy Sheehan from Seattle said, "Your father's car was found outside of Fresno. A man named Willie Purcell fixed it at his service station in Oregon. And your father's been at home in Kitsap County for the past two weeks."

And all at the same time, I said, "I'm too young to drive," and Aunt Dahlia said, "Stark didn't steal anyone's car."

Then Guy Sheehan nodded his chin at Detective Berkowitz and pointed at his right ear. It felt like all the blood was draining out of my body. I just stared at Detective Berkowitz's enormous mustache.

"Nobody said you stole anything, son," Berkowitz said.

Sheehan's mustache wasn't as intimidating. He had zits, too, which kind of took the edge off his scariness.

But I didn't like the way Berkowitz called me "son," and then he leaned forward, so his knee actually pressed against my bare thigh. "You know a girl named April Van Hecht?"

I shifted away from him. "I know a girl named April. I don't know her last name. She was Willie's cousin. She cut my hair last week. On my birthday."

"So I guess that makes you fourteen now?"

"Uh-huh."

"But you told her your name was Bosten McClellan. That you were sixteen."

"I didn't think I'd get into any trouble if I pretended to be older."

"Nobody said you're in trouble," Sheehan said.

"Then why are there four cops from three different states here at my aunt's house?"

I knew I shouldn't have said it as soon as the words came

out of my mouth. It was the kind of thing that would get me slapped at my house.

Berkowitz leaned back in his chair. "You ready to tell me what happened at that houseboat?"

I waited; took a couple breaths.

"I don't know what happened at that houseboat. I was hiding in Willie's room. I heard five gunshots. Exactly five. I was too scared to come out. Anyway, I was scared of Willie and this other guy, an old man named Brock. They were doing cocaine all night, so I just hid in the room."

I didn't tell them the other stuff Brock tried to make me do or how he stole money from me.

Then Guy Sheehan got really close to me, trapping me against the edge of the table, between him and Berkowitz. "Did you do cocaine with them, Stark?"

I heard Aunt Dahlia inhale as soon as he asked.

And I lied, "No."

Well, it wasn't technically a lie. Willie forced it into my mouth.

Then I said, "I don't do shit like that. Nothing."

I looked at Dahlia. "Sorry. I didn't mean to cuss."

I turned red.

She patted my hand.

I heard the diesel rumble of a school bus churning down the street in front of the house. I wanted so desperately to run outside, even in my underwear, and beg Evan and Kim to get me out of there. Into the water.

The detectives stayed for almost two hours. When they finished asking me questions, they had me write out a statement about what happened in Scappoose. As I signed it, Guy Sheehan said, "Your father didn't want us to take you in for driving his car without a license."

I finished writing my statement. I should have saved that grocery bag for them. It had the same words trapped on it.

"I'm sure it's not worth his trouble."

I peeked through Dahlia's front window until I was certain the cops were gone.

When they disappeared down Ocean Avenue, I got dressed.

Aunt Dahlia looked worried. It hurt to see her like that, because I knew I was the cause of her suffering. I swore then that I would never do anything again to bring trouble into her house. I hugged her and told her I was sorry, and she rocked me back and forth in her arms and said, "Don't be foolish, Stark. You didn't do the first thing to be sorry about."

And even though I was dying to get out to the beach and see Kim and her brother, I sat at Dahlia's kitchen table with her and, together, we filled out the registration papers for my new school. Aunt Dahlia never had children. She asked me what an "athletic supporter" was, and why it was that only boys were required to have one to go to school.

So I told her. But I told her my version—the "Stick" explanation—not the myth that the Mr. Lloyds of the world expected you to believe.

We both laughed about it, too.

When I sat in the cool sand, digging my fingers in like I was trying to hold myself in one spot—finally—on the earth, watching Evan and Kim struggle to catch the chopped-up waves next to the jetty, I decided I'd ask Aunt Dahlia if I could call Emily that evening. Just the thought of hearing Emily's voice put a weight on my chest, and I honestly wasn't sure I'd be able to talk to her without crying.

But I had to make myself not cry, I thought.

Because things were different now.

Evan finally noticed me sitting there when his leash came off and he had to chase his board all the way into the sand, about fifteen feet in front of where I sat.

"Holy shit!" He dropped his board, then turned back toward the water and hollered, "Kimmy! Look who's here! Stick came back! Holy shit!"

Evan pulled me up by my hand and then slapped my shoulder. "What the fuck? I thought you guys were back in Washington."

I kept looking past Evan, watching Kim as she came out from the surf.

"My brother's not here yet. But it looks like I'm moving back for good."

"School and everything?"

"Yeah."

"Shit. Then I'm ditching tomorrow. Let's go to C Street."

Evan got closer to me. He cocked his head like he was looking at something under a microscope. "Did I say something wrong? Is something the matter, Stick?"

"It's . . . I got a really long story to tell you guys."

"And where's your wetsuit?"

Kim was out of the water now. She bent down and unfastened her leash and climbed the last few feet up the sand bank to where we stood. Then she was there with us. If it was possible, Kim Hansen looked even better than I remembered, even better than I imagined, those times I'd fantasized about her since my Easter vacation ended.

"I have it at my aunt's. I'll come out with you tomorrow, okay?"

"You came back," she said. Kim sounded genuinely happy to see me.

And before Evan could say anything else, his sister wrapped her arms around me and gave me a kiss, right on the mouth.

I would have drank an ocean of salt water at that moment, as long as it tasted like it did on Kim's lips. But it was a quick taste. After all, her brother was right next to us. Still, it left me feeling a little weak and winded; and plotting for some time in the immediate future when Kim and I might be able to do it better.

EMILY

"Hi, Em."

"Oh my God, Stick, are you okay?"

"I miss you so much."

Aunt Dahlia cleared her throat and made it obvious she was leaving to go outside.

"I love you, Emily."

"I love you, Stark McClellan."

Make yourself not get choked up.

"Please tell me you're coming home."

"I love you so much, Em. I wish I could hold you, and just hold you forever."

"Stark?"

"I don't belong there with Dad."

"Please come back."

"I have to live here now, with Aunt Dahlia."

When I said that, Emily began crying.

"You will like her, Em. She promised you could come stay

with us this summer. And I will sleep out on the couch. Unless nobody notices I'm not there."

"What will I do without you?"

"Summer's not too far away."

"I know you can't come back. I hate this."

"I love you."

"You promise I can come?"

"Yes."

"Will you wait for me?"

"I think Aunt Dahlia wouldn't care if we took a bath together."

"You better not do that with anyone else."

"I promise."

When Aunt Dahlia came back, she carried strawberry ice cream from the Corner Store—a place that sold bait, surf wax, and beer—that was just at the top of the Strand. She put a birthday candle right in the middle of the carton and lit it, and she promised that she would never forget my birthday again.

Then, after we watched television until we both started dozing off on her couch, Aunt Dahlia tucked me into bed and kissed my forehead.

"I suppose now that you're fourteen years old, I've missed out on an entire lifetime of chances to tuck you in and kiss you good night, Stark."

"Not too much," I said.

She flicked off the light and closed my door, and the words that Emily said tried to eat their way out of me.

I know you can't come back.

On a Friday
before Saint Patrick's Day,

Emily Lohman planted a miracle in me.
When I woke up

when I woke up

in the morning
my chains were loose.

I know you can't come back.

MOM

The following Monday I started school at Anacapa Junior High.

I wore my Steelers cap.

I was afraid.

Aunt Dahlia drove me there. We sat in the parking lot together. It was almost an hour before the first class, and hardly any kids had shown up yet. I was nervous about this new situation. I didn't know anyone at all. Evan and Kim went to high school. I couldn't imagine feeling more out of place than I did at this new school.

But that was only part of it.

I had been in California for a week now, and we hadn't heard anything about Bosten. Aunt Dahlia knew what was happening to me. I felt like I was dying, like I was completely losing my connection to the most important thing in the world.

. . .

They did not put me in the mentally retarded class.

I don't think they had one in Oxnard.

But during homeroom, they called me up to see the school nurse, a big brown woman named Mrs. Mendoza, who had very warm hands and big teeth that showed when she smiled.

She asked me to take off my cap.

I knew what this was about.

"I'm not mentally retarded."

Teeth.

She put her big, warm hand on my shoulder.

"My goodness, I'll bet you're six feet tall. Do you play basketball?"

I shook my head.

I imagined they'd be measuring and weighing me in gym class today.

"And who ever said you were mentally retarded?"

I shrugged.

I took off the cap.

Mrs. Mendoza gave me some candy. It wasn't bad at all, I mean, having her look at me. She was very nice, and it felt warm when she touched my neck, feeling around for things that I didn't know were in there.

Anotia.

She said a name for it: being born without an ear.

Anotia.

All this time, I never knew it had a name.

That it was something.

The word went in my head, and stayed there.

It sounded nice.

It felt comfortable.

Like I was something.

It made me feel so good that I wanted to hug Mrs.

Mendoza. She knew who I was, like I was just another kid, and maybe for the first time in my life, I started to feel like it really was no big deal.

I wondered if she knew the name for being born with three nipples.

"You aren't the first boy I've seen who was born this way."

There were others.

"Really?"

"Really. One day, maybe you and your aunt can come in together and we can talk about it."

I nodded. "Okay."

"You just let me know if it's giving you any trouble doing things in class, and we'll work on it. Okay, Stark?"

"Okay."

"And welcome to California. I hope you like your new school."

"Oh. I do."

When I went back to class, I felt taller.

Anotia.

I wrote it down, so I could see what it looked like.

Anacapa Junior High School was different in just about every possible way from the school I went to in Point No Point. To begin with, the kids were all kinds of colors. There were Mexicans, Filipinos, and black kids; and even the white kids weren't as Elmer's-Glue white as the kids in Washington.

Up in Washington, just about everyone was the color of fish stomachs.

And the PE coach didn't wear dark glasses that hid his eyes. Maybe he was inexperienced, but he didn't carry around anything to keep records in, either. And we played *outside*, too.

The kids called him "Coach Mo." His real name was Mr. Mortenson, but I guess Coach Mo was easier to say. Anyway, it sounded good. It sounded like *anotia*.

During gym class, Coach Mo told a boy whose last name was Sage to take me into the locker room and have Jerry stencil my T-shirt and shorts. All the boys had their last names stenciled in black on their gym clothes, and Jerry was the guy who worked in the locker room, in charge of running the showers, passing out towels, and stenciling stuff.

The kid named Sage had thick black-rimmed glasses and lots of freckles.

"Come on. Follow me."

Then he said, "What's your name?"

"Um. Stark."

"*That's* your name? I thought Coach Mo called you McWilliams or something."

"Oh. Stark's my first name. My last name's McClellan."

"That's your *first name*?"

"I know. It's weird."

"Well. Not really. My first name's Miles, but nobody calls me that. They call me Ed. My middle name's Edward. What's your middle name?"

"Alden."

"Eww." Miles Edward Sage was obviously not afraid of being honest. "Well, I won't tell no one. Stark."

"A lot of people call me Stick."

"That's dumb, too."

I shrugged.

I was getting used to being called Stark, anyway.

Jerry worked behind a wire mesh cage. I don't know why they had to put wire up as a kind of window onto his towel-shower-stenciling office. Maybe the boys threw things, I thought.

I took off my shirt and slid it beneath the cage. I could smell the paint fumes as Jerry stenciled my name across the chest. It smelled like cocaine. Then he folded my T-shirt and slid it back to me. It said MC CLELLAN.

I don't think they used lowercase letters in the alphabet of gym class.

I put it on, and it made me feel like more of a regular kid here.

When I slipped my shorts off, I was half convinced that Ed Sage was going to force me outside and pin me against a wall in front of the girls' classes, so I was prepared to make him become the first guy I'd punch in California—if it came to that.

But I guess Ed was an okay guy.

He just shook his head and said, "That's totally seventh grade."

Jerry began painting my shorts.

"What?" I said.

"Wearing a jock this late in the year," Ed explained. "Get with it, Stark. In eighth grade, guys wear them maybe on the first day. The first week, if they're pussies. Nobody checks after that. What are they going to do? Put you in detention hall for not wearing a jock?"

I didn't know what they would do. I never wondered about it in Mr. Lloyd's class. It was a rule, and Mr. Lloyd kept records.

Ed went on, "Coach Mo tells us he doesn't care what we keep our nuts in as long as we don't have boxers hanging out of our shorts. Then he gets mad. But wearing a jock in the middle of April? Total seventh-grade move."

"Oh."

Jerry slid my shorts back under his screen.

"Well, I don't have boxers," I said.

"Then you should go change. So the other guys don't make fun of you."

"Okay."

I started to go back to the row where my locker was.

"And hurry up, so we can play," Ed said.

"Okay."

"And throw that fucking thing in the garbage."

Miles Edward Sage was my first friend at Anacapa Junior High School.

"I like it here."

I could see the worry wash clean off Aunt Dahlia's face when I sat down in the Dodge and shut the door. I slid across the seat and kissed her on the cheek. "I really like this school. A lot."

"I've been so worried for you, I thought I was going to be sick. You don't know how happy I am to hear you say you like it here, Stark."

"It was no big deal. No big deal at all."

After school was surf time for the kids on the Strand.

I was out in the water, floating between Evan and Kim, and everything felt healed. Perfect.

There weren't any waves. We just floated.

Evan bumped my arm. "Hey. There's your aunt."

I turned around so I could see the shore.

In the afternoon, when you're out on the water and the sun is angled lower behind you, everything on the shore looks like a Technicolor movie—so clear, painted as bright as a carnival midway.

A blue dress with parrots and bamboo stood on the sand beside Aunt Dahlia.

Mom had come for me.

She was smoking a cigarette.

Even out there on the water, I could suddenly smell it.

I put my face down on the deck of the surfboard.

I wanted to float away.

"What's up?" Kim said.

"That's my mom."

"Oh."

Evan and Kim both knew enough about how things had been for us back home. I'd told them about Mom and Dad, the Saint Fillan's room, and they knew Bosten left home after the last fight he'd had with Dad.

I didn't tell them the whole truth about why the fight happened or anything about Paul Buckley. It wasn't like I was ashamed of Bosten or anything. I could never be ashamed of my brother. I just felt something like that—Bosten being gay and everything—if anyone else needed to know about it, my brother would tell them himself when he decided it was the right time. Just like he did with Aunt Dahlia.

If he ever came back.

"You need a haircut."

Just like that. It was the first thing she said to me when I got out of the water.

Since the last time she pinned me steady in the freezing air and buzz-cut my scalp on the front porch that morning after Bosten, Paul, and I set off the UFO that attacked Seattle, my hair had grown so much that it covered the spot where there might be an ear.

I drive at night.
I blow things up.
I have anotia

and long hair.
Now go away,

Mother.

And what could I say to that, anyway?

"No, he doesn't." Dahlia answered for me.

I looked back one time. Evan and Kim were still in the water. I waved at them and pointed at the board I was carrying. I wanted Evan to know I was going to put it back in his yard.

"I need to give my friend his board back. I'll be home in a minute."

I stabbed those words at her like lances,

friend
home.

Aunt Dahlia and Mom waited in the living room while I got dressed. Mom smoked. I could smell it crawling in under my door. Nobody ever smoked in Aunt Dahlia's house.

I wanted to break something.

It was the same as being stuck in that room on the houseboat. There was no way to escape. There was only silence, and smoke, on the other side of the bedroom door.

And I hated myself for doing it, but I was every bit as afraid here in California as I'd been on the river in Oregon; so I put on a white undershirt and tucked a collared shirt into my jeans.

Mom and Dad carried their rules around like invisible swords.

I saw how Dahlia looked at me when I finally came out. I could tell. She was disappointed because I'd been beaten. I sat on the end of the couch, so Aunt Dahlia was between us.

Mom lit another cigarette.

"How have you been, Stick?"

"Good. Do you know where Bosten is?"

Aunt Dahlia kept her eyes on Mom.

"No."

"Why are you here?"

"That's not very nice. I thought you wanted me to come back."

I looked down at my jeans. They were new and stiff. I should have taken them off right then and there and left them with Aunt Dahlia. I didn't deserve such things.

"I did."

"I came to see if you want to go home now."

"I don't know what that is."

I saw Aunt Dahlia's eyes. They looked so heavy. I couldn't hurt her. I wouldn't let Mom treat her that way.

Like she didn't matter.
Like we were both empty suitcases,
and Mom was there to pick over
the unclaimed stuff that came
out of us.

There was nothing
holding me and
Mom
together.
I sat there
feeling the things that held me
together
my brother
Dahlia
together.

"I have a comfortable place. In Seattle. In a big brick building."

"I started school here today."

I was not going to cry.

I was not going to cry.

I tried to not think about it.

I could feel it.

Mom put her cigarette out.

Then I stood up. I had to do something before I started wailing like a goddamned little kid. And for some reason, all I could think about was how Jerry had stenciled MC CLELLAN on my clothes, and didn't that mean that I couldn't just go away?

"This was my first fucking day at school here! My first fucking day!"

Mom got up.

Aunt Dahlia said, "Please."

I looked out the window. Evan and Kim stood in the street beside Mom's blue rental car, dripping, in their wetsuits. They looked like they were waiting for something. Maybe smoke to come out of the house. I don't know.

And Mom was going to hit me for saying that, but I stood my ground. I did not shrink back, like I might have done some other time.

I raised my hand, and she froze. I saw how weak and withered she had made herself. I think it was the first time I noticed.

"You're not big enough anymore, Mom."

She sat down.

Then I spun around and ran back into the room. I slammed my door.

I took off the clothes Aunt Dahlia had bought for me to wear to my new school. I folded them, following the creases pressed into them so they would fit in perfectly with the other things on the shelves of the store.

I realized my face was wet. I was a stupid, ugly little kid.

And I lay down on my bed and put my face in the pillow. I was not going to cry. I was not going to scream. I just stayed there and waited.

When Bosten was in grade seven,
I remember how he was taller than me
and I was in the normal kids' school,
but I didn't do anything very good,
and the kids called me retard.

Three bigger kids,
and one of them tripped me
outside of Mr. Lohman's store.
And Bosten said
nobody fucks with my brother
you piece of shit
but I should have told him
lots of people do.
Bosten got his nose busted
and kicked in the stomach.

I came to see
if you want to go home now.

Here are five bullets for the boys on the boat.
Here is one more for the saint.

I fell asleep.

And I dreamed again that Bosten was dead. It was back in the house, and I was lying on my bed with my ear pressed up against the pipe so I could listen to Dad and Bosten fighting up above while I kept my eyes pinned to the little window, the golden rectangle of night. I saw Dad carrying Bosten outside, down the path to the well. He put Bosten inside the little pumphouse and shut him in there. And he closed the door on him and said here is one more for the saint.

And when I woke up, I was still crying. Aunt Dahlia sat on the bed next to me. It was very dark, and she pressed soft circles with her palm between my shoulder blades.

"Don't worry, baby. Don't worry. You're not going anywhere."

Mom had taken her rental car and gone.

But the house still smelled like her.

THE ANGEL

"Maybe you should stay home from school today," Dahlia said.

"I don't want to."

That afternoon the waves had come back to the Strand. I surfed with Evan and Kim, and I was getting pretty good at it. Sometimes, Evan and I would trade boards out past the breakers and I'd try his shorter one. He was teaching me how to turn and cut up and down the face of the wave.

Well, at least, he was watching me when I'd crash.

Short boards let you steal everything you could from a decent wave, like you were picking the pocket of a blind man.

But when we were out there, switching off for the last time, I saw Aunt Dahlia on the shore. She was actually up to her knees in the churning water, waving her arms and shouting at me. I couldn't really tell what she was trying to say, but I did hear one word clearly.

Bosten.

"Hey." Evan shook my arm. "She's saying something about your brother."

But I was already paddling frantically, on my way in to the shore.

Aunt Dahlia stepped backwards out of the whitewash foam.

Evan and Kim were right behind me when I got my feet planted stable enough where I could stand.

"He's on the phone."

I tore the leash from my ankle and dropped Evan's board. I couldn't think about anything else, except that it was Bosten.

Finally. He was alive.

I ran across the sand toward Dahlia's house, cursing, my feet slipping, the muscles in my legs aching with fire.

It seemed to take forever, like running through wet concrete.

I raced around the rotten fence to the front door. Tracking sand and dripping water, I half stumbled into the kitchen and grabbed the receiver that was lying atop the table.

"Bosten!"

"My man, Sticker."

My chest began heaving, like I was having hiccups. I was so happy, thrilled, to hear my brother again. I couldn't even tell whether I was laughing or crying.

Bosten. Where the fuck were you?

Shit. Everywhere.

Where are you now? Are you okay?

I'm all right, Sticker. I'm in L.A.

We're going to come get you.

We're going to come get you right now, okay?

Hang on.

What do you mean?

I need to find another dime or something.
The operator's saying my time's up.

Where are you?

I don't know where this place is.
Somewhere by Hollywood, I think.

Where can we come get you?

I don't know.
Look. Tomorrow, I'll be in a place called Angel Street.
It's in downtown, by Broadway and Third, or maybe Sixth.
I know how to get there.
It's a place for kids.
Street kids.

Okay. We'll come.

Sticker?

What?

I don't think you should bring Dahlia there.

Why?

Just don't. Please?

Why?

See if you could maybe bring me twenty dollars.

I guess Bosten ran out of dimes. That was the last thing I heard my brother say.

And I called his name three or four times into the dead mouthpiece, but there was nothing on the phone.

When I looked out across the living room, I saw that Dahlia and Evan and Kim were just standing there, outside the door, in the sand of the front yard, like they had to have permission from me to get close to what was happening.

I sat down at the table, holding my chin in my hands, staring at the phone.

I could hear Aunt Dahlia telling Kim and Evan that it

was all right for them to come inside, even if they were wet and sandy, but Evan kept saying, "That's okay, we can wait out here."

She picked up the phone, held it to her ear, then hung it up.

"What did he say?"

I tried to think.

It was like I couldn't remember what he said.

It was as though everything had been completely pulled apart again.

I swallowed. I was suddenly aware that I was sitting in Aunt Dahlia's kitchen, wearing my wetsuit, dripping sand and seawater everywhere. "He's okay."

"He wouldn't say where he was. He asked if you made it here, and then he told me he needed to talk to you. That was it."

"He ran out of money for the phone."

"He'll call back, baby."

Aunt Dahlia rubbed my neck. I could feel how my wet hair curled over her hand when she did it.

I looked back at Evan and Kim, then got up and went into my room to grab some dry clothes that I wadded up and carried toward the front door.

"I'm going to help my friends take care of the boards and stuff," I said. "I'll be back for dinner."

And then I left.

Evan exhaled thin clouds of pot smoke with every word. "Dude. Just ask her. You can't steal your aunt's car."

I steal cars.

I changed into my clothes at the twins' house, and the three of us sat out in the sand, sheltered from the afternoon wind by the enormous boulders piled there to create the jetty.

"I don't know what to do. I don't want to hurt her feelings, but my brother has to have a reason why he doesn't want her to come."

Kim sat so close to me that our knees touched. "What did he sound like on the phone?"

"To be honest, it was all kind of a blur. I was so choked up just knowing he was alive. I can't even tell you how scared I've been that something horrible happened to him."

Evan sucked at the last bit of his joint, and threw the soggy end at the rocks. "Do you want me to go with you?"

I shook my head. "Bosten doesn't want anyone there."

Kim put her hand on my leg. Our eyes met, and I knew we were going to kiss again; and it was going to be that day, too. And I hated myself and felt guilty, like I was letting down my brother, because at times she made it impossible to think about anything else except the taste of her mouth.

But everything was so different now.

My mouth watered.

She said, "You have to be fair to your brother, and you have to be fair to your aunt. They both love you."

I swallowed.

She followed me out when I went home for dinner. I knew she would, and we hid behind the Corner Store, between two trash cans, for at least fifteen minutes, kissing with our tongues all over in each other's mouths.

She whispered, "I think you're brave."

I steal cars.

I pushed against her. I was out of breath, and Kim even put her hand down and rubbed between my legs. Nobody ever touched me like that before. I slid my fingers up inside her sweatshirt and felt her breasts. They were cold and hard.

Then I pushed away from her.

"I need to stop this."

"Why?"

"Because I'm stupid."

"What   are you talking about?"

"Fuck!"

I turned away and hurried down the street toward Aunt Dahlia's.

I didn't turn around once to look at Kim. I didn't want her to see how stupid I was.

Because I suddenly began thinking about Emily, about Bosten. And Mom and Dad. And I felt horrible and dirty.

I am ugly.

I couldn't look Aunt Dahlia straight in the face after that. I felt like I was stealing something from everyone I cared about, and I couldn't stand myself for it. I decided to tell the truth.

"I'm sorry, Dahlia."

"What for?"

"For not telling you the truth."

"Oh."

She put down her fork. She'd made spaghetti for dinner. Mom never cooked spaghetti at home. Aunt Dahlia was a good cook. Everything she made tasted perfect.

"Bosten wants me to come see him. He's going to meet me tomorrow at a place in Los Angeles called Angel Street. It's where kids who run away from home go. But he told me to come by myself. He's scared about something."

Aunt Dahlia waited a long time. Then she said, "You're not going to leave me, are you?"

"I would never do that."

"Well."

"I can drive."

"You told me that once."

"I'm big enough."

"You're bigger than me by a good bit."

"I promise I will come home."

"I'll call the school in the morning. Tell them you're staying home, sick."

"Thank you."

"You better get that boy to come home now, too."

That was the thing that kept bothering me. I didn't exactly know if Bosten wanted to come home again.

"I'll try."

The morning came gray and heavy, like the Strand was wrapped up in a damp wool coat.

I didn't sleep much during the night. I don't think Aunt Dahlia did, either, because her house was never so deathly quiet in all the time I'd been there as it was when we sat together and ate our breakfast of scrambled eggs.

"If you tell me no, I won't go."

"I'm not going to do that."

She gave me a map of Southern California.

It looked like one of those painted Visible Man models, with red and blue blood vessels running all over the surface.

The night before, we studied a course for me to drive from the beach in Oxnard to the center of Los Angeles, and I memorized it as much as I could, but my brain was never good for stuff like that.

Of course I was scared.

And she gave me thirty-five dollars, too, which I folded inside Bosten's wallet. I didn't even ask for it, but somehow, Dahlia knew we might need the money.

I guess she did her own math.

I waited inside until all the kids from the Strand had gone past the house and caught their school bus. I saw Evan and

Kim leaving, too. I know Aunt Dahlia wondered why I wasn't excited about talking to them, but I just couldn't make myself face either one of them on that morning.

I was convinced something terrible would happen to me when I left. It was more certain than the feeling of danger I had when I hid inside that floating room and counted off five gunshots.

Ghosts of their noise still rang, at times, inside my head.

Aunt Dahlia squeezed me so tight before I left. Secretly, I hoped she wouldn't let go, or that she'd change her mind and forbid me to do something as foolish and reckless as I was going to do. But I was lying to myself if I thought even for a moment that she'd ever be like that.

So I got in the car and drove away up Ocean Avenue.

Just like that.

By noon I was in Los Angeles. I was completely lost, too.

I realized that maps can't be read while you're driving, and the one Aunt Dahlia had given me didn't show anything about the one-way streets that trapped me, herding me along in the wrong direction, floating on a nonstop river of cars carrying people who appeared to be going exactly where they wanted to go.

Finally, frustrated that I was aimlessly going to be swept along until I ran out of gas, I pulled the Dodge into a flat, open parking lot that was surrounded in chain-link fencing. I had to pay a man three dollars to leave Aunt Dahlia's car there, but I was glad to be on my feet and out of the pulsing traffic.

I didn't wear the cap Emily gave me anymore. My hair had grown long enough that people didn't immediately zero in on that side of my head. They still noticed, though. When you're born like me, that telltale twitch of the head, the widening of the eyes you see from strangers, become almost like predatory warning signals for a game animal. Anyway, I saw that same startled look when I paid the parking lot owner with a five and waited as he stumbled through counting off my two dollars in change.

I guess it's hard to do math when you're looking at someone like me.

He was short and thick, with very stubby fingers and a bristling gray mustache that rivaled the monstrousness of the one on the cop who took me out of bed in my underwear.

I had torn off the corner of Aunt Dahlia's map and held it in my hand, hoping he'd be able to decode it for me. On the page was a magnified street view of downtown L.A.

"I'm kind of lost," I said.

The man handed me my change.

He had a strong accent, but I had no idea where he could have been from. He waved away the torn map corner like it smelled bad. "This is Flower."

He pointed, and my eyes followed his plump finger. "There Wilshire."

I liked the way he said *Wilshire*. It sounded like *Weelshider*.

I looked at the map. I saw the corner of Wilshire and Flower on it.

"Which way to Broadway?"

He swung his arm toward the left. "Broadway. Down there. Maybe six block."

"Oh. Uh, thank you."

I started off toward the street, spinning the map in my hand so it was going the same way as I was.

"Hey. Kid."

I stopped and turned around. The man came and stood directly in front of me, like he thought I couldn't hear.

Or something.

I'd seen that enough times to know what he was thinking.

“I lock the gate ten pee-em. Ten pee-em is closed.”

He clapped the edge of one hand into his palm.

Nice try at sign language.

I nodded and made the same gesture back at the parking lot man. “Okay. Ten p.m.”

He nodded.

Downtown Los Angeles reeked of piss, vomit, and smoke. I imagined hell wouldn’t smell too much different. It was like the entire city was coated with the same filmy goo you try not to step in around the floor of a boys’ urinal. The soles of my shoes stuck to the sidewalks. I thought they would probably stick to the ground in hell, too.

The area that lined Broadway was wild and noisy. The buildings there were so tall and close, the streets only got moments of sunlight, even though the sky had totally cleared since the morning. And all along the sidewalks were rows of ground-floor shops that sold stuff I never thought people would want to buy, or at least not shop for in the combinations I saw displayed in storefronts and windows.

One of the markets had a perfectly arranged pyramid of limes that was stacked next to a table with plastic-sealed packages of socks and underwear, all lined up neatly beneath a shelf of transistor radios and batteries.

Most of the shops had signs written in Spanish.

I think a lot of the people I passed didn’t even speak English at all.

I had been to Seattle a few times, and I always thought it was a big city. But I never imagined any place could be as intimidating, or buzz with such a constant vibration—movement, sound, smell, light, and shadow—as Los Angeles.

And I must have looked dumb, walking, spinning my head around to see everything as I moved through the crowds of people who shopped and mingled and bumped into one another everywhere on the street.

When I turned the corner onto Broadway, I stepped straight into the path of a little boy who was running down the sidewalk away from his mother.

His forehead hit me square in the balls.

I moaned and clutched my stomach.

I wondered why getting hit in the balls always felt like having your liver and intestines sucked out your navel through a straw.

The boy rolled away from me without breaking stride. He kept running as though nothing happened. His mother, carrying a sleeping infant in her arms, ignored me and brushed past, floating along after the kid with the dangerous head.

I just stood there and waited for the pain to start receding and my guts to migrate back toward their starting points.

This was the corner of Broadway and Sixth.

And I didn't see any place called Angel Street. But there was so much to look at, so many details, all compressed together like some kind of wild painting.

I moved up along Broadway.

In front of one of the stores, a man sat behind a folding card table. He rattled off word after word in Spanish to a small crowd that had gathered around him. A woman at the edge of his table clutched a wad of wrinkled dollar bills in her hand, while the man shuffled walnut shells in overlapping circles in front of her. He lifted one of the shells and dropped a small yellow bead beneath it. Then he went on, talking and talking, his voice like a song, or a poem, making a dance of sounds in my head.

I watched his hands and listened to his narration.

The movement and tone of his voice hypnotized me, and sometimes the entire audience would laugh in unison. The man running the game was apparently very funny, while he worked at crossing and looping those walnut shells.

I didn't think people actually did things like that, either, except maybe in movies about other times and places. But here it was, in the shadow of skyscrapers, this dance and spectacle taking place in front of my eyes, right on a sidewalk in Los Angeles.

It was amazing to me.

I thought it was beautiful.

I watched the game for a while. Money changed hands. The man rarely looked up from his shells. When he did, he'd take only the quickest glance, like his eyes were snapping machine-gun flash photographs of the spectators. Then he noticed me, and stopped shuffling his hands.

He pointed to me and said something.

It sounded friendly. He had kind eyes.

But everyone around the table turned and looked at me. They were waiting for me to do something as an answer to the man running the game.

Then he pointed from me to the shells on his table.

I felt myself turning red. I didn't know what to do.

People began talking, saying something to me, calling me *joven*.

Joven.

I shook my head, backed away, and tried to disappear up the sidewalk, into the drifting sea of the crowd, but I could never just blend in. Not anywhere.

Especially not in Los Angeles.

And as I got farther up the street, my escape route was blocked by a wall of people that cut across the sidewalk and created a pathway in front of the stairs that led through the front doors of a church. I couldn't get around the pack of bodies. The street was choked, at a standstill, too. Cars had pulled up to the curb, decorated with streamers and paper flowers, their doors standing open.

Four little girls in yellow frilled dresses, and wearing pale white leggings that wrinkled around their ankles, with black shoes polished like mirrors, came through the doorway. Each one of them carried a basket of flowers, and they scattered petals and blooms down onto the sidewalk where they walked. Then eight little boys, Mexicans, stepped out from the church, lined up like soldiers, and all dressed in matching green suits and ties, their hair slicked down across the tops of their heads, shining like the shoes worn by the flower girls. More men and women, young and old, all brown-skinned, shining, swaying in their dresses and suits, walking proudly like hunters carrying a trophy, and waiting beside the open cars with their gleaming eyes fixed on the façade of the church.

Finally the bride and groom emerged through the doorway, and the voices of their party rose in happy and musical salutes. The man looked scared. I knew how he felt, with all these people watching him. He was thin, with barely a trace of mustache, and he wore a very simple suit with a yellow shirt. His eyes met mine, and it was like we both knew something about the other.

He looked to be about seventeen.

And I thought he looked brave.

But I didn't feel bad or out of place watching as the groom nervously led his bride into their car. And when the people forming the lines caved in behind them, a pathway cleared through the crowd, so I continued up the sidewalk, looking for anything I could find that said Angel Street on it.

I stopped in front of a shop with the word CARNICERÍA painted in blue across its wide glass storefront. At some time, the letters had been rained on, and they dripped down the window like melted wax.

Inside, I saw a glass case that was filled with meat, pale

sausages, and parts of animals. A beautiful girl in a white apron stood behind the counter, and an old woman with her back to me pointed and waved her hand, "no," at things she wanted the girl to turn over, lift.

No, again.

At the back of the shop, a stocky man, bare-armed and wearing a T-shirt smeared with blood, hacked away at a leg joint, swinging a wide and flat cleaver while a lit cigarette dangled from his lips and smoke curled back into his eyes.

Even from where I stood on the sidewalk, I could hear the drumming whacks of the cleaver, and I could see the bone dust and marrow that flecked out across his wooden block.

And in front of the girl, at the very center of the meat case, was an enormous pig's head, blanched white, smiling at me, his eyes squinted like he was laughing, as if he was so happy I had come there to see him, surrounded as he was with curved platters of cow brains, tongues, and tripe.

I thought he was like the king of all the dead things, the ruler of all the pieces that had been so carefully arranged around him, all the missing parts everywhere in the world.

I had never seen anything like this before—certainly never seen an entire pig's head for sale—and I tried to calculate if there was a price you could pay for something like that.

His ears looked nice, too.

I wondered if anyone could just buy one ear.

A scale with a stainless metal pan hanging beneath it dangled over the counter. It reminded me of a prop you might see in a horror film. The girl who worked there dropped something red and wet into it, and she watched as the needle danced its clockwise, twitching response. Her dark hair fell over her shoulders, and she was saying something to the old woman customer, who nodded. I was mesmerized by her mouth, the whiteness of her teeth.

She was perfectly beautiful.

She must be the daughter of the butcher, I thought, because she couldn't have been much older than I was. And I wondered if she had ever kissed a white boy from the state of Washington before.

One with anotia.

I looked at the pig head again.

When I lifted my eyes, I noticed that the girl had seen me. Maybe she knew I'd been watching her; but we just stared at each other for a while. She didn't smile. Neither did I. It was like she knew me.

She pulled a piece of brown paper out from beneath the case and scooped the contents of the metal scale onto it. As she tucked the paper around the piece of meat, flipping it over, turning it around, I saw that her slender left arm ended just below her elbow.

But she worked quickly, like missing a hand was nothing to her.

The butcher kept chopping.

The old woman counted out money from an orange wallet.

I watched the girl behind the counter, and I wondered if Mrs. Mendoza had a word for this girl, too.

She looked at me again.

I left.

I was sorry I watched the girl. It made me feel like I'd stolen something from her.

Maybe she thought the same thing about me.

Maybe that's what the pig was smiling about.

I almost walked right past Angel Street without noticing it.

Well, there wasn't much to notice in the first place; just a crooked, hand-painted sign nailed to the top of a heavy door with a small, grated window cut into its center. The door was squeezed inconspicuously between two storefronts, and when I pulled it open, the only thing on the other side was a dark and worn, narrow flight of stairs that led straight up to another doorway.

It reminded me of the way up from my basement. The stairs that would take me to Saint Fillan's room, to Mom and Dad. But these stairs at Angel Street smelled like piss.

I stood in a puddle of it at the bottom landing.

A bare, yellowed lightbulb hung down from the ceiling above the stairs. It dangled on a blackened cord of wire. When the door shut behind me, it was like I'd stepped into another world, or maybe another time.

The stairs creaked under my feet.

I looked back and saw the patterns of my shoe soles printed in piss on the lower steps. When I got close enough to the upper doorway, I could read the words that had been stenciled in black with spray paint:

ANGEL STREET YOUTH SHELTER

I didn't want to wait anymore. I imagined pulling open that door and looking right into my brother's eyes, seeing him the way he was the last time we were together and happy, on that Easter morning when we surfed together at the Strand.

But the door opened onto another dark and quiet room.

I went inside.

It smelled like smoke. I stood with my hand on the door, inside an old lobby, very small, with a torn sofa and a table that had equally torn magazines and coverless books on it. A mute television sat on the floor beside one wall. It had only one rabbit ear. The other was missing; and I thought, *I have come home.*

At the back of the room was a curved, wooden registration counter, like you'd see in an old run-down hotel.

A man smoking a cigarette leaned behind it, like a tired bartender.

He didn't have any hair on top of his head, which helped spread the light from the flickering artificial-flame glass bulbs in the fake electric candles behind the desk. But the hair on the sides of his head hung down to his shoulders.

He said, "You're the last one."

"Uh. I am?"

It was all so surreal, like the guy had been expecting me. And for just a moment I thought that maybe I was dead, and maybe this was where you go to get sorted out or maybe to find your missing parts.

I watched him, hoping he might give me some kind of clue. Like we were speaking in code or something.

As my eyes adjusted, I could see a hallway behind him, and a door with a brass number nailed onto it.

He took another long drag from his cigarette.

"The last bed. You never been here before?"

I shook my head, and kept my back pressed against the door out to the stairs.

"Room two has three beds. Two boys checked in today. You're the last one."

The bald man pinched his cigarette between his lips and pulled a clipboard up from beneath his registration desk. He started to write something on it, and checked the time on his wristwatch.

I looked at the door again.

"You're new on the streets, aren't you?"

I shook my head.

"Um. I don't think I'm on the streets." I cleared my throat.

There was no window in the room, and I became aware of how much smoke had filled up the space between me and the guy at the desk.

"I'm looking for my brother. He called me yesterday and said he was going to be here."

I took a cautious step forward.

On the wall in back of the man, there was a sign. It said, ANGEL STREET RULES.

I guessed it was there to make boys like me and Bosten feel at home.

NO DRUGS.
NO SMOKING IN THE DORMS.
IF YOU ARE UNDER 18,
CALIFORNIA LAW REQUIRES
ANGEL STREET TO CALL
A PARENT.
YOU MUST LEAVE AFTER 2 NIGHTS.

At the bottom of the poster, in what looked like red crayon, someone had scribbled, "No Sex," and, below that, in pencil: "Especially not with Steve."

I assumed Steve was the bald guy smoking the cigarette—the guy who ran this place. He put down his pencil.

"My brother's name is Bosten McClellan."

"I know Bosten."

For some reason, just hearing Steve say he knew my brother made my heart start beating faster. "Is he here?"

Steve shook his head. Ashes dropped onto his desk and he swiped them away with the underside of his forearm. "Nuh. He checked in today, but he's out on the street right now. You know that kid. He needs to straighten his shit up.

Slow down a bit.

He's going to end up dead.

Everyone's tried talking to him."

"Oh." I didn't know if it meant I should leave. "Is he going to come back?"

"He knows to come back before midnight."

I thought about the man who was going to lock the gate at ten pee-em.

"My brother is only sixteen."

"What's that supposed to mean?" Steve sounded annoyed. He pressed his cigarette butt down into the lid from a pickle jar and twisted it around.

I didn't know what it was supposed to mean. I just wanted Steve to tell me Bosten was going to be okay.

I shrugged.

"Look. Every time your brother's come in here . . ." Steve flipped back through the pages pinned to his clipboard. "Three times in the past two weeks. He stayed here three times, counting showing up this morning."

Steve did the math.

He pivoted the clipboard around so I could read it.

"See that phone number?"

Steve bit his nails. And his finger was yellow. He put it down right under the phone number next to Bosten's name. It was our phone number in Washington.

I nodded.

"Look familiar, kid?"

"It's ours."

"Every time he's been here, I've talked to your dad. We have to. To get permission. I talked to him about an hour ago."

"My dad knows Bosten's here?"

Steve let out a heavy sigh, the kind people would make when they were about to call me *retard*.

"You know the drill, kid. Your dad doesn't want the boy to come home, anyway. Why wouldn't he give permission?

If he didn't give permission, we'd kick your brother out.
You're not dumb.
You know what happens to
boys like Bosten
on the street.

Your old man even sent him some cash a few days ago."

I didn't know what happened to boys like Bosten on the street.

So I supposed I *was* dumb.

"My dad sent money?"

"And you know what boys on the street do with their money. Or the things they'll do to make money.

And Bosten needs to slow it down a bit at both ends of the cash-flow gig."

I didn't know anything.

I decided not to ask him any more about boys on the street, because I thought he didn't know how stupid I was about things yet. And maybe I was afraid of finding out too much about Bosten.

I swallowed.

"I came to take him home."

"To Washington?"

"We stay with my aunt now. In Oxnard."

"Well, good luck making that happen."

"Does he have any stuff here?"

"Bosten? That kid never has nothing but the clothes on his back."

Steve took another cigarette out. "Smoke?"

He held the pack out to me.

"No."

"Yeah. You're not a street kid."

"I know."

Steve lit the cigarette. He squinted his eyes when he dragged in the smoke, like it was painful. I thought that looked cool.

I said, "Can I stay here and wait for my brother?"

Steve pointed at the rules on the wall. "You can wait for two nights, if you want to."

I didn't want to.

I sat down on the least-ripped part of the couch I could fit on, and Steve added, "And the TV doesn't work."

Then he put his clipboard away.

I stared at the wall, at the TV with a missing ear.

I could feel that Steve was just standing there, staring at me, but I didn't want to talk to him anymore. There was a plastic lid from one of those really big coffee cans sitting on top of the torn books and magazines on the table. It was filled with all kinds of cigarette butts. I tried counting them, identifying the brands.

I picked up a book.

The cover was torn off. I turned it and looked at the spine of the book. For just a moment, I thought, with the cover gone, it was like the book was missing an ear, too. Down the spine, it said, *The Catcher in the Rye*.

I never heard of it.

"What's your name, anyway?"

Steve was still watching me.

I guess when all you have is a broken television set and a bunch of torn books, you might as well watch the back of an ugly kid's head.

And I almost said *Stick*, but stopped myself.

"Stark McClellan."

"Do you want to talk to your dad?"

"No."

I put the book back, spun the lid of butts around, counted.

"What happened to your ear?"

"Nothing." I said, "I have anotia."

"Oh."

Steve said it like he knew what I was talking about.

He probably thought something else would fall off me if he just watched long enough.

I thought about
the girl in the *carnicería*.
How she might be an angel.
And I fell asleep,
sitting there on that torn couch
in Angel Street.

BOSTEN

I know

I am floating.
And I see all the people
that come and go,
and come and go,
carried by tides we can't swim against.
Sometimes we reach out
and our touch is a passing thing.
Paul Buckley, Willie, April,

Sutton,
Emily.

Only the sounds
and words
stay trapped in my head.

Here are five bullets.
Here is the saint.

Bosten and I could never let that sea
separate and drown us.
We were all we ever had.

Someone's arm wrapped around my shoulder. There was warm, thick breath against my neck.

"Stick?"

My eyes were shut, and I expect this will sound strange, but I smelled Bosten.

I know my brother's smell, whether he's clean or dirty, wet or dry. Before my eyes opened, I knew it was Bosten, there, next to me, and the words in my head pleaded

don't let this be a dream.

"Sticker?"

And then I saw him.

"Aren't you going to say something?"

Bosten grabbed both of my shoulders, his eyes were just inches from mine.

I couldn't talk.

He looked different. I guess I did, too.

Because everything had changed.

Bosten was thin and pale, gray. His eyes were so dark, and he looked like a man. There was a patch of golden fuzz growing out from his chin, and more down the turn of the jaw in front of his ears.

And he was wearing the same clothes he had on that day Mrs. Buckley drove him home, but they were filthy. His T-shirt had gone brown, and his flannel had holes in it.

But it was my brother.

I grabbed on to him and put my face against his neck. And I didn't talk; and I didn't let go, either. I realized Bosten was crying.

That was something my brother never did in front of me.

"I'm sorry, Sticker. I didn't mean to scare you or nothing."

I put my hand in his hair and rubbed his head.

"I was so goddamned scared."

Then I really *was* scared that maybe this was a dream, so I pushed him back and looked at him again. His eyes were wet, and I wiped at them with my thumbs.

"Goddamn it. Fuck, Bosten."

I started crying, too.

"I like your hair." Bosten combed his hand over my head.

"You need some clothes. And a bath." I pulled at the soft hair on his chin. "You need to start shaving, too."

I looked over my shoulder. Steve was gone. There was nobody in that small lobby room except for me and my brother.

"Did you bring any clothes for me?" Bosten sat back on the couch. He had his arm around my shoulder, so it made me lean forward with him when he reached out and grabbed the cigarette he'd been smoking.

"No. And you don't smoke."

Bosten shrugged. His eyes smiled at me, but his face was so tired.

"Just watch me, Sticker."

Then he took a big drag from his cigarette, and he didn't even make any expression at all. I thought that was even cooler than how Steve smoked. Bosten exhaled a cloud through his nostrils.

"How about money?"

"I have money. But you're coming home with me. To Dahlia's."

Bosten pulled his arm off me. He put out the cigarette and wiped his palms on the grease-slicked knees of his jeans. He wouldn't look at me.

I knew what that meant when my brother wouldn't look at me.

"How did you get here?"

"I drove."

I drive at night.

"I got lost, too."

Then I remembered. "Shit. What time is it?"

"About midnight."

"Shit. The guy at the parking lot locked Dahlia's car in."

"Steve said you could have the third bed in our room. There's a kid in there named Jericho. He's a good friend. We kind of watch out for each other. We stay together."

"I have school tomorrow."

"You go to school?"

"I like it."

Bosten didn't say anything. He put his fingers down inside the pocket on his shirt and pulled out a wrinkled pack of cigarettes. He lit one.

I had two pieces of paper tucked into the same pocket where I carried Bosten's wallet: the corner of Aunt Dahlia's map of Los Angeles, and the newspaper clipping from Kingston that had a photograph of the handpop flare we launched, our UFO attack.

I unfolded it and watched Bosten's face. I still saw wonder in my brother's eyes, but I could see it had been shadowed over by all the things that had happened to us since that night of the basketball game.

Bosten smiled. "That was a long time ago."

He held his lit cigarette in one hand, the same way Mom did, pinched back in the curl of his palm.

"Not really."

My brother just stared at that image, like it was a movie or something, like you could see it changing, burning, right there in his hand.

"Do you know what happened to Buck?"

"No."

I thought about what I should say, and I could still hear the words from Ricky Dostal and Corey Barr in the locker room as they laughed about Paul Buckley trying to kill himself with a pair of sewing scissors.

"They put him in a hospital."

And Bosten said, "You don't need to tell me."

"Sometime I will."

"Okay."

"Let's go home, Bosten."

I watched him smoke. He put the newspaper clipping down on the table with the torn books. I could see him thinking about things.

I said, "You're all I have."

"That's not true."

"Please?"

Bosten balanced his cigarette on the edge of the table, so the ashes hung out over the floor. He unbuttoned his shirt and took it off. His undershirt was covered in filth, and there was a slashing tear right across his belly.

"I don't think I should go with you."

And Bosten turned up his left arm so I could see all the marks on it, the ones by his wrist and the others at the crook, all made by the uncareful needles that boys on the streets spent their money on and traded their bodies for.

One of the needle marks oozed pus. It was right beside one that looked like it was just done that day.

Bosten just stood there, watching my face while I looked at what he'd done to himself. And he had this expression like he was saying, "I told you so."

I thought about Paul Buckley's arms.

I tried to remember if there was ever a time in my life when I'd gotten mad or disappointed with Bosten.

"Are you trying to fucking kill yourself or something?"

Bosten shrugged. "I don't know."

He smiled, like it was no big deal at all.

He slipped his arms back into the sleeves of his shirt.

Before he could sit back down and pick up his cigarette, I launched myself from the couch and grabbed my brother around the collars of his shirt.

Bosten was startled. "Hey—"

I pushed him all the way across the floor, jammed him against Steve's registration desk, so the small of his back was pinned. And I'd never fought with my brother, not one time in my life; but I didn't know what else I could do. I was afraid he was going to kill himself.

I imagined him ending up like Willie.

And I knew Bosten could fight. I was being stupid if I thought that he wasn't going to punch me in the face for what I was doing, but my brother just kind of went limp and gave up in front of me.

"What the fuck, Bosten? You can't do this to me. You can't leave me like this."

Bosten just stood there, his arms hanging loose at his sides.

"What are you going to do? Beat the shit out of me? Like Dad?"

I let go of him and turned around.

"Fuck you, Bosten."

"See?

I always knew
one of these days
you'd stick up for yourself."

My brother walked across to the table and put his cigarette in his lips.

"Steve would be pissed   if we burned the place down."

"I'm going to leave."

I didn't turn around. I was too disgusted to look at Bosten.

I went to the door and opened it.

"It's locked,   so you can't come back in until tomorrow at   noon."

"I'm not coming back. I'm going home."

It was like a dream. I couldn't believe this was happening, but I heard the door latch shut behind me and next thing I knew, I was on the stairs, going down, smelling the reek of piss in that dark hallway.

And the door opened behind me.

"Hey.   Wait. You forgot the   UFO picture."

I stopped.

Bosten said, "Let me   wake up   Jericho. He's the best at breaking into places. We're going to need to get Aunt Dahlia's car out   if you plan on taking me home."

The boy named Jericho was small and rat-like, with a faint mustache of amber fuzz over his lip. He wore horn-rimmed glasses, which made him look even more like a rodent. He told me he was seventeen and that he ran away from his home in Utah to come to Los Angeles.

And he said it would be a piece of cake getting Aunt Dahlia's car out of the lot.

When he said "cake," it made me hungry.

We walked down Broadway to Fifth Street and turned

right. Jericho knew exactly the lot on Flower Street where I'd left the car.

"The guy who runs it's from Greece or something. He's a dick, but sometimes, he'll let us bum a cigarette," Jericho said.

Jericho's head twitched when he walked, and he sniffled constantly and rubbed the snot from his running nose across the back of his sleeve.

"You can come to our house," I offered. "I mean, if you need a place to stay for a while."

"Shit," he said. "Do I look like I need a place to stay?"

Jericho wiped his nose again.

He did look like he needed a place to stay, but I was afraid I'd make him mad.

"Sorry."

"Shit. You're all Big Brother talks about. Like you're his hero or something."

Bosten said, "Shut up."

Jericho twitched and sniffled. "Okay. Sometimes he talks about slamming shit up in his arm, too."

Then he laughed and slapped at Bosten, but he only fanned the air.

"And what do *you* talk about all the time?" Bosten said.

"Getting high. And my sweet Bosten."

I decided I didn't like Jericho, but told myself if he knew a way to get the Dodge out of the Greek guy's lot, then I'd better shut up.

There were people—big people—wrapped in blankets or anything they could bundle themselves in, lying on the benches in Pershing Square. Their pungent smell was like an incense of filth and defeat.

One of them lifted his head when we walked by. He called after us.

"Jericho and two of his pretty boys. You got anything for us, J? Jericho?"

Jericho didn't say anything. We just kept walking.

It was warm. It must be easy to last out on the streets in a place like Los Angeles, I thought.

On Flower Street, Jericho said, "When am I going to see you again? I'm going to miss you, babe."

Then he kissed Bosten right on the mouth.

Bosten looked at me. I could tell he was embarrassed. But I didn't care. I wanted to punch that rat-faced kid.

I said, "I'll write down our address and phone number in Oxnard, in case you're ever out there."

Jericho laughed. "Baby, I'm always *out there.* I'm just never out. There."

He had his twitching arm around my brother's waist.

"There it is."

The three of us stood at the back of the lot. Aunt Dahlia's Dodge wasn't the only victim of the ten-pee-em lockdown, but maybe the Greek guy stored cars there, too. Jericho curled his fingers through the chain link and studied the layout like he was a general planning a surprise attack.

"There's too much light up front. The cops would see us. I think we'll just take it out right here."

I wondered how Jericho thought we'd get a Dodge over that fence.

He said, "You. Little Brother. Stand down there and watch for cops."

He pointed his snot-streaked hand at the corner of the lot.

I didn't mind watching for cops, even though I wasn't really clear about what to do if I found any, because I didn't want to see what Jericho and my brother were going to do about freeing Aunt Dahlia's car.

In minutes, though, it was obvious enough. Jericho carried some heavy wire cutters in his back pocket, and it wasn't long at all before the back line of fencing had been completely separated and a gate wide enough to drive a tank through had been opened up.

Just like that.

I drive at night.
I blow things up.
I steal cars.

We all three sat in the front seat, with Bosten in the middle.

I was kind of hoping that Jericho would just jump out at the first stoplight, but he didn't.

And the frame of the Dodge scraped a little when I drove it off the sidewalk and over the curb. Luckily, there wasn't any traffic, too, because I went for an entire block in the wrong direction down a one-way street.

Once I straightened out and got the car heading in a legal direction, Jericho declared himself the navigator, and guided us west on Sunset until we were driving along Santa Monica Boulevard, looking for a place where we could get something to eat.

We ate breakfast at a Denny's in Hollywood at one in the morning.

The people who worked there were not nice to us at all. I could tell they'd had Jericho and Bosten as customers before. And while we ate, Jericho proudly announced, "This is probably going to be the first time I don't get thrown out of here."

Bosten smiled, then glanced down at his pancakes and said, "Maybe."

By two o'clock, we were outside an abandoned building where junkies and street kids stayed. It was where Jericho asked me to drop him off. Bosten knew the place, too, but I didn't want to hear anything about it.

So when Jericho pushed the door open and slid out of the car, I grabbed on to Bosten's wrist as he started to scoot away from me.

"Don't go out there."

"I'm not going to leave you, Stick."

I let him go.

I didn't watch what they did. The only thing I cared about was getting Bosten back in the car and taking him home—going home again, like we were supposed to. I heard them talking to each other, but I didn't want to know what they said. I guess I felt mean, bad for taking Bosten away from somebody he cared about, but I knew my brother couldn't live the way he'd been going.

Bosten burned too bright for that.

He was a wild horse running at a full gallop straight for a cliff he knew was there.

My brother got back into the car.

I breathed again.

He noticed.

"Look. I told you I won't leave you."

"Okay." My voice shook.

"I'll try to be good."

"Okay."

I waited for him to shut the door.

"I think you should give Jericho some money for helping us out."

I knew I promised that I'd never do anything to make Aunt Dahlia suffer again, so I could hardly look at her when we finally got home to the Strand. It was almost four in the morning, and Dahlia had fallen asleep on the couch in her living room with all the lights turned on in her little house.

She trembled when we walked through the door together.

Then she started to cry.

Dahlia put her hands on my shoulders and kissed my ear. She whispered, "From the first time I saw you,   I always knew you were someone.   I always knew you were."

Then she grabbed on to Bosten and kissed him all over and put her hands in his filthy hair and told him, "I am so   happy you're home. You look so   good. Baby, you look so   good."

And Bosten squeezed her back.

I went into my room and took the clean clothes I'd been carrying for my brother out of my suitcase. I brought them into the bathroom, put them down next to the sink, and then I ran the shower for him.

Things change.
Sometimes things heal.
Bosten's arm got better,
but there was something in both of us that remained empty,
and it wasn't something anyone could give a name to,
and we knew that,
so, together, we kept it chained
inside a room somewhere,
waiting for morning.

It's always foggy along the beach in California during June.
The school year is nearly over.
Bosten is enrolled in continuation school,
but I don't think he has learned how to continue very well.
Kim and Evan are waiting outside.
Bosten and I still sleep in the same bed at Dahlia's house.

We are going into the sea.

Thank you for reading this FEIWEL AND FRIENDS book.

The Friends who made

STICK

possible are:

Jean Feiwel
publisher

Liz Szabla
editor-in-chief

Rich Deas
creative director

Elizabeth Fithian
marketing director

Holly West
assistant to the publisher

Dave Barrett
managing editor

Nicole Liebowitz Moulaison
production manager

Ksenia Winnicki
publishing associate

Anna Roberto
editorial assistant

Kathleen Breitenfeld
designer

Find out more about our authors and artists
and our future publishing at macteenbooks.com.

OUR BOOKS ARE FRIENDS FOR LIFE